The

HEART

A NOVEL

MAKEDA SILVERA

does not

BEND

RANDOM HOUSE CANADA

National Library of Canada Cataloguing in Publication Data

Silvera, Makeda, 1955-
        The heart does not bend

ISBN 0-679-31134-3

        I. Title.

PS8587.I274H42 2002   C813'.54   C2001-903455-5
PR9199.3.S51766H42 2002

www.randomhouse.ca

Text design: CS Richardson

Printed and bound in the United States of America

10 9 8 7 6 5 4 3 2 1

For Lucille

There Are No Honest Poems
About Dead Women
AUDRE LORDE

Prolegomenon

WHAT IS SAID OVER THE DEAD LIONESS'S BODY COULD NOT BE SAID TO HER ALIVE

EVERYONE IS SITTING at Grand-aunt Ruth's breakfast table in Kingston—Uncle Peppie and Aunt Val; Uncle Mikey; Glory, my mother and the executor of my grandmother's estate; the grand-aunts, Ruth and Joyce; cousins Icie, Ivan and Vittorio; and my daughter, Ciboney, and her eleven-month-old baby. Uncle Freddie is the only one missing.

The muttering around the table gives way to the crackling of the papers in Glory's hand. Except for the three youngest, we are nervous. Ciboney, just fifteen, looks bored, but the hint of malice around her mouth makes me wonder what she is thinking. Vittorio, handsome at nineteen, idly plays with his brick-coloured, shoulder-length dreadlocks. Aunt Val has an arm protectively around Uncle Peppie's shoulder. Uncle Mikey crosses and uncrosses his legs. Grand-aunt Ruth wipes sweat from her face with an old washrag, and Aunt Joyce fans herself profusely with a rattan fan she brought back from America. Cousin Icie and Cousin Ivan sit like tin soldiers. My thoughts are a muddle, and my heart is thumping so hard that I am convinced everyone can hear it.

"Okay, we all here?" Glory asks.

"Uh-hum," we respond as one.

"Well ah think we should just get it over wid," Glory says as she straightens the papers once more.

"'I, Maria Maud Galloway, of sound mind and body, make this my Last Will and Testament.'"

"'I hereby revoke all my former wills and other testamentary dispositions of every nature and kind whatsoever hereto before made by me.'"

Glory pauses, inhales heavily and says, "Dis is not Mama's first will. Dis is about de tenth. De lawyer dem love her."

"'I nominate, constitute and appoint my daughter, Glory May Galloway, to be the sole executor of this my will.'"

She pauses again. "Ah skipping some of de legal talk."

"'To my grandson, Vittorio Oliver Galloway, I bequeath the properties known as 100 Pear Avenue, in the Municipality of Metropolitan Toronto, Canada, and the fifty-five acres of land in the township of Muskoka free and clear of all liens and encumbrances whatsoever, for his own use absolutely.'"

"'To my grandson, Vittorio Oliver Galloway, I also bequeath the property at 3 Wigton Street, in the City of Kingston, Jamaica, free and clear of all liens and encumbrances whatsoever, for his own use absolutely.'"

A loud gasp escapes from Uncle Peppie; Aunt Val strokes his shoulder. Glory sighs. Uncle Mikey uncrosses his legs and plants his feet firmly on the ground, his face an ugly mask. Uncle Peppie slumps further into his chair.

"Lawd God Almighty!" Aunt Joyce shouts.

"Calm down. Quiet, Joyce, mek we hear de rest of de will," Grand-aunt Ruth commands.

Glory's mouth is clamped tight as she reads the rest of the will silently.

"Go on, Glory," Grand-aunt Ruth says, gently resting her hand on Glory's arm. Glory takes a sip of her coffee, as if to help loosen her mouth.

"'To transfer my hope chest to my great-granddaughter, Ciboney Galloway, for her own use absolutely.

"'To transfer all other household items on the properties to my grandson, Vittorio Oliver Galloway.

"'To transfer all moneys from my bank account in the Municipality of Metropolitan Toronto and in the City of Kingston, Jamaica, to my grandson, Vittorio Oliver Galloway.'"

Glory is still reading. By now I am only half listening. I see Maria, Mama to me, in the hospital bed, me changing her soaked diaper. She grips my hands, her eyes pleading, the words coming out with difficulty.

"Molly, tek mi outa dis iron coffin. Tek me out, carry mi home. Mek mi dead in mi own bed."

"'Should my said grandson predecease me, or die at the same time or in circumstances rendering it uncertain which of us survived the other, or die within thirty days of my death, then I direct my Trustee to give my grandson's share of my estate to charity, for the charity's use absolutely.'"

Glory's voice breaks. Her body sags from the weight of the will. Uncle Mikey offers her a glass of water.

"Here, Glory, drink dis."

"Dis is madness. Dis is plain, outright madness," Glory says. "Ah should have certified her a long time ago." Her voice is full of contempt and she is trembling.

"Ah wonder if Maria was in her right mind for truth?"

Aunt Joyce adds, shaking her head in disbelief.

Uncle Mikey's voice is bitter. "Mama is a wicked, revengeful 'oman. How she could do dis? Wherever she gone, she won't find peace." He pushes his chair back, ready to leave the table.

"Mikey, tek it easy. Sit down. Yuh not massa God. And only Him can judge," Grand-aunt Ruth says. He opens his mouth to argue, but one look from Grand-aunt Ruth and he changes his mind.

"Ah try mi best all dese years to be a good daughter, and for what? Ah use to parcel up de whole of Canada and send home to her."

"Yes, Glory, yuh give her your best, and she did love you very much. Don't cuss and don't harbour bad feelings. God not sleeping and Him work in mysterious ways. Dis is why life and death is a mystery to us all," Grand-aunt Ruth says.

I remember Mama at the hospital, her eyes wild, her panicked whisper pleading with me to take her home.

"De man calling mi, Molly. Him ready to tek mi." Her breathing was harsh, her mouth caving in without her dentures.

I didn't have to look across the table at Uncle Peppie to feel his shame. He was Maria's first-born, the faithful, obedient son. It's as if she's in the room, sitting at the table, and he won't say anything bad about her. Like me, he never stood up to her, and her death changes nothing. When Uncle Peppie finally speaks, he doesn't mention the will.

"Well, at least she get her final wish. She bury right next to Mammy, in Port Maria Cemetery."

"You too kind-hearted, Peppie," Uncle Mikey jumps in, sucking his teeth.

Glory, in full agreement, cuts her eyes across the table.

"Is Peppie save her. Is him give her a second life."

"Dis is her idea of revenge," Mikey spits out. "She was always harbouring some anger. Freddie right fi nuh come."

"Molly remember de dresses," Uncle Peppie quietly reminds me.

They have forgotten Vittorio. It's as if he weren't there. Grand-aunt Ruth comes to his rescue.

"What time is yuh flight, Vic?"

"Soon, Aunt Ruth. I should get back to packing." He pushes back his chair, eager to get away.

"Let we hold we head in prayer before yuh leave, Vic. Dis bickering and bad feeling toward de living and de dead nuh good," Grand-aunt Ruth says, determined to bank the fire. "Okay, let we all hold hands. 'Please, dear Father, help us to bury dis hatred and to ward off de temptation of Satan. Let us receive not de spirit of de world, but de Spirit which is of God.'" Her eyes are closed. She doesn't need her Bible for this. "Praise de Lord and may Him Spirit and de goodness of Him heart be wid us."

Uncle Peppie slowly pushes back his chair and excuses himself. Aunt Val follows. Vittorio mumbles something about finishing his packing. Uncle Mikey says he needs fresh air. Glory follows. The grand-aunts retire to the kitchen. Cousin Icie and Cousin Ivan escape to the backyard.

I nurse my cold cup of coffee. Just Ciboney, the baby and I are left sitting there. We stare out the window, oblivious to the flies swarming the table. She looks like me when I was her age: tall and willowy, molasses complexion, full lips and ackee-seed eyes. I want to fold her in my arms, tell her I love her, but it seems too late.

How could Mama do this? How? I was her only grand-daughter. I was there. I was always there. Vittorio never was, and what did he know of Wigton Street?

Outside it's bleak. It rained all night and the clouds are just hanging. I don't know what I expected from my grand-mother, but if I am not careful, I might say things I'll regret, especially to Vittorio. But I want my daughter back and he is the only person who can get her back for me.

Early the next morning I leave the house, hire a car, take the dresses to the cousins, and then drive out to the cemetery.

EARTH IS THE QUEEN OF BEDS

I AM WEARING your old lady's dress today, Mama, one of the many you left behind. You asked for us to take them to the country and give them to your cousins, but I kept two for myself. One is sea-blue with white hyacinths threaded together, floating in the blue. The other is salmon-pink with white roses on a spread of green leaves. Both dresses have buttons all the way down to the hem and a pocket on each side.

I am here sitting on your grave, wearing the blue dress. It's all washed out; it was your favourite. Your grave is only a few weeks old, and your scent is still in the dress that feels so soft on my skin. I want to take in every hint of your old lady's smell. I didn't wash the dress, though Grand-aunt Ruth said that every dress, every blouse, every slip, every piece of drawers had to be washed, then put away for ten days before wearing.

I wish there weren't this concrete between us, wish I could slide right into your silver-blue coffin. We got it custom-made in your favourite colour, the lining a softer blue, folded in accordion pleats. Glory lay two *Daily Word* pamphlets inside. Ciboney and Vittorio placed a single white orchid in your hands. I lined the inside of your casket with pepper-red hibiscus flowers. A cross of white carnations and a bouquet of blue Bengal trumpets and lavender chrysanthemums are wilting on your grave.

Your mother, Mammy, my great-grandmother, is buried in this cemetery, only a few yards from here, next to the poinciana tree; its clusters of red blossoms shade her headstone. Your father, Pappy, is buried here, too. He has no headstone, he's covered over in crabgrass and bush.

You couldn't have chosen a nicer place to rest. This is quiet country, peaceful, away from the posses and the city. No gunfire here, no thieves to watch out for, no one shooting up.

Here birds fly easy and butterflies drink from morning glory vines. Woodpeckers and doves chatter. The grounds are patchy with crabgrass and ferns growing between broken rocks. Flowering trees shower the dirt with their sweet blossoms.

The gravediggers are out in full force, shirtless, sweat running down their backs, pickaxes digging into the hard, dry dirt. They talk loud and laugh hard, but they take no notice of my old lady's dress.

The land you grew up on isn't far from here. The wooden house is gone, swept away by the sea after Mammy died. I think of when we used to go there, about the waves coming up on the sand, washing back just a bit, then coming up again, covering my little girl toes, then up my legs. I was afraid of the waves carrying me back out with them. You held me, steadied me so I could float till I wasn't afraid anymore. I always started off in your arms, even after you had taught me how to swim. Sometimes you'd pile the rust-brown sand over me, covering me till only my face peeked out, you counting backwards from twenty as I thrashed my way free.

It's just past noon and the gravediggers' women come with hot cooked lunches and ice water to drink. One woman brings a bottle of white rum and five enamel mugs.

A mourning dove twitters above your grave, and the sunlight streams through the trees. Beyond them is a funeral procession. I can hear the loved ones wailing, disrupting the quiet of the graveyard. Still, seeing and hearing them is a relief. I don't feel so alone.

Watching them, I try to figure out who died and how. The mourners are young, their clothes bright, and the women's hair a rainbow of colours. Everyone sports dark sunglasses. I suspect they might be burying a young man, maybe around eighteen, who was gunned down. A loud screech comes from a girl no more than sixteen. I think briefly of Ciboney. The girl is wearing a black dress that fits her body tightly, the neck scooped so low I can see the dance of her breasts as she sobs and jumps toward the open grave. Three people grab and pull her away, but she is strong and they have a hard time holding her.

"Patrick, Patrick, nuh lef mi! Mi and de baby need yuh," she wails. "Patrick!" Confusion abounds as she tries again to jump in with the coffin. All this time a video camera records the mourners' rites to the dead.

Glory wanted one, too. She wanted us to record your funeral, Mama, but with all the confusion, we forgot. It's just as well. What would it show us? How would it comfort us?

We dressed you and made up your face at the funeral parlour for the mourners to view—Glory wanted it that way. It was not the custom of the funeral parlour to allow relatives to dress the dead, but Glory wore the attendant down, and she finally gave in. She stood in the doorway and watched. Uncle Peppie, Uncle Mikey, Ciboney and Vittorio were also there. Glory and I sponged you clean. We powdered you from neck to toe with Johnson's Baby Powder, put on a brand-new white pair of drawers, then took them off because the attendant said we had to fit you in a diaper first. She said that was the way God wanted to receive the dead. We didn't question her, though we suspected her advice, like Grand-aunt Ruth's instructions about washing Mama's clothes before wearing them, was an old wives' tale. Glory had brought a lovely slip of a white dress, and we fitted it over your body, along with a pair of white silk stockings and soft, white pull-on sandals. I plaited your hair for the last time.

Ciboney and Vittorio put long white gloves on your hands. Glory applied Pond's makeup to your face. Your lips were shut tight as a zippered purse, but with the help of some tweezers we arranged them in a half smile—that's all you would give. Still, your face looked rested, so different from those last days in the hospital bed when you were shouting, "Tek mi out of dis iron coffin!" Glory added a bit of lipstick to your mouth, and Uncle Peppie helped me pin a flower of hibiscus in your hair. We put a touch of flowery perfume at each ear. You never wore makeup, you didn't like lipstick, but Glory said it would be a beautiful farewell gesture.

We took photographs with a throwaway camera: you in your silver-blue coffin, me plaiting your hair, Ciboney and Vittorio each slipping on a glove, Glory and Uncle Peppie's hands holding yours, me kissing you for the last time.

The videotape has run its course and the young mourners are gone now. All is quiet again, except for the sound of the gravediggers' pickaxes and their occasional laughter. The sun is beating down on me, but I don't want to leave you. I want to crawl into the cool earth and snuggle up right next to you. A gravedigger passes by, watches me and says, "A so sun hot pon dis island, but a little ease soon come, darlin'." The sweat pours down my face like sea water and onto my old lady's dress.

Yes, I know this is only a holding ground—a place for the living to mourn, to remember.

~ ~ ~

My first memory is of our house on the dead-end street. I went to live with you there in 1957, two days after my birth in a Kingston hospital. My mother, Glory, was fifteen years old. She named me Marlene, Molly for short. My birth certificate reads "father unknown." My mother left for Canada two and a half years later to seek opportunity, to get an education, to better herself. She never did come back to live here.

The house was painted sky-blue, trimmed in soft baby-pink, with steps leading up to a balcony. Some nights when the air was still, we'd climb the steps and sit on a bamboo bench, my head in your lap, counting the stars until the distant croaking of toads, the chatter of crickets and the familiar singsong voices of the neighbours lulled me to sleep. You would pick me up gently, carry me off to bed and tuck me in.

I remember our yard, a jungle of trees, sweet-smelling mangoes ripening, a rose-apple tree, banana, coconut, papaya trees, avocados, grapefruits, ackee and a great big almond tree. Magnificent beds of zinnias, crotons, spider lilies, birds-of-paradise, dwarf poinciana and roses spread in front of the verandah. Hedges of red hibiscus lined the path to the balcony steps. Overgrown bougainvillea in flamboyant colours weighed down the barbed-wire fence that separated our yard from the neighbour's.

The kitchen smelled of mouth-watering sweet cakes, puddings, spicy Jamaican foods. I never ever wanted to leave that house, but I mustn't blame you.

Part One

You Cannot Shave a Man's Head in His Absence

MARIA GALLOWAY DIDN'T GO to the Palisadoes Airport to see her son Freddie off. She never went to airports, not even when her son Peppie left in 1958 and then her daughter, Glory, in 1960.

The day Freddie left she sat on the verandah in the same chair she always sat in, a blue wicker one, smoking Craven A cigarettes, with the morning newspaper fresh in her hands. Back then she wore no old lady's clothes. Her sleeveless, brown jersey dress made her breasts a soft mountainside, her hips rolling brown hills. She sat there, quiet, looking on as friends and family came to bid Freddie goodbye.

It was hard to know what she was thinking. Her sure calm never left her face. Freddie knelt in front of her, gave her an open smile, flashed perfect white teeth, then lowered his eyes, like a small boy reciting his prayers. But he was nineteen and leaving to find his fortune abroad.

It was 1966 and I was nine years old. He was like a big brother to me, and I knew I was going to miss him something terrible. Freddie was my grandmother's youngest son.

"Come, nuh mek de plane lef yuh behin'. Hard-earn money buy dat ticket, and remember, nuh bodder go a white-man country and get inna any trouble. Act decent and show respect."

Her left hand was holding her cigarette tight. I saw tears well up in her eyes, but she didn't cry. "Gwaan, nuh mek de plane lef yuh," she repeated.

Freddie shrugged, smiled at her and kissed her cheek. "Tek care. We will see each other again if life spare." The December afternoon was humid, and the sun was like a yellow beach ball hanging in the sky. We crammed into cars and vans to say our final goodbyes. The smell of raw fish followed us as we raced along the seashore to the airport.

The waiting area was like Christmas morning in downtown Kingston. I kept expecting to see Junkanoos on stilts, their faces smeared in mud, horns on their heads, wire tails, dancing to drumbeats. Mothers and aunts and cousins laughed and cried, kissed their loved ones goodbye. The talk was hopeful and full of promise.

"Write mi when yuh reach."

"Don't forget mi."

"Mama, ah going to send money home soon as ah can."

"Ah hope de ackee and de fruits last de trip."

"Lloyd, 'member yuh have a 'oman an' a child here, don't tek up wid no foreign 'oman."

Vendors hawked their wares, selling everything from food to hair clips.

"Sweet bread, grater cake, bustamante backbone, paradise plum."

"Fish and bammy over here."

Uncle Freddie was all smiles and promises. "Yes, Dennis, yes man," he said to his best friend. "As soon as mi reach, ah send dat pair of Clarke's shoes fi yuh."

Freddie's girlfriend, Monica, admonished him not to forget her. "Nuh go up dere an' feget mi yuh nuh."

My uncle Freddie hugged and kissed her, whispered something in her ear that made her laugh. Then he smoothed his hands over her growing belly.

"Tek care a mi son. Ah going to send for de two a yuh soon. Send mi a picture when him born."

He promised the grand-aunts, cousins and friends everything foreign had to offer. He promised Monica that he would write and send money. For Dennis's ten-year-old sister, Punsie, he promised a camera. He saved his last good-bye for me. He lifted me high off the ground, squeezed me tight against his big chest. "Ah going to miss yuh, Moll." He kissed me from ear to ear, then whispered, "Ah won't feget yuh, yuh my special girl."

Uncle Mikey hadn't come to see him off.

My grandmother was still sitting on the verandah when we got back. Inside the house the air was thick with the smell of roasted yellow-heart breadfruit and yam, ackee and saltfish and golden-brown flour dumplings.

The grand-aunts took their plates to the verandah, while the rest of us sat around the table eating, drinking and talking about the good times we shared with Freddie. Monica was all teary-eyed. Cousin Ivan and Dennis and Freddie's other friends said they would miss him for his skilled kite-flying, the soccer matches at the end of the street, crab season and street dances.

Punsie said she'd miss the Chinese sweeties and the paradise plums Freddie bought for her. And me, I was losing the best and kindest uncle in the world.

I couldn't begin to think what life would be like without Uncle Freddie. He was the heart of the street. All the guys liked and respected him, even the older ones, for his easy manner and his contagious laughter. He took me to my only cockfight, in Dennis's backyard.

When everyone left the table, I went out to the verandah to join my grandmother and grand-aunts.

"Ah going to miss mi little nephew. No more Mr. Freddie. He was such a sharp dresser, and a ladies' man," Aunt Joyce said, a faraway smile gracing her face.

Aunt Joyce was the youngest of the sisters and the most fun. She laughed at everything, said whatever came into her head without thinking. She seemed to live only for the moment, so carefree. Joyce was three times divorced and had a string of suitors at her beck and call, but they never came close to her passion for clothes and shoes and gold jewellery.

"If dressing was all dere was to life and having whole heap of 'oman, him would be king," my grandmother replied sourly, dragging on her Craven A. "Ah only hope him remember poor Monica and de baby," she added.

"Nuh talk like dat, Maria, him love de girl," Aunt Joyce protested.

"Yuh mark my word, when him reach foreign all will be forgotten."

"Nuh mind, Maria. Him will change. Remember the Lord is within all of we," Grand-aunt Ruth added.

My grandmother didn't answer, but the tightening of her mouth and the steel in her brown eyes was enough. Nobody said anything for a while. I stared at the comic strip in the newspaper. Dennis's mother's voice travelled from several houses down the street, reaching our verandah. "Dennis, come water de yard."

Then my grandmother spoke. "Well, put bad and bad aside, ah will miss Freddie. Him really use to help me wid de garden," she said, softening slightly.

I decided it was safe for me to speak.

"Mama, yuh won't miss him for de crab season?"

She nodded. "Ah suppose so. Mm-hmm."

"Nuh bother even talk 'bout crab," Grand-aunt Ruth said. "Mi restaurant will really miss him, de crab soup and de crab fritter."

"Ivan can go wid Dennis and de rest a boys fi catch crab, him old enough," Mama said.

Ivan and Icie lived with Grand-aunt Ruth; they were cousins four times removed. Their mother was my grandmother and the grand-aunts' second cousin, who lived in Port Maria; she had several children and not enough food to go around. Icie was thirteen and Ivan fourteen.

"Dennis!" Aunt Joyce shouted across the three yards.

"Yes m'am?" he shouted back.

"Ah putting in mi order now fi next crab season, since mi favourite nephew gone."

"Don't worry, Miss Joyce, you and Miss Ruth and Miss Maria covered."

"All right, don't forget," Aunt Joyce shouted back.

"No m'am."

I remembered crab season. Uncle Freddie and his friends dragged crocus bags full of crabs into the backyard and threw them in huge drums. Punsie and I would watch them trying to climb out. Everyone on the street came to our yard to join in the excitement. There were always crab races. I hear Uncle Freddie now, shouting above the voices of his friends as he egged his crab on: "Run, run, crab, run fi yuh life!" During the season, we ate crabs so often we forgot the taste of other meat. We ate crab run-down cooked in coconut cream, and crab fritters spiced with curry powder, and my grandmother's favourite, crab shell stuffed with callaloo, sautéed onion, minced fresh hot peppers, then baked in an open wood fire. Uncle Freddie and his friends played music late into the night as we filled our bellies with crab.

Aunt Joyce brought my mind back to the verandah.

"Den, Maria, it won't cold when him get dere?" she asked.

"Ah think so, but Peppie and Glory will have clothes for him."

"Ah really going to miss him. Ah can't lie, him is mi favourite nephew," Aunt Joyce said.

Mama sucked her teeth. "Yuh know how much money dat bwoy tief from mi? If me never smart and one step ahead of him, ah would be in de poorhouse."

"Nuh mind, Maria, him gone. Try forgive him," Grand-aunt Ruth said.

"Ah because you two never have no children or unnu would be singing a different tune. Yuh think it easy fi raise four pickney alone?" Mama's voice was bitter. Neither of the grand-aunts answered, but a look passed between the two.

I never found out whether they couldn't have children or chose not to have them.

I stole a glance at Mama. She took another drag of her cigarette and went on as if she had not said something vexing.

"Mikey get a job, yuh know. Him working at Paul and Paul Fashion. Him get a job sewing dresses," she said proudly.

"Ah hear is a lot of fancy people go dere to get clothes mek. Ah wonder how much dem would charge to mek a dress for me?" Aunt Joyce asked excitedly.

"Yuh can ask Mikey when yuh see him, ah sure yuh would get a good deal," my grandmother said, her voice lighter.

"Dat's real nice, ah glad for him. Now wid God's blessings all him need is to find a girlfriend," Grand-aunt Ruth said, little enthusiasm in her voice. Then she added in the same lifeless tone, "How come him wasn't at the air-port?" I had never heard that tone in Grand-aunt Ruth's voice. As far back as I could remember, she was the paddle in the boat. She never spoke much, but when she did, her words were always balanced and encouraging. She was as slight as the shoot of a tree, and hedged about five feet tall, yet she carried command. She had a long face and a straight nose, a big head of coffee-coloured hair and a honey com-plexion. She was also a God-fearing woman who went to church every Sunday.

"Him have him business fi do." My grandmother drew on her cigarette again, and a look of defiance crossed her face. I wanted to hug her, even though I didn't understand. "Him did tell Freddie goodbye from last night. Him couldn't go to de airport, him had to prepare for him job. Freddie understan'. Dem understan' each other," Mama said. I winced, for I could not remember ever seeing her so sad. I muttered that I had to tell Punsie something and disappeared through the front gate.

When night was almost down, I heard Mama calling me. I washed off the dirt and excitement of the day, ate dinner, and then we went to bed. We didn't wait up for Uncle Mikey.

In Mama's big mahogany bed, I snuggled next to her. She stroked my hair. Her cigarette breath was warm and soothing on my face. She squeezed me tight in her arms and I felt a tear fall on my cheek. I buried my head in her bosom, and in the dark she sang to me.

My Bonnie lies over de ocean
My Bonnie lies over de sea
My Bonnie lies over de ocean
Oh bring back my Bonnie to me.
Oh bring back, oh bring back,
Oh bring back my Bonnie to me . . .

It didn't matter to me what she'd said to the grand-aunts about Uncle Freddie. I knew she loved him.

~ ~ ~

I awoke to the smell of scrambled eggs and bacon fried to a crisp. The house was too quiet. No music blared from the room next door. Uncle Freddie wasn't here anymore. It was a week to the day since he'd left. Mama had already come back from Coronation Market. I dressed myself and went to the kitchen to eat. Miss Gatty, our washerwoman, was already at work. I could hear the sound of clothes being rubbed against the scrub board through the open kitchen door. Mama was back there with her. They were gossiping like they always did when Miss Gatty came around. They were the same age, forty-two. Miss Gatty was a tall, thin Maroon-looking woman, with a face full of worry and fuss. She wore her hair in neat plaits, tied with a piece of cloth. I remember her fingers, long and bony, and the thick gold band that she never took off her left hand. She and Mama had been friends ever since I could remember.

"Gatty, is de best thing dat could happen. De bwoy woulda stay right here and drive mi to destruction."

I should have known that Freddie would be the talk; Mama hadn't seen Miss Gatty since he left.

"Him seh him wan' learn trade. Send him go learn trade, him nuh go. Send him go learn mechanics, him seh him nuh like lie down under dutty car. Cabinet-mekin', him seh cut up him hand; and is not seh him head tek to book, so him can tek learning fi doctor or lawyer. Him no have no job and yet him was de biggest spender and dresser pon de street."

"Miss Maria, yuh don't got to tell me. Is seven of dem me got, six bwoys, and not one a dem turn out good. Ah wish ah did have smaddy abroad fi get dem off de island, maybe dere would be a chance, especially fi de younger ones. Already mi have more grandpickney dan mi can count. Some of dem ah don't even know dem names."

"A Peppie why dem up dere. Him encourage and help mi to send dem. Dat bwoy is as dependable as salt inna sea.

Ah only hope Freddie find work and behave himself. Sometimes ah wonder if him woulda did benefit from a father, him so wild."

Mama ended the conversation. "Gatty, mek mi leave yuh to de washing. Ah have a set of baking to do for de Chinese pastry shop."

Mama worked at home from her kitchen, making pastries, delivering them twice a week to the two Chinese shops in our neighbourhood and to Grand-aunt Ruth's restaurant. I finished eating just as Mama came into the kitchen.

The dogs were barking at the gate and I knew it would be Baboo. I raced outside, my braids flying, not wanting to miss him. Baboo was a short, wiry Indian man dressed from a bag of rags. Torn pants, torn overshirt, running shoes with so many holes they looked as if rats had mistaken them for cheese. His long, knotted hair was in a clump. He came with his hand-drawn cart from the local bus stop to deliver market provisions to the houses on the street, and for that he was paid a few shillings.

Punsie and I and the rest of the gang on the street waited outside for him to make his last delivery, so he could give us a ride in his cart. It wasn't just the ride we enjoyed, it was Baboo himself. He was a walking storybook, painting colourful pictures of people dressed in finery, jewels and gold, of royalty in a faraway land—Calcutta, India. He spoke in a nasal voice, which made us laugh as we pressed against each other in his cart. He told us the scratchy sound of his voice came from smoking ganja, the "wisdom weed." But this Saturday held a different attraction. A new family was moving into the house next door. It had been empty for a long time. Trees and bushes had overgrown, hiding the house from passersby. We used the yard as a playground when we got tired of the street. It was the only yard around with a stinking toe tree, a jumbelin tree and a gineppe tree, and during the season we'd climb them and shake the fruit down. Sometimes Punsie and I would dare each other to stand and try to piss against the walls of the house like the boys did.

What caught our attention that morning was the girl moving into the old house. She was about my age, but that was where the similarity stopped. As we passed in Baboo's cart, I realized that I was staring into the face of a *dundus*. We all saw her at once and pointed in amazement—we had never seen an albino before. We hurried back to my yard and peeked through the red bougainvillea bush hanging from the barbed-wire fence, but we could see very little.

Mama shouted for me to come in. "Girl, yuh forget yuh Saturday chores. Come in here now. Yuh romp too much!" I sucked my teeth in protest and reluctantly sent the others through the gate. Mama was still baking, and Miss Gatty had finished the washing when I told them about the dundus girl next door.

They didn't seem too interested. Mama only cautioned, "Watch yuh mouth and don't start teasing de pickney." I paid no attention to her warning. I was too excited to care.

The smell of burnt molasses, fresh-ground nutmeg, slivers of fresh ginger floated in the air. I loved to watch Mama turn plain white flour into plantain tarts, gizzadas with sugared coconut inside, totos, bulla cakes, molasses almond tarts and rose-apple cupcakes with yellow icing on top.

That day she wore a cotton print dress covered with a

flour-bag apron. Perspiration ran down her face as she lifted baked goods from the oven. She was a handsome woman, not given to easy smiles, but when she did smile, it was like the warm glow of candles on a birthday cake.

"Come, Molly, start de dusting, de day almost done."

It was my job every Saturday to dust the furniture and wipe the living room's tiled floor, the verandah and the bedroom we shared. Our living room and dining room were combined in one very large room, set off from the kitchen by a wide stone counter where Mama rolled out the dough for her pastries. Two bedrooms and an indoor bathroom were down the hall. The dining room contained a mahogany table with six chairs. A vase with fresh-cut flowers sat in the centre on one of Mama's crocheted pieces. There was a built-in wall cabinet that stored our good glasses and our china plates, cups and saucers.

The living room, which opened onto the verandah, had a couch and two armchairs, a coffee-table in the centre. On its surface was another crocheted piece with pineapple designs, and little porcelain figurines of grandly dressed men and women nicely arranged. Close to the window sat our record player.

"Gatty, before yuh leave, yuh want a taste of de whites?" I heard Mama asking Miss Gatty. But the question was just a formality. Every Saturday afternoon, after the washing and baking, they turned to women talk on the verandah, their throats eased by a flask of white rum, ice and a bit of water to chase it.

"So, how Mr. Mikey doing?"

"Him doing good. Him get a job wid some big-shot dressmaker-designers."

"Dat real nice," Miss Gatty said, pouring herself a shot of rum. "Dat nice."

Then Mama lowered her voice. "Ah only hope to God him find a nice girl soon. Ah can't tell nuh lie, ah really worry sometimes. . . ."

Her voice drifted off. Then I heard her say, "Molly?" I stayed behind the curtains, not wanting to be discovered, and she went on. "Gatty, ah don't know how him turn so. Ah love him wid all mi heart, but ah wish him was more like Peppie. Even like Freddie, God forgive mi. Yuh know, a little more manly, especially in de voice."

"So him never interested in girls, Miss Maria?"

"Never. From him born him different. Him tek him whole physical features off Mammy, same small bone, all him have from him father and me is de blackness, nutten else. If mi never give birth to him meself, ah would a think him is a jacket. But mi know mi never unfaithful to Oliver Galloway."

"Miss Maria, look at it dis way: it might all be a part of God's plan."

"Gatty, don't talk nonsense, what kinda plan? Mi sacrifice too much already to be curse wid dis. A mi son and mi love him, but mi not Mary and him not Jesus. Mi nuh want him fi bear any cross, for de mother always feel it, and mi load too heavy already. From mi born mi bad luck." With that, my grandmother poured herself another rum.

"Him different from him born," she repeated. "When Peppie a fly kite and knock marble, Mikey playing dolly house wid Glory. When him turn teenager, him tek to de sewing machine more than Glory."

"Him will change," Miss Gatty reassured her. "In time him will see is not a normal way to be."

"But Gatty, de bwoy near twenty-one, what chance him have to change?"

"Miss Maria, sometimes things have a way of turning. Him young, him have him whole life in front of him and as me Maroon granny use to say, 'What nuh dead, nuh dash wey.'"

"Dat is true," Mama said, but she was not convinced.

I'd never thought about Uncle Mikey's lack of interest in girls. He and Uncle Freddie never got along. They often fought, but I thought that was just what brothers did.

Miss Gatty left shortly after, her hands clutching two cloth bags filled with ackee, avocados and fruits from our yard.

~ ~ ~

The first letter we received after Uncle Freddie left came not from him, but from Uncle Peppie.

> *Dear Mama,*
>
> *I hope this letter find you in good health. Freddie arrive safe and sound. He got a part-time job as a packer in the same factory as Glory about a month ago. I am still working in the autobody repair shop and that going good, I learning a lot about European cars.*
>
> *Thank you for the escoveitch fish. Glory and me eat it off in less than a week. As always the fruitcake was nice-nice, it make me miss home even more. Enclose you will find a money order to*

*help with things. Give my love to Mammy, Aunt
Ruth, Aunt Joyce, Molly and everybody else.*
   I remain your faithful son,
   Peppie

Mama folded the letter and the money order and tucked
them in her bosom.

"Freddie get a job," she said proudly. "Ah think foreign
will do him good." Then in a disgruntled tone she added,
"But you think him would at least write mi." She shook her
head and lit a cigarette.

"Come, let we go change de money order. God bless
Peppie, him is really a good son, him and Mikey."

That night we went to the movies, our usual routine on
a Friday. The Ritz Theatre was just a mile away, an easy walk.
Kingston was a safe city back then. Sometimes we went to the
Majestic Theatre instead, but tonight it was the Ritz and
Sophia Loren, my grandmother's favourite actress. *The
Millionaires* was playing. We took our seats in the front row,
ate warm peanuts from the shell and waited for the lights to
go down. I fell asleep in her lap before the movie ended, but
it didn't matter what the storyline was, for like Mama, I had
fallen in love with Sophia. We made our way out of the theatre,
hands folded into each other's, and stopped off at Olive's
Hideaway for refreshments, rum for my grandmother and a
pineapple drink for me. Uncle Mikey was already home when
we got in. Mama talked endlessly about Sophia Loren and her
beautiful dresses. My uncle indulged her with his wide, beautiful smile, but he didn't care much for Sophia Loren. Audrey
Hepburn was his all-time favourite movie star.

I fell asleep that night in Mama's lap, listening to their chatter. I could see how different Freddie and Mikey were. Freddie loved Audie Murphy, Alan Ladd and John Wayne and outdoor sports. Mikey stayed indoors and was partial to sewing and planning dinner parties. The one passion they shared was music, but even in that they had different tastes. Freddie loved rocksteady, Duke Reid and Sir Coxsone, Prince Buster and street dances. Mikey loved American R&B, Johnny Mathis, Jackie Edwards, Little Richard and Frank Sinatra ballads.

It was only after Freddie left that Uncle Mikey started having parties at our house on the first Sunday of every month. They were small, with only ten or so guests. I stayed in my Sunday-school clothes and my grandmother was always dressed to kill. The meals were elaborate, served in hulled coconut shells and on banana and papaya leaves.

Paul, the dress designer Mikey worked with, was my favourite guest. He was a tall, thin, handsome man who kept his straightened black hair pulled back in a ponytail tied with a red silk scarf. He wore big colourful capes over his street clothes. Helen, Paul's sister, who also worked in his dress shop, came too. She was tall and slender like Paul and always dressed in a red or black kimono. She piled her hair high on her head in swirls, two chopsticks holding it in place. Her skin was flawless, almost raven black. She was one of the most beautiful women I'd ever seen.

There was Nat, a guitarist and singer, and Richard, a short, muscular dancer who looked like a black Yul Brynner. George, a chef at a Chinese restaurant, sported two gold crowns in his mouth. Ken was an actor in pantomimes at the Ward Theatre in downtown Kingston. He was a very pretty man, thin and fragile, like a girl in the movies. There were the twins, Tom and Rex, who dressed in matching clothes, a couple of photographers, a painter and June, the only other woman who was a regular guest.

Mama's favourite was Nat. He was older than the others and resembled Uncle Peppie, cool coal-black. He played songs she knew, the mento, and the rhumba, the mambo and the bolero.

Mama loved to dance; it was one of the few times her face relaxed. I watched her dancing to a mento beat, the hem of her dress floating above her knees, her dress hugging her Sophia Loren breasts. I wanted to dance like her when I grew up. I wanted her breasts and floating hips.

On these occasions Uncle Mikey was happy and relaxed, too, more so than at any other time. Mama moved easily among his friends. If she had any anxieties, they surfaced when she was sitting alone on the verandah, or when Miss Gatty came on Saturdays to do the washing.

~ ~ ~

I didn't meet the dundus girl until weeks after she came to live next door. She was a quiet girl, who never left her yard to play. The other kids were unrelenting in their teasing. "Dundus gal, dundus gal," they'd singsong in front of her gate or when she walked home from school. Because of that, her father built her a treehouse in their backyard, which was the envy of the street.

We met through the fence one day when I was watering my grandmother's flower bed.

"Hey, gal, what yuh name?" I asked, spraying the hose on her.

She didn't flinch, just stood there staring me down. I sprayed her again and then ran off. She made me uneasy with her white-white face and pale, wide-open eyes.

A few days later she came to the fence and called out to me.

"Petal, mi name Petal. Yuh want to come over?"

I shrugged as if I was quite indifferent.

"Yuh don't want to see de treehouse?"

"Yes, ah guess so," I answered lazily, and crawled under the barbed-wire fence into her yard. We climbed up to the treehouse using a ladder made of thick rope. I was sitting on the floor thinking about what it would be like to have the treehouse for a bedroom when she asked me, "Yuh want to see something?"

"Mm-hmm," I answered, only half-interested.

"Yuh promise not to tell?"

"Tell what?" I asked.

"Yuh have to swear on yuh granny grave dat yuh won't tell."

I hesitated, but curiosity got the best of me. "Ah swear."

"Swear on what?" she insisted, staring into my face.

"Ah swear on mi granny grave."

"Now swear on yuh mother grave. Wey she deh?"

"Canada."

"Well, swear on her grave."

I swore. Petal took out a matchbox from the pocket of her yellow calico dress. Slowly she opened it, revealing a live grasshopper feeding on grass. She stared at me again, shutting the box.

"Yuh mek mi swear on mi granny grave for dat?" I asked angrily. I sucked my teeth like my grandmother did and got up to climb down the rope.

"Wait, ah only joking wid yuh." She grinned. "Yuh 'ave nice eyes."

I couldn't find anything complimentary to say about hers, so I just looked into them. She fiddled with the match-box, and the grasshopper tried to escape as she opened and closed the lid; all the time she looked straight at me. I didn't like it one bit. I wanted her to be like Punsie, who filled our yards and our street with screams and laughter.

"Open yuh mouth," Petal commanded.

"For what?"

"Jus' open it," she insisted, the grasshopper dangling between her fingers.

"Yuh is a mad gal!" I shouted.

"Is brain food, it will mek yuh smart, and it taste good."

I was not convinced. "Who tell yuh dat foolishness?"

"Mi see it on television, is brain food in America."

"Dat is nasty," I said, disgusted.

"Yuh like the treehouse?" she asked, and before I could answer, she told me I could climb the fence and use it whenever I wanted.

"Yuh going to eat it now?" she pestered, knowing full well that I liked the treehouse.

"Awright, only after yuh!"

She pulled the right leg off the grasshopper and crunched it to bits between her teeth.

"Mm-mmm," she said, satisfaction all over her dundus face.

She pulled off its other leg and waited patiently until I gathered enough nerve to open my mouth. Reluctantly, I bit into it. It was surprisingly crunchy and tasted almost like grass. We ate the rest of the grasshopper bit by bit. I never did tell Punsie and the others. I just said that we played games in the treehouse. I begged Petal once to let Punsie into the tree-house, but Punsie and the others had teased her too much in the past. For the next two years, until I turned eleven, Petal and I secretly ate live grasshoppers.

~ ~ ~

Uncle Freddie had been gone almost a year, and he had never written to his mother or to Monica. He had sent Dennis shoes and a felt hat, along with a miniskirt for Monica and a pair of red booties for his baby son, a pair of pedal-pushers for Punsie and black patent-leather shoes for me. The gifts came in a Christmas parcel my mother and Uncle Peppie sent to our house. The first time Uncle Freddie wrote, it was to me. I'd just turned ten that August. I was playing marbles outside the front gate with Punsie and some of the boys from the street when the mailman rode up to our gate on his bicycle.

"Mail from foreign, Molly!" he shouted. I scooped up the marbles I'd won and ran to take the letters from him. One was from Uncle Peppie, one from my mother and the last a birthday postcard for me from Uncle Freddie. Mama opened the two letters and separated out the two money orders, which she put in her bosom.

"Yuh mother seh to give yuh a big kiss. She seh another parcel on de way."

I proudly showed her the birthday card from Uncle Freddie, with its picture of Niagara Falls. Mama's face was glue tight, and she roughly asked, "Yuh can eat dat?"

With that she rose from her wicker chair and stormed through the gate. I sat on the verandah, staring at her empty chair, then I crawled under the fence to Petal's yard. I searched the grass under the treehouse for grasshoppers, found four and ate them like they were my last meal. I climbed to the treehouse and sat alone, confused by Mama's response to the card. Petal joined me sometime later, and I let her fill my head with stories of America's wildlife, which she'd watched on TV.

It was pitch-dark outside when I crawled under the fence and back to our verandah. The house was empty. I waited in the dark, frightened of the bats that stuck to the ceilings. This was the first time Mama had left me on my own. Uncle Mikey soon came home.

"Come here, Dutty Bus," he said softly, using his special name for me. "What happen? Where Mama?" I began to cry as I relayed the story about the postcard.

"Dat bwoy going to be her ending," he said, more to himself than to me. "Yuh eat anything dis evening?"

I shook my head.

"Come let we mek a egg sandwich, and then we go find her. Don't cry."

We ate scrambled eggs with hard-dough bread and a glass of milk, and then we went to Olive's to look for Mama. She wasn't there. Later we found her in Shady's Hideaway. She was sitting on a chair, her head slumped on one of the Formica tables.

Uncle Mikey pulled her to her feet, and with his hand around her waist, we walked her home. Later, as we all huddled together on the living-room couch, Mama began to talk.

"Mikey, you and Peppie really good to mi, and we go through whole heap together. Ah remember when ah had dat restaurant downtown years before we buy dis place, is you and Peppie helping me. Unnu scrub pot, wipe de floor, carry de heavy meat, de big crocus bags full a green banana and yam. Freddie and Glory was still in Port Maria wid Mammy. Dem never know 'bout dem hardships, for ah mek sure ah send money every month fi dem. De only thing ah couldn't provide fi any of you was real education, ah never have dat kind a money, and ah needed you two bwoys to help me. Unnu come to town when unnu just turn teenager and unnu never fail me yet . . . you bwoys help mi and treat mi better dan a husband. Nutten nuh come free or easy especially fi poor people. Unnu father was a wutliss wretch, and a same way Freddie turn out. But old-time people always say when a tree bend from de beginning, it grow twist up, and him just like him father."

"Never mind, Mama, don' think about all dat. We don't want for anything now. Dat is de past," my uncle said. His hand travelled across her back and massaged her shoulders. She began to cry, and we both hugged her.

Much later, in bed, Mama's hands searched for mine as she began to sing softly, her breath burdened with Wray & Nephew white overproof rum.

My Bonnie lies over de ocean,
My Bonnie lies over de sea,
Oh bring back, oh bring back . . .

Mama got up early the next morning. She looked tired, especially her eyes, but neither I nor Uncle Mikey said anything about the night before.

"Mama, de garden need a little care," my uncle said, looking through the living-room window.

"Yes, ah know, ah try keep up wid it, but wid de baking, sometimes mi too tired. Ah will have to get somebody to look after it."

"Ask Grand-aunt Ruth nuh, she have 'nuff people coming in and out of her restaurant."

"Yes, dat's a good idea." She went to the window, looked out at the garden and said, "Ah miss Freddie, truly, if only fi dat." My uncle didn't respond.

~ ~ ~

The summer of 1968, when I was eleven, I saw my first restricted movie. Mama never ever missed a Sophia Loren movie, and she was not going to miss *Two Women* when it played in Kingston. We walked to the Ritz Theatre and saw RESTRICTED: 18 YEARS AND OLDER plastered on the billboard right beside Loren's sultry lips and big breasts. Mama held my hand firmly, looked the cashier straight in the eye and bought our tickets. As usual we took seats in the front row. Before the movie started, Mama nodded at the screen. "Nutten wrong wid seeing dese movies," she said. "There is good and bad in de world, and yuh have to see both to mek sense of things."

The big curtains parted and when Sophia Loren came on the screen there was a hush in the theatre. Her lips were tomato ripe, her body generous, her eyes hungry. We rode with her as she and her young daughter fled on a dirty, over-crowded train from Naples to the countryside. She was shab-bily dressed, with bags and bundles on her head, but even in the midst of war, she was beautiful. Her daughter was by her side. For a moment I imagined Mama and me running from war. Sophia Loren looked so strong, she could protect her daughter from everything. Her hips swung just like Mama's did when she carried the pastries in a cardboard box on her head to the Chinese shops.

Suddenly Sophia Loren and her daughter were being raped by Nazi soldiers. I wanted to look away but couldn't. Instead I held tightly to Mama's hand. I felt the young girl's fear and panic. Mama held me tight, saying, "Cover yuh face, put yuh head in mi lap."

But it was too late. I had already seen too much. As we left the theatre, a little breeze rustled and a brown-and-white stray dog yelped in the dark. I held on to Mama's hand. The movie stayed with me for a long time.

~ ~ ~

Grand-aunt Ruth's restaurant was at the corner of Maxfield Avenue and Lyndhurst Road, in a piazza at the southeast cor-ner. Mama delivered baked beef patties there twice a week, in return for a small sum of money when they were sold. The Chinese pastry shops that she supplied were nearby on Chisholm Avenue and Waltham Park Road. Sometimes, she walked over with the pastries in the morning after I had gone off to school, but it was not unusual for her to deliver them after I got home from school. Grand-aunt Ruth's restaurant was always our last stop. We would sit outside on the piazza while Mama and Grand-aunt Ruth caught each other up on other people's business and talked unendingly about the left-over colonial government and corrupt politicians. Aunt Joyce, who stitched uppers at Maressa Shoe Factory, often joined them after work. She never took much to cooking, so she ate her meals at the restaurant, where she often met her suitor of the month. Mama claimed that eating out every night wasn't healthy, even though the food was cooked by Grand-aunt Ruth herself. "Normal people eat at home around a dining table."

Mama would ask her, "Joyce, when yuh going to settle down? It nuh good to run round so, yuh know." Then Grand-aunt Ruth would add, "Is true, Joyce, yuh need to settle." Aunt Joyce always answered with a mouthful of laughter, and her body, not unlike my grandmother's in its generosity, threatened to bounce right out of her tight cotton blouse and pencil-straight short skirt. Then she'd say, "Ruth, yuh is like the kettle calling the pot black. You settle down?" She'd laugh again, looking around to capture her effect on any man passing by. "But mi have God," Grand-aunt Ruth would answer. "Mi nuh need no other man."

"Well, there yuh go," Aunt Joyce answered, laughing again.

Truth was, Grand-aunt Ruth owned her house and had taken in Ivan and Icie as her own. "Yuh nuh change at all, eh?" Mama responded. "From we growing up as gal pickney, a so yuh stay, and mi end up wid de pickney dem and wutliss man." Mama never failed to say that, and it always made me sad, but Aunt Joyce never let it bother her much. Again she'd say, "There yuh go." But I hated when Mama got like that. How could she regret having children when she loved me so much? I would not have been there with her had it not been for her daughter, Glory.

Grand-aunt Ruth had no children, but she'd do her best to comfort my grandmother. "Nuh mind, Maria, yuh have dem already and dem a big pickney, remember God have a plan for all a we."

That particular night stands out even now because of a man named Myers, who came into the restaurant to buy a meal. Oxtail and rice, he ordered, then later a beef patty. When Grand-aunt Ruth told him that her sister had made them, he bought another one, praising their spices. He was a friendly man and he seemed to know a lot about everything. He bought us all a round of drinks: white rum for my grandmother, a beer for Aunt Joyce, soft drinks for Grand-aunt Ruth and me. Aunt Joyce invited him to sit with us. We learned that he was a gardener at Hope Road Botanical Gardens. Mama's eyes lit up.

"Ah looking for somebody to help out wid mi garden. Yuh have de time?"

"Yes, ah can find de time," he said. "Give mi de address an' ah will come by tomorrow afternoon." He was an ordinary-looking man, tall, medium-build and clean-shaven, younger than Mama by a few years. Aunt Joyce tried to interest him in other talk, but it was clear that he was concentrating on gardening and on my grandmother.

He came to our house the next day, and I was glad that I was on summer vacation. Mama and I were sitting on the verandah.

"Miss Maria, nuh worry. I can have dis garden back in top condition in no time. Dis is de kind of work I been doing all mi life."

"Yuh can start tomorrow?" Mama asked.

"Can start right now if yuh please, Miss Maria."

"No, tomorrow okay, de sun too hot."

"Yes, it too hot to dig up de beds and transfer plants, but not hot enough to stop mi from pulling some weeds and raking de grass," he offered.

"Dat okay. Start tomorrow. One more day won't mek any difference. And call mi Maria. How much yuh going to charge mi? And how often yuh will work?"

"We can discuss that tomorrow," he said sheepishly.

"No, mek we do it now," she said.

He turned to me. "So how yuh doing, little Miss?"

"Fine," I said shyly.

"Still on holidays?"

"Yes."

"Good, den yuh can be mi little assistant in de garden." His nut-brown eyes danced and I no longer felt so shy.

"Yes, ah can help, ah can pick out de weeds," I said, my excitement building.

Then he turned back to my grandmother. "Ah can uproot some of those bird-of-paradise plants. Dem want to tek charge of de garden," he said, smiling.

Mama sent me inside to get him a glass of ice water.

"Start tomorrow den," Mama said when I returned with the water. Then she added, "Some garden tools round de back. Yuh can look at dem. Mi son use to help mi wid de gardening, yuh know, but him gone to foreign."

"Dat nice," he replied. "Good opportunity. England or America?"

"Canada," she answered. "Molly, show Myers where de garden shed is."

I ran ahead of him to the shed. He turned the tools over in his hands as though they were prizes. He felt the point of each to examine its sharpness. He looked around the backyard, took out his measuring tape and wrote some figures on a piece of paper. Then we came back around to join my grandmother on the verandah.

"Everything is dere. Ah will start tomorrow early before de sun come up." He sat down again and asked me for another glass of water.

"Yuh have a nice backyard, Maria. Ah can get some okra and tomato seeds, callaloo sucker, cho-cho vine, scotch bonnet pepper, green onion and some other provisions to start a vegetable garden in de back." Mama smiled, encouraged by his enthusiasm.

I was up early the next morning. Myers was already in the garden, had dug up the weeds from the four garden beds, fertilized the plants and soaked the beds with water. He was shirtless, his body toned but not muscular. He wore old khaki pants, cut off at the knees.

"Sleepyhead," he teased. "Want some jelly coconut? Ah going to climb de tree after dis."

I spent the day following him around, my belly full of coconut water. He gave me rides in the wheelbarrow all around the yard. I laughed and screamed as I bounced from side to side. His laughter was loud and deep and honest.

Later that day, he piled dried coconuts in a crocus bag and put them in a corner of the kitchen for Mama to make her coconut drops and gizzadas for the Chinese pastry shops.

Uncle Mikey was pleased with the way the yard looked. He commented on the new buds coming up, the large beds of cannas that Myers had introduced and the orchids he had transplanted from the Hope Gardens. "Mama, dis Myers man is a blessing, look how de garden look rich!" Uncle Mikey exclaimed. My grandmother agreed.

Myers came once a week and spent the entire day in the yard, digging weeds, introducing new plants, cutting back the hibiscus and the bougainvillea, picking coconuts and repotting plants. He and Mama grew into a slow companionship. They sat on the verandah or in the backyard, smoking cigarettes and drinking rum, sometimes quietly husking dried coconuts until dusk. Later he'd ride off on his motorbike. Some evenings he took me for rides through other neighbourhoods, around Hope Gardens, where the houses were vast and giant trees protected the owners from curious eyes. I was always glad, though, to get back to our dead-end street, where you could peer into houses through doors and windows that were wide open, and where my friends ran barefoot, flying kites, playing marbles or dandy-shandy.

~ ~ ~

Summer came to a close, and my grandmother and I took our annual end-of-August trip to Port Maria to see Mammy. I loved those visits and always looked forward to them.

Mammy was waiting at the station when we rolled up in the bus, her thinning grey hair tied in a bright square of cloth, her eyes two blue buttons. She was a wisp of a woman, her pass-for-white skin told the story of her mother's mother's journey from Africa and her plight on a sugar plantation in Jamaica. We were loaded down with canned goods and cloth, stockings, hairpins and hairnets. She hugged and kissed us, turning me around to examine how much I had grown.

"Gal pickney, yuh still all skin and bones. Where de flesh?" she teased me, her mouth crowning her toothless smile. "Come let we hurry home, unnu must be hungry."

Mammy's house was a wooden one by the sea. It was perched high on stilts, had a galvanized zinc roof and was painted sky-blue. Her verandah edged out of the yard and almost into the street. Fretwork in the shape of palm fronds framed the windows. The floors were kept shiny with a coconut brush.

There were no fruit trees in Mammy's backyard, except for a coconut palm, and no vegetable garden. The sea was the backyard. My great-grandfather had built the house on a small patch of leased land. That was where Mama grew up and where my mother and Uncle Freddie spent most of their childhood.

As we ate, my grandmother told Mammy all the news from town and read her two letters from the grand-aunts. Mammy couldn't read or write, but she was one of the most spirited and intelligent women I've ever known. She had a memory that wouldn't quit, she seemed to know people's motives, and she knew the Bible from Genesis through Revelation.

"How Peppie? Freddie write yuh yet?" Mammy asked, her voice almost apologetic.

"Write! Write. Dat a de beast of ungratefulness a walk round pon two foot," Mama replied bitterly.

"De Lord is de final judge, Maria, and nuh give up on him. Mi know yuh heart heavy now, but a yuh pickney and mi know yuh love him. In yuh heart yuh grieve, but don't turn yuh back on him, for as de scripture say, what man among you, if him have a hundred sheep an' him lose one a dem, don't leave de ninety-nine in de open pasture and go after de one which is lost?"

"Get mi some water, Molly," my grandmother said. I took my time getting the water and kept my ears open.

"What 'bout Mikey now, any sign of change?" Mammy asked.

"No. The Lord knows ah wish him never have those feelings."

"A change will come, Maria, nuh worry. Just remember fi go down on yuh knees and praise God, Him will tek care of things."

Mama didn't answer. She was not a church-going woman, though she always sent me to Sunday school. Grand-aunt Ruth was the only one who took to going to church like Mammy. It was an open secret that Aunt Joyce went to church to show off her fancy clothes and jewellery.

We made plans to go sea-bathing the next day and to church Friday night, Saturday and Sunday. For as long as I knew her, Mammy had been a member of a revivalist church whose members were known as Pocomanians. Services were held in a boarded-up building with a dirt floor, and were very different from those at the Anglican church I went to in Kingston. Mammy's was a livelier church, and spirits came upon the congregation, sometimes making them dance and jump and talk in tongues. Once, when I was seven, the spirit had come upon Mammy. Her seventy-year-old body had moved in a frenzy, and she'd shouted out her praise in tongues. I'd been frightened. Mama had comforted me, told me not to worry, it would pass, and it did. By the end of the service, my great-grandmother had become Mammy once again.

That night she let me play with her hair, running the comb through it, plaiting it, pulling it loose and plaiting it again. Mama sat close by, listening to her mother's hum and to the changing sea, looking at me with pride on her face.

For the rest of the holiday, we sea-bathed, ate fresh fish, sang and listened to Mammy talk of her girlhood. I'd fold myself in the comfort of Mama's lap and listen. Some days the sea was a deep, quiet, shimmery blue, but other times it would turn restless and dark, whipping against the house. On one such night, Mammy began to talk about slavery times.

"Is about 1890 mi born yuh know, so mi pon dis earth long time. Mi see whole heap, mi born not far from here, Port Antonio. Dem time whole heap of ship use to come in from all over de world and dock dere. Is right dere dem dock mi grandmother, tek her from Madagascar, bring her pon slave ship to here." Mammy shook her head, spit in her handkerchief and continued. "Mi never know her, never even know mi own mumma, she dead when mi a baby. But she give birth to thirteen before mi, nine sister and four brother, all mi sisters raise mi after she dead. Ah never school, but mi do wid what mi had, and God never left mi." She smiled and looked up at the sky, her hands raised and trembling in the air.

~ ~ ~

That September I went back to school. I was a good student
and my report cards showed it, but I hated having to sit all day
in a classroom, hated having to be nice and clean in my
starched uniform.

Myers often came to our house. Sometimes he was like
a shade plant in the garden, so quiet that I didn't know he'd
come till he was gone. I often rushed home from school just
to sit with him in the garden. Myers didn't take Uncle
Freddie's place. We didn't fly kites, and there wasn't the same
excitement during crab season, though Dennis still brought
by plenty for us. I think I must have decided back then, sitting
with Myers, that I would work with plants.

"Dirt is life, yuh know, everything grow," he said, covering my small soft hands with his calloused ones. He gently
circled my fingers in the dry dirt. "Wid just water, a little
care, yuh can create beauty wid flowers, grow vegetables and
fruit, yuh won't go hungry. Ah going back to de country one
of dese days, leave de city life."

One evening shortly after I had returned to school, I
came home to find that he had dug and raised a tiny bed for
me. "Molly, ah got some suckers fi yuh to plant," he said
excitedly. "Water dem every morning before yuh go to
school, and in de evening when de sun go down. Yuh should
never water in de sun-hot, it not good for de plants." He
handed me a small hoe to dig into the water-soaked dirt.
"Yuh going to use yuh hands as a measurement to decide
where to plant de other suckers. We don't want dem too close

to each other, and not too far apart." The dirt between my fingers and the smell of the damp earth pleased me no end. Were it not for the tiny suckers, I would have rolled like a pig in the dirt.

"How long dem will tek to come up, Myers?" I asked.

"Patience, little Moll, dat is what it will tek," he said mysteriously. "Yuh just water dem, spend time wid dem, and we will dig for weeds once a week." Later that night, as was our custom, we sat on the verandah with my grandmother, having a cold drink, listening to Uncle Freddie's friends playing soccer and breathing in the scent of mangoes and rose-apple blossoms caught in the night's heat.

A few weeks later, in the middle of the night during a heavy rainfall, I heard Mama crying Myers's name over and over, and hoarse whispers coming from Myers. I tried to wake from my sleep but couldn't. I felt the big bed rocking from side to side, but with the heavy rain outside, it was easy to believe that I was in the sea, safe in the bosom of Mama's arms, and the hoarse whispers were like waves in my ear and Mama's cry a lullaby.

A glorious morning followed the rain, and I awoke to blue skies with streaks of burnt orange and crimson and Mama calling, "Molly, wake up, is school morning, get ready." Her pastries were already in the oven, and she had a steaming bowl of banana porridge and slices of hard-dough bread waiting for me. I wanted to ask her about the night before but thought better of it. After school let out, we went to deliver the baked goods. The box of pastries was perfectly balanced on my grandmother's head and her hips swung under her cotton dress as we walked up our street to Maxfield Avenue.

~ ~ ~

Christmas was always a busy time for Mama and she thrived on the season's demands. There were cakes to bake—the ones she sent abroad to my mother and uncles, cakes for the grand-aunts, cousins and Mammy, special cakes she made for Paul and Helen, Uncle Mikey's friends, and others for our house and for paying customers. That Christmas season was special. My mother had written that she was getting married a week before Christmas, and though she said it was to be a very small no-fuss wedding, my grandmother insisted that she should have no less than a three-tiered cake. Also, Aunt Joyce would be leaving the island the day after Christmas.

We were on the piazza in front of Grand-aunt Ruth's restaurant when Aunt Joyce burst out with the news.

"Dem fire mi, dem dutty shit, after mi work wid dem fi so long. Dem seh mi tief shoes."

"But Joyce, how dem can accuse yuh of dat if nutten nuh go so?" Grand-aunt Ruth asked.

"How yuh mean, yuh doubting mi?" Aunt Joyce said angrily.

"Is not dat she doubt you, but dem nuh seh dem find de shoes in yuh bag?" Mama offered.

"Smaddy plant dem in mi purse. Why mi would a tief dem?"

Mama and Grand-aunt Ruth exchanged looks.

"Even when mi seh to dem, call de police, call de police if yuh think is me put de shoes in mi bag, dem never budge. Dem did want to get rid of mi, because mi start talk 'bout union."

"But why yuh gone talk 'bout union? Mi nuh tell yuh from long time, fi lef dem injustice up to God," Grand-aunt Ruth said.

"Listen, Ruth, when mi haffi work dem long hours mi nuh see no God."

"Yuh must have faith," Grand-aunt said, ignoring Aunt Joyce's irritation.

Aunt Joyce sucked her teeth, and then she surprised us all.

"Remember Ken? De mechanic who use to eat dinner here every evening? Well him in America, in Brooklyn, New York, and him sending mi a ticket."

"Dem say 'nuff opportunity in America," Mama encouraged, "and yuh nuh have no pickney to hold yuh back. Gwaan, gal, go see life, an' nuh think 'bout dem dutty fart you deh work wid. Nuh future nuh deh deh."

"Ah going, but ah worried to death 'bout Mammy. What if anything happen and ah can't find de passage back?"

"Lawd, Joyce," Mama said, "Grab de opportunity, don't let it fly in yuh face. Mi and Ruth will look after Mammy. For yuh branded as a tief now anyway."

Joyce cut her eyes but said nothing. Mama always spoke her mind, even if what she had to say hurt the other person. To ease the wound, Grand-aunt Ruth added, "Joyce, everything will work out. Go, nutten nuh deh here, and sooner or later dem would find something to fire yuh for."

"Joyce, is de best thing to do," Mama agreed. "Yuh and Ken can mek life together, have a family and who knows, maybe in time, come back and buy a big house in Red Hills!"

My aunt Joyce smiled for the first time. "Yes, Maria, yuh right. So mek we have de best Christmas ever."

The talk that evening was celebratory. All about my mother's wedding, Aunt Joyce's departure and Mammy coming down to Kingston for the holidays.

I helped Mama a bit with her baking, mixing the sugar and butter, but I got bored. I much preferred my hands in dirt and water, sticking seeds into the earth. So mostly I sat and watched her. She never used a recipe book to bake from; every detail was kept in her head.

A few days before Christmas, Mama picked up a big brown parcel from the post office. It was from my mother, and packed with shoes and dresses and dolls, games and books full of fairy tales. Uncle Freddie sent nothing. My grandmother gave Monica money for little Freddie Jr. She took it from the money orders that Uncle Peppie and my mother sent. Each time she gave Monica money she cursed Freddie again.

Uncle Mikey had new dresses made for me, Mama, Grand-aunt Ruth and Cousin Icie, and he gave Aunt Joyce a lovely hand-embroidered linen dress as a going-away gift. Christmas left us fat with cake and pudding, turkey and ham— more food than we could finish. I danced and ate until my eyes couldn't stay open. Mama gave the leftovers to people in our neighbourhood who were less fortunate.

We didn't see Myers over the Christmas holidays, and not even Mama knew where he had disappeared to. I came home one evening after school and found him in the garden working.

"Myers, Myers," I greeted him, "where yuh is all holiday? You miss pudding and cake and everything."

"Ah went to de country, mi had some family business to tek care of," he muttered over his shoulder.

"Ah didn't know yuh had family. Who is dem, yuh mother?" He didn't answer, and a long silence hung about the vegetable garden.

Petal called me from next door, so I crawled under the fence and up into the treehouse. I felt uneasy about Myers's response and was glad to get away. Petal had two matchboxes with two grasshoppers in each waiting. We chewed on them, savouring the juices. "Don't swallow," she said to me, "ah want to taste yours." She squeezed my lips open and we exchanged grasshopper juices. She held on to my tongue and I did the same with hers. Then she pressed her body against mine and lay on top of me. She pressed me hard and let out a sigh. We stayed close together and I played with her dundus face for a long time. It made me feel better, especially after Myers acting strange. When I heard my grandmother calling, I hurried down the ladder and back under the fence. Monica had come to visit with Freddie Jr., who was almost three and a half now. He was going to be tall like Uncle Freddie. "Him is de dead stamp of him father," Mama said, smiling. "Come here, little man."

"So yuh don't hear from him at all, Miss Maria, yuh don't have a address for him?" Monica was almost pleading.

"Girl, tek mi advice and forget him. Him nuh good, him is a wutliss son of a bitch. Count yuh blessings, yuh have a nice little boy, look after him and try to better yuhself." I could see by the look on her face that Monica was disappointed with my grandmother's advice. Mama didn't tell her that he had fathered another child in Canada.

Myers appeared at the back door after he had finished

gardening and asked if I wanted to go for a ride on his motorbike. I quickly forgot I was vexed with him and ran to put on my shoes.

"Bring back some grape-nut ice cream!" Mama shouted.

We rode up to the Hope Gardens where he worked, and he named the plants that were new to me. Before we left, he took me through the maze. I got lost a few times, taking wrong turns, but Myers was right behind me. I forgave him all at once for that afternoon. On our way back home, we stopped not just at the ice cream parlour but at Shady's, where he bought a flask of rum. He and my grandmother sat on the verandah and shared it. I sat with them, eating ice cream, counting fireflies and listening to the croaking frogs and Punsie's mother shouting for her to get off the street.

"Ah hear yuh have a nice Christmas," Myers said to Mama.

"Yes, whole heap of food and drinks. Ah did tell yuh dat Molly mother was getting married?" She smiled, happy at the thought.

"Yes, yuh did tell me."

"Well, when ah get de photographs, ah will show yuh."

He sipped his drink slowly, looking as though he had something on his mind, but he said nothing.

"So how your Christmas?" Mama asked. "How everything in de country?" He fingered his drink, looked at the glass, then in a quiet, boyish voice said, "Ah getting married, going back to de country." Mama didn't look surprised, but I saw her shoulders sag just a bit. She didn't congratulate him.

"Myers, yuh never tell me!" I shouted, feeling cheated.

"Molly, it not nuh big thing. It don't need nuh whole

heap of talking." He sounded almost apologetic. "And anyway, we have enough flowers fi talk 'bout," he said, his voice
lighter.

"So when is de big day?" Mama asked.

"Not right now, ah have to save some more money, so
ah can tek care of mi family." He paused, poured himself
another drink as if for the courage to speak. "It not nuh big
wedding, is just to give de children a name."

I didn't know what that meant. I filed it away as something that I had to ask Punsie, and if she didn't know, then
Monica would. After all, I had a name, and my mother
wasn't married to my father; in fact, I didn't even know who
he was. That night the air was light and cool. I felt drowsy and
wanted to curl up in my blanket.

"Molly, tidy up and go to bed," Mama said. "Yuh look
tired, an' is a school night."

It was late when Mama came in. I had been thinking
about Petal and how good I felt when she rubbed against me.
I was sure that night that Myers came to my grandmother's
bed. I felt the bed moving, heard it creaking. I moved myself
to the edge of the bed full with sleep and pulled my blanket
tighter over my face.

On my walk home from school the next day, I stopped
by Punsie's yard.

"Ah have something to tell yuh," I whispered.

She grabbed my hands and we ran toward her mother's
fowl coop. Close by was a dwarf mango tree, crowned in
leaves, which we often climbed for privacy.

"Yuh know seh Myers and mi granny doing things?" I
said, almost out of breath.

Punsie laughed and laughed, as she often did. Then in an equally excited tone she exclaimed, "How yuh find out? Raatid!"

"Ah was on de bed, ah hear it creaking."

"Yuh keeping things from mi?" she joked. "Look how much time mi tell yuh 'bout mi mother." She laughed again, throwing back her head. "So yuh feel de bed a jerk up and down?"

I nodded my head.

"What else?"

"Like what?" I asked.

"Well, dem talk? Dem say anything, like 'go faster' or 'harder'?"

"No," I said, embarrassed now that I had said anything.

"What yuh going on like dat for, yuh don't know is a natural thing for a man and woman? Everybody do it," she boasted. "What you think Freddie and Monica do?"

"Yuh think mi stupid? Of course mi know," I protested.

"Girl, now yuh know 'bout de birds and de bees," she said. "Hey, Molly, yuh know Troy like yuh."

I sucked my teeth but felt nice inside. He was a nice-looking boy who lived on the other side of our street. "Mi not interested," I lied. "And ah have to go home now."

We climbed down the tree and I ran home.

~ ~ ~

When I turned twelve, Uncle Mikey and two of his friends, Helen and Paul, took me to see a performance by the Jamaican National Dance Theatre. After that, we went to see the pantomime at the Ward Theatre. I had never seen live actors on stage before, and I was awestruck. Mama didn't come with us. She much preferred films. "If mi want to see live people act, mi only have to sit down on Ruth piazza," she said.

My mother sent me a beautiful watch for my birthday, with Cinderella inside the glass and a pretty red band. Uncle Peppie sent a card with money. Uncle Freddie sent another postcard, this time of Yonge Street in Toronto. Grand-aunt Ruth gave me a Bible, Cousin Icie and Ivan a piece of coral from Port Maria, and Aunt Joyce gave me a lovely pair of gold sleeper earrings that were the envy of all my friends, but I didn't get a chance to flaunt them. Mama said that I could wear them only on special occasions: Sunday school and Uncle Mikey's parties. Myers gave me the best gift of all, two perfect and beautiful orchid plants.

"Dem might not tek to dis dirt, for dem is specialized plants, but we will see," he explained. "In de library dem have books dat explain dat dem have over fifteen thousand species—is a fascinating flower, but delicate." I gently touched them and promised myself I would look them up.

After my birthday Petal and I celebrated in the tree-house, rubbing on top of each other and eating grasshoppers. I didn't know it would be our last time together, or I might have stayed longer, but Punsie was yelling for me at my front gate. I had promised to play ball with her.

Uncle Mikey celebrated his birthday a week after we returned from our annual visit to Mammy's. His was a more elaborate event that took place in the Red Hills, at Paul and Helen's house, which was absolutely stunning—I had never seen anything like it. It was lit up like a Christmas tree and had a breathtaking view of the sea and downtown Kingston. There were so many rooms it was like a maze.

Mama wore a dress that Paul and Uncle Mikey had designed and sewn for her. It was made of white satin, with strips of gold thread through the fabric. She wore a pair of looped gold earrings from my mother, and her long black hair framed her face in curls. Her dress was the talk of the party, and she looked every inch like a black Sophia Loren. All of Uncle Mikey's friends who came to his Sunday parties were there, as well as others I didn't recognize. Everybody was beautifully dressed. There were more men than women, but that seemed only natural, given that it was Uncle Mikey's party.

Mama was very happy. I saw a rare softness in her face, and her lips rested in a smile. She and Helen chatted, generously helping themselves to the rum punch.

A man named Frank sat behind a grand piano in the centre of the room. He looked to be over thirty, was tall like Uncle Mikey, but had receding hair and a stylishly trimmed beard. He wore a red, open-necked shirt and black velvet pants. We all fanned around the piano and sang "Happy Birthday to You" till I was sure our voices reached past the Red Hills and down to the sea. When the singing stopped, Mama kissed Uncle Mikey on the lips. Then she made her speech.

"Son," she said, "Happy birthday, and ah hope all yuh dreams come true." Her voice broke, then she caught herself and went on. "Ah love yuh more dan words can ever say, so ah will just stop dere." I caught a tenderness in her eyes that she hadn't offered Uncle Freddie when he left the island. The crowd clapped long and heartily, as though at a political rally.

Uncle Mikey's friends also made speeches, then we ate cake, and I had my first taste of champagne. I stuffed myself with more cake and then explored the maze of rooms. Later the lights were dimmed and the stereo played Johnny Mathis, then Otis Redding, Toots and the Maytals. When Millie Small's "My Boy Lollipop" played, the party went wild. She was the first Jamaican to have an international hit song; it reached the top five in both the United Kingdom and North America. The sweating bodies gave off a wonderful heady smell. I danced with my grandmother, showing her how to do the ska and the rocksteady. Helen was next to us dancing with June and then Angela, Frank's sister.

The DJ played a Sam Cooke song, "Cupid," and again the crowd cheered. Frank went over to Uncle Mikey, took his hand and pulled him into a slow dance. I felt Mama close beside me, watching. I had never seen two men dancing so close. At our Sunday parties nobody ever touched like that, except when they held hands for a wide spin.

"Can I see yuh again?" Frank asked Uncle Mikey.

"It all depends," my uncle said in a flirtatious voice. I couldn't see his face, but I knew he was smiling. Frank squeezed him tighter and stole a kiss.

"Naughty, naughty," Uncle Mikey chided, and settled more snugly into Frank's arms. At the end of the song they left the room. I didn't follow. I was watching Helen and Angela dance. They danced slowly, their bodies pressed against each other in the heat, the hems of their dresses above their knees. Beads of sweat had formed on Helen's upper lip. I stood nearby, their bodies brushed mine, and I trembled.

Frank came to visit often, and Uncle Mikey blossomed. He became more talkative, seemed more comfortable with his small, thin frame. Frank was a real charmer. He'd bring fresh-cut flowers for my grandmother, even though we had a gardenful. I especially loved that he brought me bars of chocolate, which I handed out to my friends on the street. He was a sharp dresser and his shoes gleamed with polish. He bought a brand-new black BMW, the first ever parked on our street. We didn't know much about him except that he was the son of a successful hotelier. He told my grandmother that he worked with his father, a man she seemed to know by name and reputation. She didn't say much, just "Oh, dats yuh father?"

Frank and Mama chatted a lot on the verandah. She was, I learned, knowledgeable about the North Coast hotel business, where she had worked many years as a cook. "Is a growing and profitable industry," she often said.

Looking back, I can't say that my grandmother was unfriendly toward him, but during the Sunday parties she began to dance less and watch more. As time went by, Uncle Mikey began to spend part of every Sunday afternoon in his room with Frank. Once, on my way to the bathroom, I noticed Uncle Mikey's door was slightly ajar. I peeked in and saw them kissing each other's mouths. Frank's shirt hung neatly on a rack above the closed window. When I walked back from the bathroom, the bedroom door was shut. I pressed my ear against it and heard the slight creaking of the bed and my uncle's voice sounding like a sparrow's cry.

Hours later, Uncle Mikey's friends were still dancing and eating and talking in the living room, oblivious to his absence. Mama sat crumpled like cardboard.

~ ~ ~

Myers left for the country that September to get married and be a father to his three children. I cried for a long time, and even after I stopped crying, my throat ached each time I looked at the garden and my small bed of flowers. He promised to come back and see me, to bring his daughter who was the same age as me, but he never did.

Uncle Mikey began to spend more time away from home, and Mama took it badly.

"Is Barbican yuh live now?" she asked him one night when he came home late. She had waited up for him and I was in bed.

"No, Mama," he said in a light and happy voice. "Ah just working out some plans with Frank. Ah going to try mi hands at designing a signature set of towels, bedsheets and napkins for the hotels, so dat's why ah not around as much."

"So what 'bout yuh present job?"

"Dat going well, but ah just feel dat ah need to branch out, try different things. Frank thinks it would be a good idea, him say de hotel business profitable."

"Yuh just be careful," Mama warned. With that she left him in the living room and came to bed.

Uncle Mikey didn't heed her warning, and Mama began to drink more heavily. It was no longer an afternoon at Olive's, or a drink or two on the verandah, or a nightcap at Shady's after our movie. She'd drink for a week straight, beginning at dawn. Some mornings she left when I left for school, stopping at Olive's, Shady's or her new place, Johnny One Stop. In the evening she'd stagger down the street. Sometimes she'd be sitting on the verandah, nodding off when I came home from school. Sometimes she wasn't there when I got home. I'd fix myself something to eat, then play on the street with Punsie and the others. When she didn't come home by dark, I'd search the different rum shops till I found her.

One evening when I was almost thirteen, I came home from school and saw Mama nodding off on the bed. I changed my clothes and was about to go over to Punsie's, when she suddenly asked, "Where yuh going?" Her voice was slurred.

"Over to Punsie, Mama, ah going to look for little Freddie."

"No, tek off yuh clothes. Come lie down wid mi."

My anger stewed as I lay there beside her, smelling her rum breath, seeing her mouth drooling saliva onto the pillow. When she began to snore, I tried quietly to get up, but she grabbed hold of my hands.

"Stay, don't go out dere. Mi nuh want nutten happen to yuh. Mi have to deliver yuh to yuh mother in good condition." I could hear my friends playing hide-and-seek, throwing balls, could hear their light-hearted laughter.

"She have yuh when she just turn fifteen, and yuh not far from dat. Yuh soon turn thirteen, mi want hand yuh over to her widout any damage. Mi was fifteen when mi had Peppie, spoil mi years. Mi was a good girl, obedient, mi never bad, or run up and down, mi just fall in love too quick. But him mother had big plans fi him, and mi never in de picture, mi family too poor, and mi mother couldn't read or write.

Quick-quick she send him go England, and mi never hear from de bwoy again, not one letter, not even a postcard. When Peppie born, de woman say a not her son pickney even though him was dead stamp of him. Mi had it rough, life never easy fi mi, even now. . . ." My grandmother's voice had a regretful edge to it. She held on tightly to my skinny arms and dozed for a minute, then went on.

"A nuh likkle try mi try wid all mi pickney dem. Mi really try. An' de second man mi fall for was Oliver, and him worse. De only thing him ever give mi was a wedding ring, which mi had to sell, fi feed de pickney dem. Man nuh good, yuh can't depend on dem. Dem is just a necessary evil. Ah glad Freddie left de island. Peppie will tek care of him. Teach him responsibility. Thank God Glory gaan. It would a pain mi fi see her go through pickney after pickney wid dem wutliss man, wid not a penny in a dem pocket. All dem have is promises. . . ." She drifted back to sleep.

The binge lasted five days. Each night I had to go to bed early. I was glad when the drinking ended and I could be back out-side with my friends. Punsie had come by every night, but after getting no answer at the locked door, she gave up. It was the same with Petal, who'd called over the fence. It didn't take long for them to know why I couldn't come out to play. Sometimes when Mama lost herself to the rum, her feet would become unsteady and I'd have to hold her arms and support her as we walked down the dead-end street.

After the binge had ended, I was playing marbles with Punsie when she asked me if my grandmother was okay again. Even though she was one of my best friends, her question embarrassed me.

"What yuh mean?"

"Ah mean if she stop drink now."

I knelt in the dirt and looked steadily at the marble in my hand, unable to answer.

"Is nutten to feel any way 'bout, everybody pon de street know dat yuh granny drink and drunk and stagger up an' down de street," she laughed. "Look pon fi mi father—him do de same, except him a man."

She hadn't said it in a mean way, but I didn't care. She had no business. I got up from the ground, seized her and punched her in the mouth.

"Shut up," I said.

She punched me in the stomach and I fell down. Punsie came at me again, but I was quick and grabbed her plaits. We rolled around in the dirt until her brother Dennis pulled us apart.

"What unnu fighting 'bout? Unnu a gal pickney yuh know, it nuh look good."

Punsie flashed her hands and cut her eyes at him.

"So what de fight about?" he insisted.

"Nutten," Punsie said. She brushed herself off and strolled up the street toward her yard. I went home feeling mixed-up but justified in hitting Punsie.

After the fight, I spent less time outside. Instead, I sat watching Mama prepare pastries for Grand-aunt Ruth's and the Chinese shops. She looked so different then, no hint of the other woman who had kept me hostage, no sign of the woman who had cried and railed about life.

"How come yuh not outside playing wid yuh friends?" she asked one evening.

"Nutten, ah just have lots of homework, and ah borrow gardening books from the library to read."

"Dat good, girl, maybe yuh can tek over Myers' job," she teased.

Dennis came sometimes to help with the weeding, and I kept up with the watering, but the magic was gone and even the flowers looked faded.

Punsie and I resumed our friendship. It was hard to stay angry for long on our street. Everything took place outdoors and you had to pass people's houses to get to the main street. It wasn't the first time Punsie and I had fought; it was just the first time we'd hit each other.

One day I came home from school to hear shouting coming through the windows of our house. I lingered outside in the front yard and listened.

"Ah telling yuh fi yuh own good, it nuh right to be so brawling. If yuh a go do it, do it under cover. A danger yuh putting yuhself in."

"But Mama, what mi doing? Him ask mi to come to de country wid him for de weekend, what wrong wid dat?"

"Yuh nuh see nutten wrong wid dat? Suppose man come in wid gun and machete fi kill unnu ass?"

"Mama, it safe. Frank go dere all de time," Uncle Mikey pleaded.

"All de time? Ah sure yuh just another in a long line a man. Yuh be careful, dats all I haffi seh, because dem money man will run lef yuh at the smell of trouble. Remember yuh is a poor uneducated bwoy."

I made a lot of noise slamming the gate and went inside.

Mikey had a small suitcase beside him and he was sitting, looking up at Mama like a little boy as she stood by the stove cooking.

"Hi, Molly," he greeted me, "how was school?"

"Fine, Uncle," I said, and went straight to my room.

A car horn blew shortly after, and through the window I could see Uncle Mikey climbing into Frank's car. When we sat down to have dinner, Mama's face was a dark cloud. "A trouble him a head for, yuh know. Mi see it, as sure as God mek apple." She spoke with finality.

I didn't respond. Nobody had explained anything to me.

That evening Petal came to the fence. "What going on wid yuh granny and uncle?"

"Nutten," I said. "Nutten, yuh too fast."

"Mi know is what. Mi mother and father say him like man. Dem say Mrs. Galloway son is a battyman."

"Yuh lie!" I shouted at her.

"Yuh uncle is a battyman, yuh uncle is a battyman," she sang.

I started yelling names back at her: "Dundus gal! Dundus gal! Yuh ugly like mi don't know what. Yuh face favour when bammy eclipse. No wonder yuh nuh have no friends. Yuh would frighten God himself." I went up on the balcony shivering with anger. That was the last day I ever talked to Petal. She'd come to the fence and call out to me, and she even slipped a note through the fence saying she was sorry, but I never forgave her.

Before I turned fourteen my periods started. Mama lectured me about not getting close to any boy, not a touch, not a kiss. By then, I was spending more time with Punsie, and I was interested in a boy who lived down the street. Punsie was the first one

I told. Although we were just a year apart, she had all the answers, and she enjoyed teaching me.

"Punsie, mi granny say if a boy kiss mi or touch mi, ah can get pregnant. Is true?"

She laughed loudly, then said, "Yuh too fool. Come mek mi talk to yuh some more 'bout de birds and de bees."

We hurried around to the fowl coop where we would have privacy and sat on an old bench.

"First of all," she whispered, "a boy have to put him thing inside of yuh fi get yuh pregnant. But yuh can't get pregnant wid a kiss, or even if de boy feel yuh up."

"How you know that?" I asked.

"Mi know, mi try it already, and remember, mi have a big sister and brother. Anyway, Junior like yuh. Him say mi must tell yuh."

"Don't fool wid mi!" I exclaimed proudly. "Yuh sure?"

He was one of the most handsome boys around, and I hadn't expected him to take a second look at me. I wasn't a pretty girl. I was skinny and tall, taller than Punsie. My only redeeming features were my eyes, bright and shiny like ackee seeds, and my large breasts.

Punsie nodded. "What mi must tell him?"

"Tell him mi like him too. But him can't come to mi yard. Ah will meet him over at yours."

~ ~ ~

The more my grandmother drank the more Uncle Mikey stayed away. One day while we were eating dinner, he announced that he was moving the first-Sunday-of-the-month parties over to Angela and Frank's house. Mama's face showed no emotion. I could not tell whether she had known that it was just a matter of time before this happened, or whether it was a big surprise. Her voice betrayed her. It had all the heat of hot oil in a frying pan.

"So dis area nuh good enough fi yuh anymore? A rich-people neighbourhood yuh want now? Remember where yuh come from. I tell yuh dat all de time, so nuh fool yuhself. Remember seh de higher monkey climb, de more him ass expose."

"Is nutten to do with that, Mama, is just dat ah can see dat yuh don't tek much to Frank. And ah trying mi best not to upset yuh. Ah don't want nutten to come between mi and yuh," he muttered.

"But look how long yuh having dese party, and nutten don't come between us. Yuh don't see fi yuhself how me and de others get on good? Yuh ever see mi show dem bad face? Look pon yuh birthday party—or yuh feget?"

"Well, is just you ah thinking 'bout," he tried again.

"But me and Frank nuh have any problems with each other. Him can come here anytime, for dis is where yuh live."

"Okay, Mama," he gave in.

"Eat up yuh food before it get cold," she said, satisfied. Then she added, "Me and Molly going up to Ruth restaurant. Yuh want to come for de walk?"

My uncle said he wasn't up to it, he was tired and needed an early night.

~ ~ ~

A month later, my grandfather arrived at our house un-expectedly. It was an unusually cool February night, and my grandmother and I were in bed talking about Port Maria and her childhood when we heard a faint tap at the front door.

"Somebody must be out dere. Who could be out dere at dis hour?" Mama grumbled, getting out of bed and turning on the light. I followed close behind. "Who out dere?" she called boldly.

A man's voice I didn't recognize came through the closed door. "Maria, is me. Open de door."

"Me who?"

"Is me, yuh husband, Oliver."

"Oliver?" she echoed in disbelief.

"Yes, yuh husband," he said again. "Ah sick, ah need help. Open de door."

"What happen to hospital, dem nuh open all night?" she asked through the closed door.

"Maria, please, please have a heart, open de door," he pleaded.

She was silent for a moment while he kept tapping, kept pleading with her. I stood behind the curtains dividing the living room from the bedrooms, feeling half-afraid. I'd never met him, but I had heard enough over the years to be frightened of him. He used to beat my grandmother.

She opened the door. I heard him come in and slump onto the couch. Then my grandmother's voice: "Lawd God Almighty, a who do dis to yuh?"

She shouted at me to get a sheet and a blanket, a wet rag, Dettol, bandages. I couldn't make out anything of his fea-tures, even though the lights in the living room were on. His face was caked with blood and his elbows bruised and bleeding. His pants were torn at the knees.

"Boil a pan of hot water and bring another towel, dis need more dan a wet rag," Mama ordered.

Soon after she sent me to bed. I kept my ears open. "Yuh can stay here for a night or two, then yuh have to leave."

Uncle Mikey found him lying on the couch that night when he came home. He rapped at our bedroom door, and my grandmother got up and went into his. I heard them whispering. "Mama, him can't stay here. Nuh room is here, not for him."

"Is only till him head feel better, after mi nuh fool fi go tek up crosses."

Uncle Mikey sighed. They kissed good night and Mama came back to bed.

The next morning I awoke almost as early as Mama so that I could get a good look at my grandfather. I still couldn't see much of him though, because Mama had bandaged most of his face. As I was leaving for school, she covered him with a light cotton blanket.

That night we didn't go to the movies as we usually did on Fridays. Instead, I watched Mama feed my grandfather chicken broth and wash and change his bandages.

Miss Gatty was as surprised as Uncle Mikey when she came on Saturday and found my grandfather lying on the couch. Still, she greeted him like a long-lost friend, before she went out to do our washing. Mama sat with her outside, smoking. I was, as usual, dusting the furniture in the bedroom, with the window open, the curtains flying in the breeze.

"Him come back?" Miss Gatty asked, distrust in her voice.

"Come back?" My grandmother sucked her teeth. "Him come here, sick, sick, couple nights ago. Mi had no choice."

"Well, maybe him change, yuh can only wait and see, Miss Maria."

"Change? Change to what, Gatty? Dem only change pon de outside. You know as much as me, dat man is like croaking lizard. So how Randolph?" Mama asked, changing the topic.

"Him all right, still running wid de woman and de rum . . . it could be worse, so mi thank God, 'cause at least him bring home a little money fi help wid de house, and him nuh beat mi."

"Sometimes, dats all yuh can ask for, mi dear," my grandmother answered. "Anyway, Gatty, mek mi go bake dem pastries, for dis is what bring in mi little money."

"See yuh next Saturday."

"Yes, if life spare," Mama said

On Sunday morning, my grandfather moved from the couch into our bedroom to make way for Uncle Mikey's friends. He didn't look as bad as he had a few days back, though he still had on bandages, and he was strong enough to eat rice and meat, and to talk.

"So yuh is mi little granddaughter," he said, stretching his hand toward mine. "Pleased to meet yuh, granddaughter. Come here, come sit on de bed, mek mi have a good look at yuh."

I wanted a good look at him, too, so I sat on the edge of the bed. He was a big man, tall and muscular, like Uncle Freddie, with the same big hands and wide smile. And he was charming.

"Give yuh grandfather a hug," he said cheerfully. I did and it felt good.

"Ah can see dat yuh is definitely a Galloway." He laughed, showing straight, yellowing teeth. Then he asked the usual questions: "How school? Yuh studying yuh lesson? What yuh want to be when yuh grow up?"

I wanted to be a gardener. Now he broke into a big wide laugh that reminded me of Uncle Freddie.

"Be careful wasp don't sting yuh and snake don't bite yuh and ground lizard nuh run yuh down. Dem is some of de professional hazards." He laughed again, and I began to laugh, too. Since Uncle Freddie and then Myers had left, I hadn't really laughed much with adults.

"Tek me now," he continued. "Mi have professional hazard in mi job as a car dealer. It can be dangerous some-time, for dis Kingston have some crazy people. Dem want brand-new car and dem don't want to pay brand-new prices. So dem come to buy a second-hand car and believe dem driving out a brand-new car.

"Imagine, car bruk down and man come back fi mash up yuh face. Dat is what ah mean by professional hazard." He touched his chin, which was still bandaged, smiled and kept talk-ing. "In my job yuh have to be salesman, boxer, head doctor, everything roll up in one. If ah never have boxing potential, ah wouldn't be here to tell de story."

That evening during the party, I never left the bedroom, except to get two plates of food. Mama had made steamed snapper, cooked down in onions and thyme and a touch of pepper sauce, along with roasted yams, and rice and gungo peas. I heard Uncle Mikey and Frank talking in his room next door and worried that they might spoil my evening with my grandfather. The bed creaked and my uncle called out Frank's name. My grandfather was so busy telling his own stories that he didn't hear. But I did, and for the first time, I was vexed with Uncle Mikey.

Monday, when I came home from school, a cot and the small dresser that held my clothes had been moved into a corner of the living room for me. A lovely floral screen made a partition. My grandfather started sleeping in Mama's bed. His bandages came off and he returned to work. Each evening he came home carrying a paper bag holding another piece of his clothing. Mama spent a lot of time at the stove, cooking like she did for Uncle Mikey's parties, and we ate together as a family most evenings. Even though I had stopped talking to Petal, I still cared about what she thought. I made a point of watering the garden when she was out in her yard. I looked haughtily over the fence at her, for the whole street knew my grandmother's husband had come back.

The odd night, he missed supper and came home smelling like the bottom of a rum barrel. He'd bang at the door, because Mama hadn't given him a key.

One Saturday evening he came home from work earlier than usual and handed Mama a small bottle of perfume. In no time supper was simmering on the stove. Mama washed and combed her hair and slipped into her best jersey dress, showing off every inch of her curves.

"Maria, yuh still one well-built woman. Nuh young gal can put a candle to yuh."

She smiled, pleased. But she still sucked her teeth. "Yuh gwaan wid yuh sweet mouth, yuh cyaan fool mi." A peal of laughter followed.

We sat down to eat and Grandfather Oliver amused and flattered her some more. She fell right into his rhythm, bold as the overgrown bougainvillea hanging over our barbed-wire fence. Maybe she was thinking of the girl from the seaside town who fell in love with a handsome boy named Oliver. Later we settled in the living room, and Grandfather Oliver searched through our record collection.

"Maria, remember dis?"

It was a song I'd heard at Uncle Mikey's parties, "Man in the Streets," by Don Drummond. Then he played one by Duke Ellington, who was one of her favourites. He pulled her to her feet and I sat on the couch and watched them dance a waltz and then the cha-cha, her skirt swirling above her knees.

A soft breeze drifted through the windows, and the scent of bougainvillea swept into the room. I wished that all my friends on the street could see my grandmother.

For a time we stopped going to Grand-aunt Ruth's restaurant on Saturdays. Instead, we stayed home and waited for my grandfather to come home to supper. Mama always dressed up, and I was the bartender, serving rum and coconut water, or just plain water with ice. We still went to the movies every Friday night, since that was also my grandfather's night to stay out late with his friends.

Mama looked more rested in her face. I looked forward to evenings with my grandfather, just as she did, though I couldn't help but compare him to Myers. Myers knew the difference between the little tomfool lemon-yellow wing, he knew the patoo by its call, he knew lizards by their croaks and which ones changed colour. Grandfather Oliver didn't much care about flowers or their names, and he didn't know the difference between crabgrass and carpet grass, a hummingbird and a doctor bird. Still, I welcomed the change in Mama.

With Grandfather Oliver around, Uncle Mikey spent less and less time at home. Mama must have noticed, too, but she said nothing about it. Then one day Uncle Mikey told her that he was definitely moving the Sunday parties to Frank's place.

"Mama, ah mek up mi mind, ah think it best. Ah feel uncomfortable with Oliver around, is not de same. Him don't like mi friends and ah don't want no embarrassment."

"But Oliver have no say in anything. Him nuh own de place."

"Mama, ah don't want to argue or cause nuh strife, but him is here over six weeks, him move in him clothes. Him live here."

Mama knew Mikey was right. She knew she had fallen back on a promise, but she didn't let up.

"Him nuh own de house, so him can't come and gwaan wid nutten."

"Mama, ah just think moving de party is de best thing right now."

Her last words were biting. "Well, what is to be must be, then."

She got up, went into the bedroom, changed into a street dress and left the house. Uncle Mikey went into his room and closed the door. I was sure I heard him crying. I sat on the couch and felt weighed down and helpless. I had nothing to offer.

Punsie's loud banging at the gate was a welcome distraction. "Ah have things to tell yuh!" she said.

"Like what?" I asked.

"Ah cyaan tell yuh here, come let we go round de fowl coop."

She handed me a folded-up piece of paper. "Here, is from Junior."

I read the letter and suddenly I felt light.

"Ah feel love in the air," Punsie teased. "Read it out loud nuh. What yuh think mi is, just a messenger?"

"'Dear Molly,'" I obliged. "'I like you for a long time. I been watching you come up and down this street. I like the way you walk and I like your eyes. I want you to be my woman. With all my heart and soul your one and only man Junior.'"

I shook with excitement. Things weren't so bad, after all. "What mi going to do, Punsie, how mi going to answer?"

"Girl, come, let we go over to mi house."

I went off with Punsie, still feeling free and light. There was no one to stop me, since Mama wasn't home. We went into the bedroom Punsie shared with her sisters and closed the door. She pulled out a bunch of magazines from under her bed. I'd seen them before in the Chinese ice cream parlour, hanging on a fish line in a section with a large sign saying ADULTS ONLY. Punsie handed me three *True Confessions*: I'M CARRYING MY HUSBAND'S BEST FRIEND'S BABY. HOW I LEARNT 101 WAYS TO KISS MY MAN. I WAS A LOVE CHILD.

"Here, carry dem home and read dem."

I rolled them up in an old newspaper and hurried home. Mama hadn't returned yet, and Uncle Mikey's door was still shut. I climbed into my cot, read Junior's note again and slipped it in my panties. I covered myself up with a light cotton sheet and read the magazines. Late that night I heard Mama and my grandfather come in.

The good times ended as unexpectedly as they began. One Saturday evening we waited and waited for Grandfather Oliver, but he never came home. Sunday morning he arrived in time for breakfast. I didn't hear what Mama said to him— I was on my way to church. After that, he rarely came home for supper. Instead, he'd come in late at night, drunk. Soon there was talk on the street that he was seeing a barmaid and visiting a policeman's wife a few streets over. My grandmother paid no attention to the rumours, but I didn't like them, because Junior lived on the same street as the policeman. Mama and I started going back to Grand-aunt Ruth's on Saturday nights. She didn't say anything about my grandfather's goings-on. Instead, the conversations centred on Aunt Joyce, who was into her third job in America and dissatisfied with her new home, on my mother and her new husband, on my uncles and on Mammy.

One Saturday morning the policeman paid Mama a visit. "Miss Maria, ah don't want to show yuh any disrespect," he said, "but yuh husband running wid mi wife."

Mama didn't seem surprised. "Hold on, sah." She turned and shouted, "Gatty come here!"

Miss Gatty hurried to the verandah, drying her hands.

"Gwan, sah, talk," Mama said.

"As ah was saying, ah don't mean no disrespect, but if ah catch yuh husband inna mi yard again, ah gwine to kill him.

Ah come warn yuh, because ah know yuh long time, and mi know all yuh children dem and mi respect yuh."

Mama was calm. She lit a cigarette and invited the policeman to have a seat.

"Mr. Sergeant, ah thank yuh fi come all dis way to tell me dis, but yuh shouldn't bodder. Yuh shoulda just kill him."

The policeman was as taken aback as I was. As Miss Gatty was, too.

"But Miss Maria—"

My grandmother cut him off. "Yuh want a drink, Mr. Sergeant?"

"Ah wouldn't mind one for de road, dat is, if yuh tekking one, too," he said.

"Gatty, bring three glasses and some ice."

I was proud of the way my grandmother handled the situation. I left them drinking and went up the street to see Punsie.

~ ~ ~

One afternoon, I arrived home from school and heard Mama shouting as I walked through the gate. A few neighbours were standing on the street, straining their ears. I passed them, cut my eyes and slammed the gate behind me.

"Ah want yuh to tek yuh rass claat outa dis house!" Mama waved her arms. "Come out for yuh nuh own dis house. A nuh fi yuh blood and sweat go into dem walls."

"Yuh forget mi is yuh legal husband—yuh think yuh can just put me out like dat?" he shouted back.

"Tek yuh carochis and yuh rass claat outa mi sight. Her voice increased in volume.

"Woman, yuh nuh shame? Yuh nuh see yuh neighbours outside listenin', and we granddaughter," he said, pointing to me.

She gave a long suck on her teeth. "Shame! Den yuh think if mi did tek shame and stamp on mi forehead, ah would reach dis far? Sorry, Mr. Galloway, but mi don't know dat word. Mi nuh have no secret, so de whole street can gather round and listen."

Mama was standing next to the stove over a huge pot of boiling water.

"Come, come, if yuh a bad man, yuh dutty rass, yuh."

"Maria," he said, his voice going soft, "mek we sit down and talk. Dis is foolishness. Yuh know is you ah love."

"Love? Oliver, yuh bring mi to mi senses, because ah forget dat love is a terrible weakness dat mi can't afford. It hurt mi every time."

"Maria, mek we talk. All dis is a misunderstanding," he repeated, his voice going softer.

"Yes, de misunderstanding was to scrape up a piece a garbage like you and bring inna mi house!" Her voice was even louder.

"Maria, quiet nuh. We can work dis out."

"Oliver, de only thing we going to work out is when yuh lef mi house."

He reached toward her.

"Don't come no further, or yuh face going to look like a punctured tire." She lifted the pot of water and faced him. He backed away. "Oliver Galloway," she shouted, "get yuh rass out of mi house. Ah don't want fi see yuh when ah come back." She left the house, slamming the gate behind her.

That evening I almost wished I hadn't stopped talking to Petal. I wished I could crawl under the barbed-wire fence and up into the treehouse. I didn't want to face the street or I would have gone to Punsie's house. Instead, I lay on my cot, rereading Junior's letter and *True Confessions*.

The next day when I got home from school, the cot had disappeared from the living room, and my dresser was back in Mama's bedroom. My *True Confessions* magazines were gone and there was no sign of Grandfather Oliver's belongings. Mama never said his name again, never played Duke Ellington again.

She began to drink heavily once more. During her binges we didn't clean the house. She didn't buy the morning paper. She didn't crochet or embroider centrepieces. She didn't read Harlequin romances. Miss Gatty didn't come. The Chinese shops got no pastries, cigarette butts piled high in ashtrays, and the fridge was empty except for bottles of water to chase her rum and some fruit from the yard. Sometimes I boiled rice and ate it with butter. Rice was the only thing I knew how to cook.

I hated it when her binges fell on holidays. Lent and Easter were bad. The summer holidays were worse. On school days, I was free to roam till dinner. Sometimes after school I'd go over to Punsie's house, see Junior, kiss him and let him feel me up. But during summer holidays I was trapped. The summer I turned fourteen I decided to do something about it.

It was the night of Junior's seventeenth birthday. Of course I was invited to the party and had planned for it with Punsie for months. I wanted it to be special. If Mama had been sober, she would have simply given me a warning about men and their hands and let me be on my way. But she had started a binge three days before. The day of the party, Punsie sat with me on the verandah, watching my grandmother nod off, a cigarette still burning in her hand. I put it out and tried to get her to go to bed, but she insisted I go with her. I wanted to talk to Punsie, to plot a way out of the house. Uncle Mikey had given me a beautiful minidress for my birthday, and I wanted to show it off with the new shoes my mother had sent me. The sun was still high in the sky.

"Mi don't know what to do, Punsie," I whispered.

"Tell her yuh going to shop to buy something to eat. Give her some more to drink and den mek yuh escape."

"Den what if she find out?"

"Lie."

"Okay." Punsie left and I got Mama to bed and offered her another drink.

"Put on yuh pajama," she slurred.

"Mama, remember Junior party?"

"Mi nuh want yuh spoiled. Mi nuh want to hand over any damaged goods to yuh mother." One hand clasped mine tight. I heard sounds of laughter coming from the street, where my friends were playing hopscotch and skipping. There was nothing for me to do but stare at the ceiling, hate my mother for going to foreign, curse the father I never knew. I had one of Mama's romance novels on the bed and a notepad that I used for scribbling notes about plants, but I didn't feel like reading or writing. The windows and door were locked tight, it was hot and I wanted to shake Mama like a rag doll, stick pins in her, poke her eyes. Instead, I stared at the ceiling while tears ran down my face. I looked over at her dry and parched face, at the heavy black circles under her eyes, her lips pink from too much drinking. Her hair a matted mop. Her clothes were heavy with the smell of sweat and rum. There was nothing I could do. I thought about Junior dancing with other girls. Punsie would be there having a good time. Junior would know I was locked up in a room with my drunken grandmother. I wondered how I could face him the next day.

Throughout the night Mama woke up periodically and rose to make herself another drink. I thought of sneaking some rum into my glass of milk so I could numb my rage, but I didn't really want it to go away. That night meant too much to me. I didn't want to forget it.

I took my pen and a notebook and wrote, "Dear Uncle Peppie." I stopped. I knew what I wanted to say all right, but I was scared of saying it. I crossed out his name, tore up the page and started again. This time I wrote, "Dear Mom." Then I crossed that out and started again.

"Dear Glory, please come." I crossed that out, too. I asked myself, come for what? She'd never come back here. I looked at her photograph on the dresser, and for the first time in my life I missed her.

I tore up that page and started again. "Dear Uncle Peppie, please, we are in trouble. Please send for us. Mama drinking heavy. I am scared she will die. Uncle Mikey vex with her. He's hardly around. He spends most of his time with his friend Frank. Grandfather Oliver was living here for a time, until he and Mama quarrelled and he left."

I crossed out half the letter. There was nothing new in it. Peppie knew about her drinking. All her children knew.

I didn't want to take care of her anymore. I didn't want to be locked up in this room. I couldn't stand walking the street in shame. I didn't want to hear another fight with Uncle Mikey. I didn't want to see another man coming into our lives and then leaving. I crumpled the paper and hurled it across the room.

Everything was closing in. My throat felt hot and dry. I tore another piece of paper from the notebook and took up my pen.

~ ~ ~

The drinking stopped and our windows and doors were opened to let in the air. Our sheets were clothesline clean and Mama's hair was washed. Fresh-cut flowers filled our house. Gatty came and did the washing. Mama began to bake for the shops again. Uncle Mikey still wasn't around much, and when he was, he hardly left his room. He rarely ate with us anymore, but Mama still left a plate for him on the stove every night.

One day near the end of the summer the mailman delivered an airmail envelope to our house. I knew without looking at the return address that it had to be from Uncle Peppie. I watched Mama's face as she read the letter to herself. Then she folded it and put it in her bosom.

A few days later, she told me that Uncle Peppie wanted us to come to Canada. "Tomorrow morning, we going downtown to look 'bout we passport. Now listen to mi. Ah don' want yuh to say nutten to anybody. Not Ruth, Mikey or any of yuh friends. Nobody. When de right time come, we will tell people."

Mammy was the first to know. We visited the house by the sea one last time. The flesh on Mammy's fingers had shrivelled almost to the bone, but her voice was still strong and her body straight.

"Maria, go. It never too late to start life as new. Is time fi lef de island. It do too much damage." Then she turned to me. "Molly, when yuh go foreign, try go see Africa. Go see where mi grandmother born, and kiss de dirt fi mi. Come let we pray and bruk bread fi de last time."

The sea was calm, the sun shining against it, sparkling like Mammy's blue eyes. We held hands and Mammy prayed.

> *I will lift up my eyes to the mountains;*
> *De Lord is yuh keeper;*
> *De Lord is yuh shade on yuh right hand.*
> *De Lord will protect yuh from all evil.*
> *De Lord will guard yuh going out and coming in;*
> *Him will keep yuh soul.*

We spent the night there. When we left, we promised to write and to come back to see her again. We promised to take hugs and kisses to her three grandchildren in Canada.

"If life spare, Mammy, ah will see yuh before long," Mama said.

"If life spare, Maria, and wid God's blessing," Mammy replied.

Grand-aunt Ruth was the next to know, and then Miss Gatty. I whispered the news to Punsie and Junior, promising them both that I'd write.

Uncle Mikey was the last to know. Mama told him a day

before we were to leave. It was cruel, and I felt guilty and relieved at the same time.

"How long unnu know?" he demanded. "Dis . . . is a . . . conspiracy. Everybody turn pon mi. How unnu could do dis?" His voice a whimper.

I squirmed uncomfortably in my seat and looked away.

Mama had the last word. "Conspiracy, so yuh call it. Well, mi call it life."

He kicked one of the dining-room chairs over on its side, stomped into his room and slammed the door. Mama was unmoved. "Come mek we finish de packing," she said.

The next day we boarded the plane for Canada.

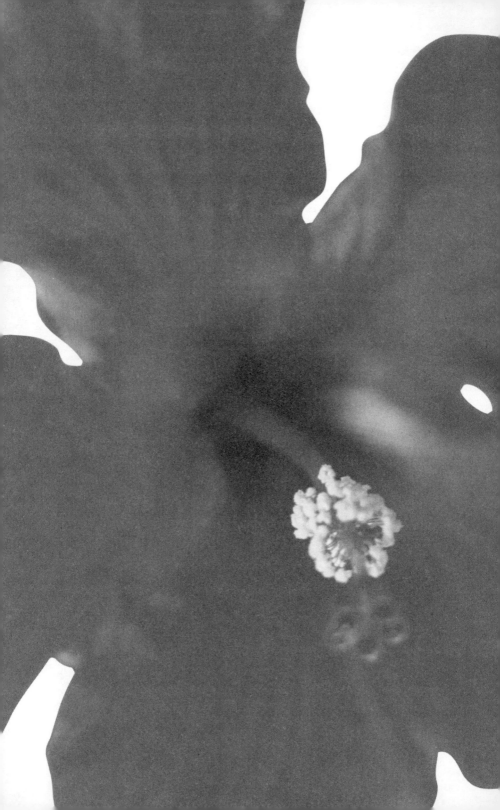

Part Two

No One Tests the Depth of a River with Both Feet

I THOUGHT OUR STREET would be easy to forget and I'm sure that Mama thought so, too. It wasn't. For the past was where we lived and dreamed our lives to perfection.

We had been living with my mother and her husband, Sid, for almost a year, and we still weren't used to our new country, our family and our apartment.

We had arrived at Toronto International Airport in the autumn of 1971 to a wonderful welcome. I was fourteen, my grandmother a voluptuous woman of forty-seven. We had packed fried fish, roasted yam and breadfruit, cassava cakes and baked goods for everyone, as well as fever grass, dried cerasee, leaf of life and other herbs for medicinal purposes. Mama was happy and proud that night; there was no trace of the unhappiness her face had held at the Palisadoes Airport when we left. We sat in my mother and Sid's living room and talked and talked, catching up on people we knew who lived abroad. My mother talked about her job as a nanny looking after three children, Uncle Freddie about his job as a bouncer at a West Indian nightclub. Uncle Peppie and Sid worked as mechanics at the same garage, and Val, Uncle Peppie's wife, was a legal secretary. I

talked about school, and Mama told stories about her pastry business and about Mammy, Grand-aunt Ruth and the others we had
left behind. There was no mention of why we'd come, and beyond
the usual pleasantries, not much was said about Uncle Mikey.

As they sat and talked, I watched. Uncle Freddie still had
his boyish charm. Uncle Peppie was everything Mama said:
solid, decent and sincere.

Val was a lot like Mama, a forceful woman who hovered
protectively around Uncle Peppie. That might have been why
Mama took an instant dislike to her.

My mother turned out to be a beautiful woman, nothing like I'd imagined. Her skin was the colour of burnt toast,
her eyes blue like Mammy's, a nose that flared at the tip like
Grandfather Oliver's, her black, shoulder-length hair
straightened to perfection. She just about took my breath
away when I saw her for the first time. I'd hoped for love and
tenderness, yet I knew she could never take my grandmother's
place. I also knew as I sat in the living room next to her that I
wasn't the daughter she'd expected. I'd wanted her to hug and
hold me, make much of me, but it was Uncle Freddie and Uncle
Peppie who fussed over me.

Glory was thirty now, tall, slender, her breasts the size of
small Jamaican oranges. Her face held the same steady, unsmil-
ing gaze as Mama's. I stared at her all night, which only seemed
to make her more uncomfortable. She hardly looked at me. I'd
only seen two photographs of her, one taken years back one winter, wearing a heavy coat, standing in deep snow against a car,
and the other her wedding photo, showing a small, slim woman
in a white minidress with a white veil slightly lifted away from her
face. In person, she looked more beautiful than in the pictures.

I was tall for my age, slim like her, but my breasts were already rivalling Sophia Loren's, and I was very conscious of them as I sat next to my mother. Sid, my stepfather, was about the same build as my mother, tall like Uncle Freddie. There was a space between his white front teeth and he exuded confidence.

The moment we arrived Mama assigned herself to the post of housekeeper, cook and adviser. My mother welcomed it. She wasn't a house-proud woman or interested in proving herself in the kitchen. She preferred to be out of the apartment, clubbing with Freddie and Sid. Mama didn't mind. She wanted to be needed. She was content to hold down the kitchen and cook, iron, listen and lend advice. Glory went to her job and did the washing at the local laundromat on the weekend—that's about all I can remember her doing. I was less content. Though Uncle Freddie and Uncle Peppie came around a lot to see us and ate with us every Sunday evening, I didn't spend the time with my mother that I'd hoped I would. I began to wonder if she really was my mother. The fact that I didn't look anything like her only made me wonder more.

"Nuh mind," Mama said whenever I complained. "She is yuh mother, in time she will grow fi love yuh. Remember she still young an' she nuh used to pickney roun' her." Mama's comfort and promise got me through those months. At school I was the odd girl out and hadn't made any real friends. I was a bright student, especially in math and science, so girls would ask me to help them with their assignments at lunchtime and before class in the mornings, but they never invited me anywhere. I wasn't cool enough. Glory didn't want me making friends anyway. She warned me to be careful of

Canadians and their undisciplined manners, and she had more stories to prove her point than I cared to listen to.

Glory and Mama got along well at the beginning because Mama was determined to make up for all the years they had spent apart, not just when Glory lived here in Canada but also before that, when Glory lived in Port Maria. She was also grateful that Sid had made Glory a respectable married woman. But despite her gratitude, Mama was quick to give Glory advice that was not in Sid's interest. One Saturday morning when Sid was at work and I was cleaning the bathtub, I overheard them talking.

"Mama, Sid serious, yuh know, about wanting a baby. Ah don't know what to do."

"Mi dear, as much as mi like Sid, ah don't think yuh should have any pickney now, is not a smart thing fi do. Yuh need education, yuh need fi uplift yuhself, and baby cyaan do dat fi yuh."

"Den what mi going to tell him?"

"Tell him? Nuh tell him anything. When him ask again, tell him yuh trying. Him don't have to know nutten."

"Ah don't know Mama, it not as simple as dat," my mother worried.

"How complicated it can be, den?"

"Ah don't want to lie to Sid. We don't have dat kind of relationship."

Mama sucked her teeth. "Girl, you a idiot? A nuh today mi know man, and dere is no such thing as a honest relationship, nuh care what dem tell yuh. So yuh try yuh best and protect yuhself. A three pickney yuh lef here a morning time fi look after, where yuh going to get time fi baby? And furthermore, yuh don't even turn mother fi Molly yet."

Glory didn't answer right away. After a while she said simply, "Is true, Mama. Is true."

My grandmother gave her lots of other advice about work, about how to handle Sid's occasional late nights out with friends and his wandering eye, and about how to take care of money.

"Mek sure yuh knot up something separate. Yes a yuh husband, but dat don' mean all things equal. So put away some savings fi a rainy day. Things can turn, and when dem turn, dem usually turn bad. Give mi de money, mi will knot it up and save it fi yuh right here," she advised.

Glory was also determined to make up for the years she and Mama had spent apart, and she insisted that Mama not get a job.

Every Sunday we had a full-course Jamaican dinner complete with rice and peas, fried chicken or curried goat, coleslaw salad and freshly made carrot juice. Uncle Peppie, Aunt Val, Uncle Freddie and whatever woman he was seeing at the time would join us for dinner. Occasionally a friend of Sid's named Justin came to eat with us, too. Those Sundays reminded me of our monthly parties on the dead-end street in Kingston, but they were not nearly as exciting. Nice, yes, in an ordinary sort of way, but there was no glamour. The only one who vaguely brought any of that was Uncle Freddie, who came dressed to the nines and always had a beautiful woman on his arm. Still, the dinners brought us together, to laugh and to remember what we chose.

During our first spring in Canada, we visited Niagara Falls. Mama was awed by the natural wonder and amazed that the United States was just across the water. We took photographs, ate ourselves drowsy with a picnic of fried chicken, fried dumplings, sweet potatoes, rice and peas, corned-beef sandwiches, hard-dough bread, escoveitched fish and bottles of juice. Uncle Freddie's new girlfriend, Joanne, came with us to the Falls. She was a Canadian girl whose parents were Jamaican and had settled in Alberta long before Freddie or Peppie or Glory arrived in Toronto.

Joanne was a lovely woman, years younger than my uncle. She had a boyish grin that suited her athletic build. She was quiet, rather shy and a great card player. Her one weakness was a tendency, sometimes, to drink a bit too much. Freddie seemed happy and started bringing her with him whenever he visited us.

From time to time, Mama would talk to Freddie about little Freddie, telling him that he should help Monica raise the child. His answer was always the same: "Yes, ah intend to, Mama." He never did. I know because my grandmother and Monica corresponded, and in each letter Monica asked after Freddie. Sometimes Mama would rail about him to me. "Dat boy so wutliss. Ah never know him would treat him own flesh and blood dat way, especially him first bwoy chile."

I wasn't the only one whose ear she held. She complained to Glory and Uncle Peppie, too. In the beginning Glory listened, but eventually it became clear that Mama's complaints had worn thin. It was the same with Uncle Peppie, except he never let on to Mama.

Uncle Peppie came to see her every Friday after work and stayed for a few hours to talk or watch television with her. Mama would be sure to have his favourite meal cooked: stewed

red peas with pigtails and salt beef, white rice on the side. She'd
sit and watch him eat and look content. She took great pleasure
in cooking and baking, and always sent Uncle Peppie home
with pastries fresh from the oven. She also made sure that
Freddie picked up his cornmeal pudding every Saturday.

"Ah glad ah able fi do all of dis for dem pickney. It use to
bother mi sometimes back home when ah consider dem over
here in de cold wid no mother fi cook something fi dem."

Mama also crocheted centrepieces for the tables, arm-
rests for the couches, tablecloths, bedspreads, cushion covers, teapot covers, pot holders, sweaters and vests, and each
of her children received these items.

Uncle Freddie was the one who protested the most.
"Mama, ah don't need all dis, mi is a bachelor, yuh know,"
he'd say seriously.

"Nuh talk nonsense, den yuh don' think one day yuh
going to marry. Put dem up, yuh wife will know what to do
wid dem, " Mama said with finality. Soon everybody protested
that they had too many centrepieces, too many teapot covers
and no place to put them, but that didn't stop Mama. "Mi
soon find other people who will appreciate dem," she'd say to
me, putting them in cardboard boxes and storing them away.

Despite her activity I began to see that she was growing
bored. She was never the type to stay at home or to sit for
long. Each week, Uncle Peppie gave her money for cigarettes
and other small items, but she longed to earn her own
money, as she had on the island. I knew she wanted to walk
down the street and have people recognize her, say, "Good
morning, Miss Galloway," talk with her about the weather, or
the government, or the rising cost of food.

She had her daily routine here down to a science. She tidied the house in the mornings after we all left, then she'd decide what to cook, watch her soaps on television, have a shower and wait for me to get home from school. Then we'd sit and talk until Sid and Glory came home. She especially looked forward to Friday evenings when Uncle Peppie came to visit, and on Sundays she cooked a big supper for the whole family.

My mother and I got along very much like sisters, and not close ones at that. I had never called her Mother and still called her Glory, and she never introduced me as her daughter to her friends—I was always Molly. Mama was our mother. I hardly went anywhere with Glory except to Kensington Market and the laundromat. On rare occasions Mama and I were treated to a drive in Sid's car, but mostly we stayed home and watched the world on television. I had to be home right after school or I'd have a lot of explaining to do, especially to Glory, who figured my breasts were going to get me into trouble. I preferred Sid to Glory; he was much more easygoing and he talked to me like an equal. He didn't order me around, or treat me like I was a walking time bomb because of the size of my breasts.

I remember buying a halter top with some money Uncle Freddie had given me when summer arrived. It was a red-and-black polka-dot halter top that I had looked at longingly in the Zellers store window for weeks. The weekend I finally bought it, we were having a few more people over for Sunday dinner. Sid's friend Justin; a friend of my mother's, Eileen, and Aunt Val's nephew Jeffrey. I had bathed and combed my hair carefully and put on the halter top, feeling quite pleased with myself. Suddenly I saw Glory's face reflected in the bedroom mirror.

"Tek it off, tek it off, Jesus God Almighty, where yuh think yuh going in dat?" she screamed at me. She had never talked to me like that, and I was quite taken aback, as were Sid and Mama. Luckily the others hadn't arrived yet.

"Glory, is what happen?" Mama asked, coming out from the kitchen. Sid was in the living room drinking a Guinness.

"Nuh dis gal, look pon what she have on fi sit down round de table," she said, pointing at me.

Mama looked at me.

"What is de problem, Glory?" she asked again, this time looking at her daughter as if she had gone insane.

"Yuh don't see de top dis girl have on, Mama?"

My grandmother focused on my halter top, but there was no alarm in her eyes.

"Glory, ah don't see anything wrong wid de blouse," she said.

"Mama, you call dis a blouse, dis little piece a cloth dat barely cover up her tittie dem?"

I stood there, half-frozen with embarrassment.

"Glory, what yuh getting so upset 'bout? Yuh expect de girl fi dress up like old woman? Yuh nuh know seh she is fourteen? De top look fine to me. Yuh acting like Molly is some gal dat run up and down and catch man. Nuh bother tek no liberty wid her for me raise her proper."

Sid got up from the couch and looked in our direction. He shook his head in disgust. The look was not wasted on my mother; she ran into her bedroom and slammed the door on us. Sid sucked his teeth and went back to his Guinness and baseball game.

"Leave yuh blouse on, girl," Mama said as she turned back into the kitchen.

I went to our room and sat on the bed. My mood had turned sour. Freddie and Joanne arrived, and Glory came out of her room to greet them as if nothing had happened. I hated that about her, the way she could so easily move from one mood to another.

"What happening, brother, how yuh doing? How yuh doing, Joanne?" she greeted them cheerfully.

I sat in the bedroom stewing. Another knock at the front door and I heard Justin's voice, then Eileen's.

"Molly!" Mama called out. "Come help mi."

"A so we look nice. Yuh really growing into a looker," Uncle Freddie greeted me. Everyone turned in my direction and smiled—Glory just barely—as I went to the kitchen to help Mama.

Uncle Peppie and Aunt Val were the last to arrive, and it was clear that they'd been quarrelling. Uncle Peppie was even more low-key than usual, and Aunt Val wore a guarded look all through dinner, but that didn't take away from the food or the enjoyment for everyone else. Mama seemed oblivious and kept a running conversation going with her sons and the rest of the men, all the while encouraging them to eat more. Uncle Peppie and Aunt Val left a short while after dinner, she saying she had some work to finish.

Eileen was the next to leave.

The men were in the living room drinking rum and watching boxing. The women, me included, were in the kitchen washing and putting away the dishes. The weather was the topic of conversation. Mama kept saying that she could not believe that a place with so much snow and cold and ice in winter could get so hot and humid come summer.

Joanne lowered her voice and said, "I have something to tell you and I need your advice." Everyone looked in her direction. "I'm pregnant."

"Congratulations, girl," Glory cheered.

"Shh," Joanne said with a finger over her mouth. "Freddie is not too happy."

Glory looked at me with those eyes that said adult talk, so I busied myself and took the garbage to the side door where I could still hear but not be seen.

"What yuh mean?" Glory asked.

"Well, he wants me to have . . . to have . . ."

"Him want yuh throw it away?" Mama finished.

"Yes," she whispered, "but I really want this baby."

"Well, maybe yuh should wait a little," Glory cautioned.

"So yuh suggest dat she dash it away too?" Mama sounded angry.

"No, Mama, but is two of them in it together . . ."

"Him will never be ready. Look pon little Freddie in Jamaica."

"Shh . . . shh . . ." said Joanne. I felt sorry for her, because I knew there was no stopping my grandmother when she felt strongly about something.

"Girl, if yuh want to have yuh pickney, have it, but don't look pon mi son fi any help, because it won't be there. Yuh have to stand up on yuh own foot."

"Mama, ah don't think yuh have any right to—"

Mama cut her off. "Glory, yuh don't own mi mouth and mi have a right to speak when mi want to."

I went back into the kitchen, determined not to catch my mother's eye.

"Please, don't fight. I don't want him to hear," Joanne pleaded.

"Hear what?" Freddie asked matter-of-factly as he strolled into the kitchen to get another beer.

"Nothing, just woman talk," Glory said.

Mama confronted him. "Why yuh want de girl dash away her pickney?" she demanded.

My uncle's eyes looked mean. Joanne's looked scared. Tears dripped onto her white cotton dress.

"Yuh talking behind mi back? Didn't we agree dat dis was between us?" he shouted.

I clutched my hands and waited for the next move.

"How unnu like cow down woman so?" Mama asked. "Is a pity she tek up wid yuh and mi sorry mi never warn her, but mi think yuh change. Ah shoulda know better, for zebra cyaan change dem stripe. Look on de lovely pickney yuh have in Jamaica and not even a penny yuh would send fi buy food fi him."

My uncle's eyes flashed to Glory.

"Mama," my mother warned. But my grandmother sucked her teeth. I went to the bathroom and came out with some tissues for Joanne. The poor girl had begun to tremble. I made myself small in a corner of the kitchen and prayed that Mama would quiet, for she was only making the situation worse.

"That's enough, Mama, stop interfering in mi life," Uncle Freddie said abruptly, his eyes fire hot.

"Yuh think yuh can shut mi up?"

"To hell wid you," he blazed at her. And he pulled Joanne roughly from the chair, grabbed their things and stormed out the door. Glory ran after him, mumbling, "Calm down, Freddie, calm down."

Sid and Justin continued to watch the boxing match on television, cheering on their favourites as if nothing had happened. My grandmother sat down on a kitchen chair, a cigarette between her lips and a self-righteous look on her face. I kissed her on the side of her neck and went to our bedroom.

~ ~ ~

Uncle Freddie never came to Sunday dinner again. Uncle Peppie and Aunt Val came to a few more, then one Sunday Val called to tell us that her sister and her husband were in town and they were entertaining at home. Mama didn't seem to care, but I had lived with her for so long that I knew better. She was at the stove turning the fried chicken, Glory was at the kitchen counter helping with the coleslaw salad, and I was grating the carrots for juice. Sid sat in front of the television watching sports.

"We have enough chicken here for tomorrow dinner, and enough to mek a sandwich for yuh and Sid to tek to work, so nothing won't waste. It will save mi cooking tomorrow and ah can iron Sid shirts and a few of your things dat sitting dere in de wash basket."

"Don't worry yuhself, Mama, relax. I can do them one evening," Glory said, totally out of character. Mama didn't miss a beat.

"Since when yuh like fi iron?"

"Is not dat, Mama, ah just think yuh should be outside enjoying de summer weather. There is a nice park round de corner."

"Okay, me and Molly will go," Mama answered. She waited as if she knew the conversation wasn't finished. Glory said nothing more.

At the dinner table that evening, Glory announced that we were invited to dinner at Aunt Val's the first Sunday of the following month.

"To what do we owe dis honour?" Mama asked, her voice subdued.

"Nothing, Mama. Val just want to entertain at her place, and yuh cook for us so much Sundays dat she thought it would be a nice change."

"I see."

Sid and I exchanged quick glances.

"De rice and peas tasty, Mother Galloway," he said.

"Thank yuh, mi son," she said in a meek voice I didn't recognize.

"Yes, Mama, and di chicken too," Glory added hastily.

"Uh-huh." Mama nodded.

We got through the dinner with a bit of small talk. Sid and Glory left shortly after to visit some friends. I washed the dishes and emptied the garbage, then settled with Mama in front of the television.

"Ah wonder what dat bitch have up her sleeve now?" Mama huffed. "When dem see yuh strong, dem try everything fi bring yuh down."

"But, Mama, mi don't think she mean anything bad," I said.

"Yuh don't know de likes of people, for life nuh half tek wid yuh yet. It long and yuh have 'nuff fi learn. And mi know dis one is a bitch pon wheels, mark my word," she countered.

I said nothing after that, and then Mama got up and switched the channel to a variety show. We sat and watched the program in silence.

Mama and I spent a lot of time together during the summer, and our talk almost always went back to our old street, the Ritz Theatre, Sophia Loren, our flower beds, Grand-aunt Ruth's restaurant. We missed our home and our freedom. Perhaps I missed it even more than Mama because I longed for my crowd, for Punsie, Junior, the others on the street and even Petal.

On Sunday we went to Aunt Val and Uncle Peppie's for supper. Our first surprise was seeing Uncle Freddie and Joanne there. Since the quarrel at our apartment, they hadn't come around or even called, but neither Glory nor Sid seemed surprised to see them. Mama carried her anger well, at least in front of Aunt Val and the others. She greeted them politely. Freddie kissed her as if nothing had happened. Joanne couldn't look Mama in the eye.

Aunt Val cooked much the same food as Mama: fried chicken, rice and peas, a green salad instead of coleslaw, plus a mixed-vegetable dish, potato salad and a macaroni-and-cheese dish. That was the first time I'd ever eaten macaroni and cheese, and it was delicious. Aunt Val had also made a pineapple upside-down cake for dessert, along with a fruit salad. The food was good and we enjoyed it. Glory praised the variety of dishes. Sid, like me, loved the macaroni and cheese, and under the circumstances Mama had to say something complimentary. But she didn't fool me; I knew her words didn't come from the heart. Even I could see that by preparing so many different dishes, Aunt Val was trying to show what a good cook she was.

We stayed much longer than Mama cared to, but since everyone else was comfortable, it would have been rude for her to insist we leave. Uncle Freddie played the perfect son, encouraging her to touch Joanne's belly. "Mama, come feel yuh next grandson, is like him can't wait to come out and see life." Mama didn't; instead she lit a cigarette, pulled hard on it and said, "Ah hope de little one have a stable life and grow up to know him father," she said. Then she turned her full attention to Joanne, asking, "When is due date?"

Aunt Val and my grandmother played a kind of tug-of-war. Mama was clearly satisfied with keeping a polite distance, but Aunt Val was pushing to be the perfect daughter-in-law.

"Mama, did you like the dinner? I hope you enjoyed the rice and peas and chicken, even though that is your specialty." Mama nodded and a smile appeared on her face. It might have been genuine, but I remembered her calling Aunt Val a bitch.

"Did you enjoy the macaroni and cheese? That's Peppie's favourite," Aunt Val pressed on.

"Mi never care too much for it, too dry. Dem things suppose to be moist wid 'nuff cheese and milk," Mama said. My aunt's smile dropped. Uncle Peppie got up from his seat in the living room and headed for the steps to the basement, and Sid and Freddie followed. There was a second-hand couch, stereo, a television and a bar my uncle had built down there.

Mama got up to use the bathroom, and I refilled juice glasses and asked the others if they wanted another slice of cake. When I helped myself to a little more macaroni and cheese, Glory gave me a grateful look.

Of course it followed that there would be a quarrel in the car going home.

"Mama, dat comment to Val wasn't nice, yuh know," Glory said.

Mama laughed. "What yuh want mi fi do, lie? De something dry like cork; as fi de chicken wid all dis barbecue sauce fi gravy." Mama laughed louder.

In the rearview mirror I caught the smile on Sid's face.

"Mama," Glory chided, "it not very funny. Val is yuh daughter-in-law, and when yuh say things like dat, it mek Peppie feel bad."

My grandmother sucked her teeth. "Unnu always bet pon de wrong horse, so yuh want to come cuss wid mi now because of Val?"

"Mama, it just not right. Yuh can't go to people house and insult dem food."

"So yuh a come teach mi etiquette now?" Mama asked, scorn plain on her face.

Somewhat wearily Glory said, "Yuh know what, Mama, mek we done dis talk." Sid turned up the radio.

Mama and I didn't go back to Aunt Val's for quite a while, for even though we were invited, Mama had no desire to go. Our Sunday meals balanced themselves on one foot. Sometimes Sid and Glory ate with us and other times they went to Aunt Val's, where they were joined by Uncle Freddie and Joanne.

Uncle Peppie still visited every Friday evening, and he remained the prize of Mama's eye. Still, the summer dragged; only so much time could be spent writing letters back home. Eventually we took Glory's advice and started going to the local park. That's where Mama met her first friend in Canada.

His name was Paolo. He was short, stout and in his late fifties. We had been in the park several times, often sitting on the same bench watching the people around us: children on the swings, young people kissing under trees, others just sitting and looking about like we were. Mama often brought along a cloth bag with her crocheting or knitting and her pack of cigarettes. At first we didn't pay any attention to this man who kept passing by us in the park. Every time he passed our bench, he slowed his pace and smiled at my grandmother. One day Mama, never one to be shy, said, "Howdy do, sir?" An uncertain smile spread across his face, but he kept on walking. Then one day he brought a bunch of daisies and offered them to her. I still remember the look of surprise and pleasure on her face as he handed her the flowers. "For you," he said, smiling.

"Thank you," she said. "Sit down nuh."

He sat down next to her, obviously pleased with himself. "My backyard," he said proudly.

"Nice," Mama responded, sniffing the flowers.

He came every day with daisies, and there was no doubt that Mama was flattered. She began to take more care with her hair and the way her dresses fit. Soon they settled into a comfortable routine. They didn't talk a lot because he was Italian and did not speak English fluently. Mama had a thick Jamaican accent, and sometimes when she couldn't find the right English word, she'd use a Jamaican one. He did the same with his Italian. The peaceful silence between them spoke volumes.

At their second meeting Mama asked him if he knew Sophia Loren. He smiled and shook his head. Mama seemed surprised.

"Yuh don't know Sophia Loren?"

"Italy big place," he said with another smile.

"What 'bout movies, yuh never see her in movies?" she persisted.

He smiled again and nodded. "We go see her?"

"What him say?" Mama asked me.

"Ah think him say you and him can go see her, or maybe him mean a movie wid her," I explained. Mama nodded back.

Throughout that summer, Paolo kept our bedroom filled with flowers. Some afternoons he'd buy us ice cream, and we'd sit and eat it as we watched the people go by. Sometimes I'd leave them to themselves and walk around the park, admiring the flowers and trying to guess their names. Paolo lived a few blocks away from us with his daughter and son-in-law. He was as new to the country as we were, and just as lonely. One day he invited Mama to dinner at his house, but she flatly refused. On our way home that afternoon I asked her why she had said no so quickly.

"Molly, yuh still young. Him is not what mi need right now."

I didn't understand what she was talking about. She tried to explain.

"Molly, ah need somebody to mek life wid. Him just come here, him helpless just like mi. Yuh nuh understand yet, but mi know him daughter would a laugh when him tek mi home.

Is one thing we meet at de park, hold hands and him bring flowers, even a movie would be nice fi go to wid him, but fi tek mi home?

"Mi like him, but too much obstacles. Me black, him white. Ah know you cyaan always look at things in colour, but some things just is. And as much as mi think some a dem black man can learn a thing or two from white man, like how fi treat woman, mi nah tek de chance." She paused, wiped the sweat from her brow and added, "Molly, in life yuh will learn dat black man is a necessary evil. Mi know dat, for mi live wid dat poison all mi life."

We were quiet on our walk home. We never said anything to Glory or Sid about meeting Paolo; they must have assumed we picked the flowers in the park. One afternoon Paolo brought a serving of pasta primavera in a Pyrex dish for us. It was the first time we had ever tasted Italian food. Mama was impressed, said she found it tasty. He gave her the recipe and she said she'd try to cook it.

"Well, ah never think ah would see de day when a man cook fi me," she said to me, her face glowing from the attention. "Nuh man never really cook fi mi except Mikey," she said, and I heard regret in her voice. She went quiet after that. There had been no mention of Uncle Mikey since we'd left the island. I gently touched her hand.

We stopped going to the park shortly before the end of August. Mama told me there was no point in leading Paolo on, and it would be too hard to explain to him why the relationship could go nowhere.

My fifteenth birthday was a disappointing event. Nobody remembered except Mama. She presented me with a small birthday cake decorated with multicoloured icing and set a bottle of sparkling apple cider on the table after dinner. Glory's beautiful face was a mixture of surprise and embarrassment, but she managed to hum a few notes of "Happy Birthday to You." Later, Sid put an envelope in my hand and said, "Buy something special—from me and Glory."

~ ~ ~

Just as quickly as summer came, so it ended, and fall rolled in. The weather got cooler, and it was lovely to see the leaves changing from green to banana yellow, mango orange and blood red.

I went back to school and Mama spent her days in Glory's two-bedroom apartment. She was bored. Of course there was the cooking, the cleaning, the television and her bags of crocheting and knitting. She needed to be needed, but she also needed to show her independence. She talked longingly about the Chinese pastry shops, Grand-aunt Ruth's restaurant and our house on the dead-end street.

"Nothing like yuh own house, wid yuh things surround yuh. Yuh own key to push in de door," she'd often say. "Molly, mek sure yuh strive fi dat when yuh get older, for it nuh good fi stay too long a people place." Mama and Glory argued a lot. If it wasn't one thing, it was another, little things like whether to cook red-pea soup every Saturday, whether to clean the floors with a mop or rag, whether to use paper towels or cloth. Of course, there was also the larger problem of Mama interfering too much in her adult children's lives. Glory and Sid had numerous arguments over whether to have a baby. It was not unusual to hear loud, angry whispers coming through the shut bedroom door. She seemed ready to change her mind about having another baby, but Mama continued to insist that it would be a bad choice, which only made Glory resent me, too.

"Ah tell yuh, yuh can't go and start up wid more pickney, when yuh don't even start fi mother Molly. She need attention and love," Mama complained.

Uncle Peppie was the only one who listened to Mama without talking back or showing any hint of resentment. She continued to offer him advice about Aunt Val: "Careful Peppie, don't mek de woman control yuh. For she think she better and brighter than yuh, and dat is de worse thing a man can have hanging over him. Look how de blasted woman tek over mi Sunday dinners."

Whenever Aunt Val called, she made a point of talking to Mama, inquiring about her health. My grandmother had developed a slight smoker's cough but wouldn't give up her cigarettes. Aunt Val even talked to her about knitting, which Aunt Val did quite well, but Mama still didn't take to her.

"She cyaan fool mi," she'd say to me. "She might be able to fool him, for him mek de woman turn him weak, but mi read her cards."

I was confused by Mama's contradictions. She told Glory to be independent, yet seemed to be irritated by Aunt Val's independence.

~ ~ ~

That fall Mama decided, more out of boredom than strong religious feeling that we would attend one of the local churches.

"Come gal, come mek we go praise de Lord. We have too much clothes just sleeping in de closet, an' time we air dem out." I think my mother was glad to see us leave the apartment—it gave her more space to argue with Sid. She still hadn't said yes to the baby, and the rift between her and Sid was widening.

We began attending an Anglican church not far from the apartment. The first Sunday, we arrived a half hour before the service, Mama wearing a well-ironed, two-piece, peacock-blue dress suit, a simple gold chain and gold earrings. Her black hair was pulled back from her face and a blue pillbox hat sat on her head. I wore a white dress and a pair of charcoal stockings. My black, pressed hair was curled around my face. We sat in the front pew and watched the congregation come in. Ours was the last pew to fill up. Mama smiled at the couple next to her and they smiled back stiffly. When the service started, Mama's voice rose proudly among the others. We got a few surprised looks, but I attributed them to her powerful voice. As children, she and my grand-aunts had attended revival services three times a week with Mammy, and everyone said she had a beautiful singing voice.

After church she introduced herself to the minister while I shyly looked on. She didn't seem bothered by the stuffiness of the congregation, or perhaps she was just deter- mined to make the best of things. Our third Sunday yielded us a few smiles and inquiries as to why we had left a tropical paradise to come here to the cold. We smiled without answers. That was the extent of the conversation. We never got the closeness and the companionship that my grandmother was seeking, and by the beginning of that winter she abandoned the idea of going to church.

We pretty much spent the winter locked up in Glory and Sid's apartment. I'd go to school and come home. Mama spent most of her time knitting and crocheting and writing letters back home and to Aunt Joyce in America. Grand-aunt Ruth wrote and kept my grandmother up-to-date, but she didn't have much to say about Uncle Mikey. Glory kept in touch with him, writing at least once a month. She pretended that his relationship with Frank didn't exist.

Freddie and Joanne's relationship began to go downhill after the baby, Kevin, was born, and Mama, of course, couldn't stay out of it. It got to the point where Joanne stopped talking to her altogether and stayed in touch only with Glory. I was in the kitchen doing the dishes one evening when a call came from Joanne. Mama was having a shower.

"Lord, Joanne," Glory whispered into the phone, "ah don't know what fi tell yuh. It not right, him shouldn't put him hands on yuh but . . ." She lingered on the "but," as if she didn't know what to say next. I told Mama the minute we were alone in bed.

"Dat blasted bwoy, him is a disgrace, him come all the way in a foreign fi beat woman. Just like him father."

Joanne left Freddie a month later. Late one Saturday night she and Kevin took a bus to Calgary, going home to her parents'. Mama launched in on Freddie, reminding him how worthless he was and always had been.

Many evenings that winter, Mama looked out at the snow and sighed, complaining about the dampness in the apartment, conveying her disappointment in Freddie and her difficulties with Glory. Even though she said nothing about Uncle Mikey, I knew that she harboured some animosity toward him and his relationship with Frank.

Then we got news that my grandfather had passed away. It was Saturday night, and Glory and Sid were back on good terms and out at a club with Freddie and his new girlfriend. As usual, I was at home with Mama watching television when the phone rang. Uncle Mikey was on the other end.

His voice was strained and sounded distant. He asked for Glory first, then said, "Let mi speak to Mama."

"Mama, is Uncle Mikey," I said.

She was surprised; they hadn't spoken since we left the island.

"Lord God, ah hope is nutten wrong wid Ruth or Mammy." She picked up the receiver.

"Hello, man," she said, as though she'd spoken to him yesterday.

She was silent for a long time. I couldn't tell what was going on because her face didn't tell me anything. I was anxious to know the story.

"Well, Mikey, there is nutten we can do. So yuh live is so yuh die."

There was another pause as she listened.

"Well . . . mek de government look after dat. Him never left no provision for dat."

Another long pause.

"Where dem find him?"

"Oh Lord Almighty!"

"Nuh cry," she soothed. "Stand up and face facts like a man. Him never did anything fi unnu. Is me alone carry box pon mi head wid patties and coco-bread and pastries fi mek unnu eat, and put food on de table and roof over unnu head."

She listened again. Then I'm sure she cut him off.

"Awright, tek care. Ah will tell dem."

She sat in silence, just staring at the television. Then she got up as though I wasn't in the room, went over to the glass cabinet where Sid kept a few bottles of liquor. He wasn't a heavy drinker, only opened the cabinet when Justin or other friends came over. There was a good selection of rum, including bottles from different islands, a couple of bottles of scotch and some gin. Mama poured some rum and took a shot straight up without water. Then she poured another, filled it with ice and a touch of water. She came back and sat on the couch. The television was still going.

"Dat was about yuh grandfather. Him dead."

It was her first rum since we'd come to Canada. I waited while she swallowed it down and lit a cigarette. Her light cough sent the smoke into my face.

"Him kill himself," she said, rubbing her forehead. "Hang himself wid rope. Dem find him in somebody back-yard under a tambrind tree."

The image set itself in front of me and I wanted to scream. "When is the funeral?" I asked.

"Ah don't know." Then she got up and went to our bedroom. I stayed in the living room for a while longer, changing the channels, and then I went to join her. She was sitting on a chair looking out the window. I bent over and kissed her. She looked so vulnerable, so helpless. She squeezed me and I moved closer to her, the smell of rum enveloping the small space we shared. I trembled and all I wanted to do was be back on our street, curled up in our mahogany bed, grandfather and her dancing in the living room, the smell of the bougainvillea rushing in through the windows, me with my own dreams fluttering in my heart.

~ ~ ~

The next day when I got up, Mama and Glory were at the dining-room table, looking solemn. I helped myself to a bowl of cornmeal porridge sprinkled with vanilla and nutmeg, and joined them. Uncle Peppie arrived soon after, then Uncle Freddie. Nobody cried. Nobody had much to say, either. Peppie left, then Freddie, each kissing Mama on the mouth. Glory went off to do chores with Sid, and Mama and I were alone.

My grandmother went back to the liquor cabinet several times that day. When Sid and Glory came home, Mama was asleep—they thought it was because she was grieving. So began Mama's first binge in Canada.

Mama cooked early in the morning and then drank for the rest of the day. The dinners deteriorated as the days went by; one night the rice was soggy, then the green bananas were overcooked and the chicken and pork chops burnt. Sid ate quietly without complaining. I watched him gulp water after each mouthful, while Glory chewed each piece longer than usual.

Mama's face had begun to change with the drinking, becoming slack, like a used elastic band. Her movements were loose. She talked aimlessly, as she had on the island when she was drinking. I had almost forgotten that side of her. Now I smelled the faint sweetness of rum on her breath and clothes and wondered if Sid or Glory noticed, but no one said anything. Mama's conversation moved from Mikey to Freddie and back to Mikey again. I watched Glory's shoulders tighten as my grandmother spoke carelessly about Uncle Mikey and Frank ruining their lives, about Mikey's weakness. "Mi would still be in Jamaica in mi house if it wasn't fi him careless living. Look how de bwoy nice, could a get any woman and instead mek man bend up him heart." Her chatter embarrassed me. Glory got up abruptly and left the table with food still on her plate. Sid earnestly ate all of his and then said he had to go help a friend with his car.

By the third day, Mama had worked her way through two bottles of rum and was on to the gin. Sid wisely stayed away as much as he could, and Glory closeted herself in their room. Once or twice she tried to talk to my grandmother, but was met with something caustic.

One afternoon Glory came back from the laundromat to find me watching television. My grandmother was dozing on and off in the bedroom.

"Mama drinking?" she asked me.

"Ah don't know," I replied.

She gave me a disgusted look. I didn't care. I wasn't going to tell on my grandmother and I felt I owed Glory nothing. She hadn't been much of a mother or a friend to me since I'd come to Canada. And why was she asking me anyway, when it was her mother and it was obvious that she was drinking? Mama stopped cooking and took to her bed. Several times I heard Glory on the phone with Uncle Freddie, then with Uncle Peppie, discussing their mother's condition.

"Yuh don't have homework?" she shouted at me as I was watching television one night.

"Is Friday, ah will do it tomorrow or Sunday."

"Turn off de blasted television, pick up a book and go read."

I turned it off and went to my room. I had a book in my hand, but I didn't read. I just lay on the bed, listening to Mama snore and plotting for the day when I would leave my mother's apartment.

Sid came home soon after with his friend Justin and another man I didn't know. Justin was a small-boned, handsome man with chocolate-coloured skin. At the base of his neck was a coin-shaped patch of skin of a lighter shade of brown. Glory greeted them and exchanged a few pleasantries, but her voice didn't sound welcoming. I knew she was worried that Mama might come out of the bedroom. Mama was unpredictable when she was drinking.

"What yuh having?" I heard Sid ask.

"Give mi a shot of de Martinique rum nuh," his new friend answered.

"And gin fi me," Justin said.

The cabinet door opened. I heard Sid suck his teeth long and hard, but he didn't say much.

"It look like mi out of rum, yuh know. How 'bout some Scotch?"

The men teased Sid. "Man, how yuh can run outa rum? Nuh we mother milk we wean off on to rum," Justin joked. Glory apologized for not having any food to offer—usually Mama had food on the stove just waiting to be warmed up.

Justin asked after my grandmother, and Glory mumbled that she wasn't feeling well and was resting.

Despite the Scotch and the music on the stereo, the men didn't stay for long. Sid left with them.

I heard the telephone ring and then Glory saying, "No, him not home. Who is it? Who is it?" She slammed the receiver down.

"Molly? Molly?" she shouted angrily. I didn't answer. Dishes and pots banged in the sink. I didn't feel the least bit sorry for her.

Mama's binge lasted a full two weeks. When it ended, she tried to go on as though nothing had happened, but this wasn't her dead-end street, this wasn't her house. Glory made up excuses and began to cook the evening meals.

"Mama, yuh need a rest, from yuh come, yuh just a cook, cook so."

My grandmother looked taken aback. "Okay," was all she said.

They didn't talk much to each other, just about the weather, a bit about work, talk that went nowhere. Sid had changed, too. He wasn't rude, he was too polite. He'd eat his evening meal and go to his bedroom. The liquor cabinet was locked with a key. Glory kept in daily contact with Uncle Peppie and Uncle Freddie about their mother's behaviour.

Winter dragged on, especially for Mama, who was often stuck in the house, afraid to venture out in the snow and ice, where she could slip and fall. In early spring she visited her first Canadian liquor store and went on another drinking binge, which again lasted about two weeks. Soon after, on a bright

April morning, the family met at Uncle Peppie's house without Mama.

On her way out Glory whispered to me that they were meeting to talk about Mama's birthday. I didn't believe that was the real reason, and I disliked her even more for treating me like a child. When she and Sid had left, I told Mama about the meeting. She sucked her teeth.

"Dem think me is a fool? Yuh know how much mi sacrifice fi dem pickney? Yuh think a little floor mi clean fi put food in a dem mouth? And look now, dem all conspire against mi. Sometime ah wonder why ah left and come here." She dragged on her cigarette, hawked up some phlegm and swallowed it. "But as sure as God mek apple, mi must find a way out, mi not going to allow dem fi tek any liberty wid mi."

I wondered then whether I'd made a mistake in writing to Uncle Peppie, for I, too, felt I'd lost more than I'd gained by coming here.

"If mi did deh back home, ah would be making mi pastries and have mi little money. Now mi haffi wait fi handout. Glory don't even give mi anything. And yet she can demand dat mi nuh work." Her anger grew. I didn't know what to say. I opened the kitchen curtains and cracked the windows a bit to let in some air. A bird flew by and sat for a while on the fence.

"Mama, why yuh don't mek we go back?" I asked naively.

"We cyaan go back, girl, yuh can think 'bout de past, but yuh cyaan go back fi live in it. Too much water gone a river."

"Mama, maybe we could find a place and move. Summer coming, ah can get a job and save some money," I said.

"Gal, stop talk like idiot. When yuh mekking any move, yuh haffi plan it. Never you just get up one morning and decide yuh nuh like something and want it fi change instantly. Nothing nuh go so, and it never turn out right. Look pon we now. We never plan dis trip good. You have yuh life ahead, and thank God mi deliver yuh safe to yuh mother, so she cyaan call mi wutliss—a drunk maybe, 'cause is so dem love judge. But despite mi drinking nutten never happen to yuh. From when yuh is a baby mi have yuh. If it wasn't for mi, yuh would never see life. She have yuh when she turn fifteen. One year after mi tek her from Mammy, gal come to town and breed, an' never even know who de father was. And mi never cuss her. Mi did hurt, yes, for is mi one daughter and mi wanted de best fi her. Dat's why mi tek yuh, and save and scrape fi send her abroad.

"De only thing mi never do is give birth to yuh. Glory come outa hospital two days after yuh born, and day four dem had to admit her back wid complications. Is a little soft drinks bottle mi put nipple pon and feed yuh. Every night yuh sleep right under mi breast, and when she come out of hospital yuh still sleep wid mi, for as she come out and feel better, she start go de party dem again. Dat is why mi had to get her off de island—mi was afraid she would mash up herself wid baby after baby.

"Peppie was a good son . . . and Mikey, too, even though Satan turn him. But back den, de two of dem work and bring home dem money fi help feed yuh and Glory and Freddie. Ah use to bake more dem days, order come in from all over, every restaurant wid any name, mi bake for, sometimes mi couldn't fill de order fast enough, an' Peppie an' Mikey use to help out. Dem days we all use to knot up we money together, mi and mi sons."

Despite her anger, her face grew soft for a moment. She lit another cigarette and blew the softness away.

One damp May evening, a Friday to be exact, Uncle Peppie came to visit his mother. She still faithfully cooked his stewed red peas. Glory and Sid weren't home. Peppie ate and was more talkative than usual. Finally he said, "Mama, from yuh come to Canada yuh don't spend any time up at mi house. Why yuh don't come stay wid me and Val for a few months? We would love to have yuh."

She considered it and then asked suspiciously, "Who suggestion dis was?"

"Nobody. Ah just thought it would be nice fi yuh stay wid we, we have a house and is just Val and me alone."

There were no further questions and to my surprise, Mama agreed.

~ ~ ~

For the first time I was away from my grandmother—we had never spent a night apart. Though we talked on the phone every day, I still felt empty. At first I had secretly hoped that Mama's move would allow my relationship with my mother to change for the better, since there would be just the two of us, but it didn't. When I sometimes tried to hug her, she would pull away. We didn't do anything together. She was too busy to see a movie with me, too busy to sit in the park and admire the flowers, too busy even to watch a television program, yet she found time to go dancing with Sid and to visit her friends at their houses. I must have reminded my mother of the father I never knew. Perhaps I reminded her of the shame she felt when she discovered she was pregnant. She found fault at my every twist and turn. My English was bad. If I expected to reach anywhere, I better learn to talk good, she said. My breasts were too big, my eyes too knowing.

I took over the cooking, a job I detested. Glory had started night school twice a week and naturally I inherited the chore. Though I loved to see my grandmother at the stove, her body moving to the clatter of pots and pans, it wasn't the job for me. I much preferred to look after the plants scattered around the apartment. I spent more and more time in my room, writing letters and leafing through gardening books, dreaming of someday having a backyard where I could dig and plant.

Mama wasn't happy at Uncle Peppie's. "De woman bossy, she bossy, she cyaan done bossy," she complained to my mother on one of our visits. "Is like she know everything 'bout dis boy dat mi give birth to. One evening mi cook some escoveitch fish wid scotch bonnet pepper and de woman nearly go mad. 'Peppie don't like too much pepper.' Ah never even look pon her. What she know 'bout him? And de woman cyaan even give mi a little time wid mi son. Every conversation she have to be a part of, and always haffi show dat she have more knowledge than anybody else. But mi nuh fool, and she know it, for mi use to read mi newspaper every day in Jamaica. Sometime mi have to wonder if she lay out him underpants fi him a morning time."

"Lawd, Mama." Glory sounded embarrassed.

Aunt Val's version was not unlike Mama's. One Sunday evening when we were there for supper, I heard Aunt Val and

Glory talking in the bedroom. Aunt Val confided, "I really don't like to complain, because she's your mother and my mother-in-law but, Glory, she is a handful. There is nothing I can do right. I don't even recognize my own kitchen. She has to cook every meal, changed up my kitchen completely. It's not that I don't appreciate her help, but I love to cook. Then she told Peppie that I resent any time she spends with him. That's so untrue, Glory. Of course there are times I wish to spend alone with Peppie. Even watching television is a chore, because your mother talks incessantly. She is the authority on everything." She paused. "I hope you won't say anything to Peppie, because he does love having his mother around."

"Val, yuh don't have to apologize. Is mi mother and in the short time we live together, ah realize is not de mother mi think mi did know. In fact, sometimes she is like a stranger. Is Mammy, mi grandmother, mi and Freddie, we all grow up wid. Peppie and Mikey leave Mammy house and join her in Kingston sooner than us. Ah can count de amount of years on mi finger that mi actually spend wid her. Nuh worry yuh-self, Val," Glory offered.

I hated to hear them criticize my grandmother. Ungrateful bitches. I waited for them to leave the bedroom before I flushed the toilet.

~ ~ ~

I was in my room writing Punsie a letter when I heard Glory screaming. I vaguely remembered the phone ringing, but hadn't bothered to get up because the phone rarely rang for me.

"Lord mi God, Lord mi God." Her voice broke. "Jesus."

Then the phone hit the floor with a loud bang. I ran out to find Glory on the floor wailing like a spirit had taken hold of her.

"What wrong, Glory?" I asked. She was in no condition to answer.

I picked up the phone, but heard only the dial tone.

"Glory," I tried again, shaking her shoulders. I ran to the kitchen, got some water and made her drink it. I knelt on the floor by her, but still couldn't get anything out of her. All I could think to do was hold her. I curled up against her on the floor and hugged her.

I offered the hem of my skirt for her to wipe her tears and she took it. We rocked back and forth on the floor. My hand stroked the length of her hair, and her thin body pressed against mine.

"Call Freddie," she said at last. "Tell him he must come over now."

While we waited for Uncle Freddie, she told me that Grand-aunt Ruth had called with the news that Mammy was dead. I was shocked. I had always thought that Mama and I would go back to Jamaica with gifts of clothes and canned goods for Mammy. I felt heavy with grief. Freddie came quickly and drove us to Uncle Peppie's house to see Mama. Everyone huddled together on the living-room couch. Even Aunt Val, who had never met Mammy, was crying.

"Open de door, Molly. Ah feel faint," Mama said.

"Ah going to call Mikey," Glory said.

"Yes, poor bwoy, him must be feeling alone," Peppie added.

"Call him," Mama agreed in a trembling voice.

~ ~ ~

I didn't go to Mammy's funeral, nor did Aunt Val or Sid, but the rest of the family went. I had wanted to go, too, but no amount of begging would change my mother's mind. She said I shouldn't miss the last weeks of school and that there wasn't enough money for an extra fare.

The family stayed on the island for a few weeks, and when they returned, Mama moved back to Glory and Sid's apartment. I don't know why she came back, but I was happy to have her there. I'd missed her company and our talks.

"Molly, de funeral was lovely. Yuh see people like rice. She was truly loved, twelve busload of people gather round fi bid her goodbye. Dem come from all over de island. Mi never know mi mother know so much people," she said proudly. "Ah wish yuh was dere, gal. Everybody ask fi yuh: Ruth, Icie, Ivan, Gatty, Baboo, Punsie, Monica, Little Freddie. Him was so glad fi see him father, but Freddie never mek much of him." She paused, shook her head and cleared her throat in disgust. "Is a shame. Imagine him never even give de bwoy pickney a little sweetie, or money fi jingle in him pocket. Nutten! Is a shame, and Monica wasn't nuh better. After di man nuh fart pon her since him left, she up and down wid him like a blasted kite. I don't even know if she get any money from him."

"So what de street look like, Mama? It change?"

"De same, few people move and new people move in. Petal and her family move. Ah hear dem gwan to America. And Punsie just have a baby, but mi sure yuh know dat, for yuh correspond wid her."

"What about Uncle Mikey?" I asked. She had made no mention of him.

"Ah, girl, dat is another chapter and mi too tired fi get into dat right now." She got up and walked to the kitchen to prepare dinner.

~ ~ ~

The summer holidays came and somehow, with the help of Uncle Freddie, I managed to persuade my mother to let me work. The local supermarket was hiring part-time help and I got a job as a packer to replace items on the shelves. I'd have loved to have been working outdoors, especially in a park or nursery, but I wasn't that lucky. Still, with this job I had money to spend however I wanted, and most important, I was out of the house.

Things weren't going so well for Mama. The problem began with one of those thick white envelopes marked "To the Household." I was getting ready for work when the mailman delivered it.

"Mek we open it, Mama, because Glory will just dump it," I urged. "She don't read dese things. She say is a waste of time."

We tore it open and out fell several colourful coupons for magazines: *Homemaker's, Chatelaine, Canadian Home and Garden, Maclean's.* A few of the magazines offered free sample issues; if you were satisfied you could continue to receive the magazines.

"Ah going to send fi dem. Dem will give Glory some decorating ideas when she and Sid buy dem house, and in de days when mi home alone, mi can catch up on more Canadian news."

She filled out the forms and I mailed them for her on my way to work.

The first set of magazines arrived and we spent an afternoon leafing through them, admiring the lovely towels and sheets, the bathroom fixtures, the renovated kitchens and luxurious bedrooms. Mama cut out a few recipes.

"Mek mi try a few of dem dishes. We can't just eat island food—sometime mi get tired of cooking de same thing." I especially liked *Home and Garden* and began to plan the flower beds for the yard. Even Glory was excited about the magazines, and we discussed what flowers I'd plant in the garden once she and Sid bought a house.

"Whatever yuh do, mek sure we have place to walk, so we not tiptoeing through nuh tulips," she joked. Since the funeral she seemed more relaxed with me, but we still didn't have the warmth and closeness I'd hoped for.

Four months later the bill came. Glory was home that day with the flu and she opened it. It said nothing about a trial period. Clearly irritated, she said, "Mama, Molly, is what dis? Is what unnu do? Dese people demanding money from mi, and mi never send away fi magazine. How unnu can do dis without consulting mi?"

"But, Glory, you know about de magazine trial period," I said.

"Don't bother, ah don't want to hear nutten. Ah will just tek care of de blasted mess misself before Sid find out," she said, sounding weary and angry. She went to her room and shut the door.

In defiance Mama began to sing:

By the rivers of Babylon, there we sat down,
Yea, we wept, when we remembered Zion.
For there they that carried us away captive
required of us a song
How shall we sing the LORD's song in a strange land?

She sang and she sang, her voice rising with each verse. Finally Glory came out of her room.

"Mama, please, remember we have neighbours, dis is not Wigton Street."

She went back into her room and shut the door again.

Some weeks later I saw a notice on the bulletin board at work: "BABYSITTTER NEEDED. I am West Indian and will bring baby to your home. 9 a.m. to 5 p.m. weekdays. Older woman preferred."

I took down the number and Mama called. She got the job immediately, for the woman lived close by. At first my mother and Sid were fine with the arrangement.

"Yes, is a good idea, Mother Galloway. It will mek yuh a little change and ah know dat can come in handy," Sid said good-naturedly.

So it was settled and the five-month-old baby arrived. Sid and Glory hardly saw him. They left for work long before the child arrived, and most evenings he was gone before they came home. Mama was delighted by the success of her business, and a certain kind of light that had been shadowed since we got here was lit again. Even when Uncle Freddie got yet another girl pregnant and refused to look after the child, she didn't get upset.

Word quickly got out that there was a West Indian woman in the neighbourhood who took in children. Before our eyes, the one child multiplied into six in our two-bedroom apartment. They varied in age from three months to three years. It might have worked—Mama was a woman who could cook, clean, look after children, watch her soaps, read her newspaper, crochet and keep everything under control. But four months later, Sid went on the night shift, which meant he was home all day trying to sleep, with half a dozen children crying, chattering, shrieking, dropping bottles and spoons, running from one end of the apartment to the other.

He must have complained to Glory. It wasn't his style to confront Mama.

"Mama, yuh have to get rid of some of dem pickney, it too much, and we never have any discussion past de one baby. And now de apartment is like a orphanage! Dat nuh right, Mama, ah mean, people live here. Dis is a home, not a institution. Beg yuh please, mek dem tek dem pickneys elsewhere," she finished bluntly. Like her mother, Glory was not given to mincing words.

"Yuh right, missus, ah don't know how ah could pass mi place in yuh apartment. Nuh worry, de broom soon clean out yuh house."

The children were gone by November. Mama told the parents that she was moving to her son's place, and that's what she did. One morning she called Uncle Peppie to come get her, and she packed her clothes and left.

"Girl, tek care," she said, hugging me tight. "Mi not deserting yuh, so nuh worry, is just time fi mi leave here."

~ ~ ~

Mama remained at Uncle Peppie's and stayed unhappy. She wouldn't move back to Glory's apartment.

Things were not going well for me, either. Glory and I barely spoke to each other. She complained when I played the radio loud or watched too much television. "Yuh can't find something useful fi do? Mi nuh know what you coming to." I cursed her in my mind, hoping I would soon be out of there. I became defiant, and some evenings when I left for the library or the strip malls on Eglinton Avenue West, I didn't return until midnight. Sid, too, had grown even more quiet and withdrawn, often staying out late at nights.

The only cheerful one of the lot was Uncle Freddie. One Sunday afternoon he came by with a new girlfriend, Bella, a white girl, fine as a needle and golden-blond. She was pretty, with large green eyes and an easy smile.

We found out later that she was Italian. I didn't believe it, with her thin, wiry body and the colour of her hair. Everyone knew Italian women looked like Sophia Loren.

"Meet Bella." He smiled proudly. "Dis is mi future wife, and baby modder." We were all a little taken aback. None of us had seen her before, except Sid, who greeted them with familiarity.

"Nice man, nice work. Sit down mek we drink a toast," he said, smiling.

"What we toasting?" Glory asked.

"Yuh don't hear yuh brother? Dis is him future wife."

Glory looked dumbfounded. Uncle Freddie laughed. "We going to do it soon, in de spring. We decide on April first," he said, watching Glory.

"Yuh joking, right?"

"No, me and Bella decide on de date."

Glory looked at Bella and then back at her brother.

"Ah don't mean to put mi mouth in dis, but why April Fool's Day? Why not another date without dat deh kind a meaning?"

"Glory, yuh too conventional, and if we going to get married we might as well have fun, right, Bella?" he said, turning to her. She smiled, squeezed his hand and laid a kiss on his ear. Glory rolled her eyes.

"Time fi a toast," Sid said, pouring two shots of Scotch.

"What about us ladies, we nuh count?" Glory asked.

"Yes, man, yes, of course," Sid said. "What yuh having, Bella?"

"Coke or ginger ale, if you have some."

"I'll get it," I offered. "Glory?"

"Yes, bring the same for me," she said.

"Yuh tell Mama and de others yet?" I heard Glory asking.

"No, not yet. Ah will tell dem next week over the Christmas holidays."

I brought back the drinks and we toasted Freddie and Bella.

On their way out, Glory pulled Freddie aside. "Yuh better tell Mama first, yuh know how she can get," she advised.

Freddie sucked his teeth, kissed Glory on the head and walked to his car.

"See yuh all over de Christmas."

"Don't bother saying anything to Mama," my mother said to me after they drove off.

"Why would I do that?" I asked.

She gave me a cut eye and walked back into our apartment.

~ ~ ~

The Christmas holidays came with snowstorms and bitter winds, but nothing could dampen my happy mood. Glory had given me permission to spend the days leading up to Christmas at Uncle Peppie's house. I was pretty sure it was for her own reasons. She and Sid were having problems—the rough, hushed voices coming through their closed bedroom door made that clear. Sid drove me over to Uncle Peppie's; Glory didn't come. On the way there Sid seemed preoccupied and we hardly talked. I was happy just to get out of the apartment.

Mama was in the kitchen buttering cake tins.

"Girl, yuh nuh 'fraid snow blow yuh weh?" she joked. "Mi up from dawn a bake." We could have been back on Wigton Street, except for the snow and cold outside.

Uncle Peppie and Aunt Val were still at work. I watched Mama mix the cake batter with a big wooden spoon, her great breasts heaving up and down.

"Molly, girl, get a pen and paper and come write down dis recipe. Yuh mother nuh interested in dem things, but yuh fi learn. A Mammy teach mi how fi bake and even if yuh nuh like fi cook, it good fi know how fi bake. And a cake is a thing of beauty, jus' like de flowers yuh love fi plant."

I wrote down the recipe for the Christmas cake in a lovely hand-bound notebook Aunt Val had given me for my last birthday. All I had ever written in it was my name, because I hadn't wanted to spoil its pristine beauty.

"Remember, before yuh get to dis stage here of mixing, yuh have to follow de first rule, it very important. For yuh just don't get up one morning and decide yuh go mek

Christmas cake. De fruits dem haffi soak, yuh haffi give dem time to mature. So dat is de first thing yuh do. Yuh can soak dem for two months, but fi get de best cake, soak de fruits eight to ten months before fi yuh use dem."

I wrote in my best handwriting:

Preparations before baking Mama's Christmas pudding:

Soak fruits: about two pounds of raisins, one pound currants, half a pound prunes (chop them up into small pieces). Put them in a big wide-mouth bottle or an earthenware jar, cover with equal measures of rum and port wine, add spices (nutmeg, cloves, vanilla essence, almond essence).

Seal the jar tight, put it away to steep.

"Ah remember when we was children in Port Maria, as soon as Mammy use up de fruits, she put couple more bottles to soak. De cake dem come out rich and black. In dem days we use a touch of molasses in de mixture," Mama said. "When yuh ready fi bake, yuh tek out enough of de soak fruit according to how much cake yuh going to mek."

Cream the butter and sugar (about one and a half pounds sugar, one pound butter) until there is no trace of sugar grains. Add eggs, beating them in one at a time (about 8 to 10 eggs). Rest it aside. Heat the fruit mixture over a low heat with a cup of water and a drop of molasses for about five minutes. Stir constantly. Add a bit of powdered cloves

and a touch of almond essence. Add about a pound
of flour and mix it in thoroughly with a teaspoon of
baking powder and a pinch of salt.

"When mi was growing up, Mammy never use recipe fi her cake, so we never know 'bout nuh exact measurement fi anything. Remember seh she couldn't read, and we nuh know 'bout cookbook. So most of mi learning tek place under mi Mammy skirt tail. Glory just like Joyce, she never tek to de cooking and baking, is me and Ruth watch Mammy and run up and down a help her. Joyce was younger dan us, all de same. She was Pappy favourite, then Ruth. Mi come last in fi him book, him nevah really count mi, but mi had de love of mi dear mother." Mama's eyes grew misty with remembering.

Bake the cakes in a slow oven (that's the secret to
a moist cake), about 250°F.
Bake for two and a half hours. Test the middle
of the cake with the tip of a sharp knife.

"Mammy cakes use to be de talk of Port Maria. Everybody want to know how dis little white woman wid de blue eyes could a mek dem breed a cake." Her eyes were still misty as she spoke, but the swirling wooden spoon in her hand never lost a beat.

"Yuh great-grandmother was a strong woman. Very strong, she mi tek after." Mama laughed as she recalled a story. "One time when Mammy pregnant wid Joyce, things was hard wid us, for we never have 'nuff money. So Mammy go down to the little grocery shop to go ask for credit. Ah went wid her dat day, and as she open her mouth to ask Mr.

Taylor for credit, him say to her, 'Miss Galloway, yuh husband have a box of groceries here.' Mammy open de box and what yuh think she see? All kind of luxury food. Can sardine, herring, bully beef, mackerel—in those days dem was luxury items for poor people, and here him was buying up groceries for a woman him had over de other side of de bay. Well, Mammy never do a thing but tek up de box and put pon her head, thank Mr. Taylor and we go home."

Mama shook her head. "When him come home, him nearly dead, for Mammy tek out all de canned goods and set dem on de table. Ah tell yuh, him was no match for Mammy. She was a white-skinned woman, but none of dem black woman in de Bay was a match for her. People had tendencies to think that she was a weakling, but all who know her, know dat she wasn't a woman to mess wid. She use to mek us laugh, for she was a woman who tek serious things and turn joke, like dat same day, we laugh and talk all de way home, and when we reach home, we give Ruth de joke."

She laughed again, remembering. "Mi father did think him strong, but him was a weak man. Him had de physical strength, yes, for him was a well-built black man, wid good looks . . . but weak, dat's why him fall prey . . ." I closed the notebook quietly, not wanting to break this special time with her, so rare since she'd moved away.

"Nuh close de book yet, you might as well tek de recipe for icing de cake, it short and simple enough," she said, turning to me.

Use about a pound of icing sugar (again use common sense, depending on the number of cakes.

Practice is the key to a perfect cake. Trial and error brings success). About two or three eggs. About one teaspoon of lime juice (try to use fresh lime juice). A tip of almond essence.

Beat the egg whites until they look like soap suds. Add half the sugar and beat again. Slowly add the rest of the sugar and continue to beat. Add the lime juice. Beat. Add the almond essence. Beat until the mixture stiffens.

Smooth the icing on the cakes. Let dry. Add the second layer of cake.

I spent the rest of the afternoon writing down recipes. Mama moved from cakes to preparing the sorrel drink.

"Mek mi give yuh de recipe for sorrel drink, for yuh cyaan eat Christmas cake widout sorrel. Remember we use to grow it in de yard back home? Man, when you consider how it use to grow so plentiful, and here it cost a small fortune in de West Indian shop."

To make a sorrel Christmas drink:

Take 3 cups of the red sorrel leaves and about an ounce of crushed green ginger. Throw in 6-8 cloves. Add one half pound of sugar or to your taste. Also add orange peel and a cinnamon stick.

Put the ginger, cloves, orange peel, cinnamon stick and sorrel into a large jar. Add six cups of boiling water. Cover and leave it for three days. Then strain everything through a white muslin cloth. Add the sugar and chill.

Serve it with ice.

"Well, girl, yuh can't say yuh granny never give yuh any-thing. Yuh won't use it now, but put it up—ah know a time will come when yuh going to crave a cake, and yuh will be proud when yuh mek it yuhself and it turn out."

On Christmas Day there was enough food for three holiday feasts. Mama really outdid herself. The table was laden with sliced, honey-marinated ham garnished with grilled pine-apple slices, roast turkey served with English potatoes, fried chicken with fried plantains, curried goat, steamed snapper in ginger and thyme sauce, gungo peas and rice, coleslaw salad, potato salad, Aunt Val's macaroni-and-cheese pie, cornbread and a baked sweet-potato dish. A large selection of beverages occupied a side table: fresh carrot juice, ginger beer, sorrel drink, eggnog, rum punch, punch à creme. And finally there was Mama's black Christmas cake and plum pudding.

We couldn't have asked for a better Christmas. At three o'clock our guests began to arrive. First Glory and Sid, then a couple from Aunt Val's workplace, her two sisters and their husbands and her nephew Jeffrey, then Justin. When Uncle Freddie and Bella arrived, he introduced her to everyone, including Mama. This time he said nothing about the wedding or the pregnancy. My heart pounded and I looked over at my grandmother, but she said nothing.

Bella sat next to Mama on the couch while the others mingled. Freddie went down to the basement with Sid, Justin, Uncle Peppie and the rest of the men. Glory, Aunt Val and the other women chatted in the kitchen. Mama and

Bella looked as comfortable as a pair of old socks. She asked a lot of questions about Jamaica and about Uncle Freddie. Mama was careful with her answers and said nothing about his bad habits. Instead she talked about crab season, flying kites and all the wonderful things I thought she had forgotten about him. Bella enjoyed Mama's stories and whispered to her about the wedding and the pregnancy.

"Don't say a word, he wants to announce it at dinner." She giggled shyly. "Can I call you Mama?"

"Sure, darling," my grandmother said, looking pleased.

As we were about to sit down to eat, there was a loud knock at the door. Uncle Peppie opened it and in burst three more people whom I didn't know. It was obvious that Glory, Uncle Peppie and Uncle Freddie knew them well.

"Come in, come in, come out of de cold," Uncle Peppie bellowed. "Mek mi tek unnu coat. Val!" he shouted merrily. "Come look who de wind blew in."

Uncle Peppie served them drinks and introduced them to us. They were Aunt Val's uncles, Washington and Melbourne, and her aunt Gwendolyn. The uncles were both over six feet tall. Melbourne was older—I guessed by a good ten years. Washington was closer to Mama's age. He was the slimmer, less balding and more neatly dressed of the two. Melbourne looked clean but shabbily put together, and he had a beer belly.

"I'm very pleased to meet you, Maria. I have heard so much about you from Val," Washington, the more handsome of the two, said. Melbourne looked on, smiling, as his sister, Gwendolyn, struck up an animated conversation with my grandmother.

Dinner was a boisterous affair. Washington turned out to be quite a comedian, and Melbourne was a man full of stories about his years as a lightweight boxer.

Freddie announced his wedding plans and Bella's pregnancy, to which we drank a toast. Mama surprised us all by not making a scene. Perhaps it was because she liked Bella, or because of the attention she was getting from the two uncles. Whatever it was, I was grateful.

After dinner the music started. Washington and Melbourne kept Mama on her feet dancing all night long. She wore one of the beautiful Sophia Loren dresses Uncle Mikey had made, and her gold earrings shone against her lovely dark face. She looked like the Queen of Carnival; her body rivalled that of any thirty-five-year-old woman. As the night wore on, I watched, fascinated, as the two men competed for her attention. Washington drew her out, made her laugh, flirted outrageously with her, but in the end Melbourne won. Years later she confided to me, "Is Washington me like first, him so funny and mek light of everything and him have looks, but Melbourne a di one mi set mi eye pon. Looks not everything. Pretty man a trouble. Look how yuh grandfather did handsome and . . . A 'oman fi tek man uglier dan her, and blacker too."

That night I wore a red turtleneck pantsuit, compliments of my mother's closet. In trying to hide my large breasts, she had forgotten that I wore two sweater sizes larger than she did. By the time she saw me that evening, it was too late for me to change. I spent the evening watching the adults, helping serve the cake and drinks. I also helped myself to a glass or two of rum punch. Bella caught me at it once. "I won't tell," she laughed. "My sisters and I used to do that all the time, only it was wine—my father made it by the barrel."

Jeffrey asked me to dance a few times, but he was a clumsy dancer. Then Justin asked me to dance to a slow song and he pulled me close. I felt his chest snug against my breasts. Mama was dancing with Washington, oblivious to everyone else in the room. Glory and Aunt Val were cleaning up in the kitchen, and the rest of the men were in the basement. Bella sat on the couch, a permanent smile on her face, watching. Justin pressed his mouth against mine and slipped his tongue between my teeth. When the song finished, he squeezed my hand and went downstairs to join the others. I sat next to Bella on the couch, savouring a delicious feeling of love. She hugged me and whispered, "Be careful, dearie."

Mama was jovial for the rest of the holidays. Melbourne, Gwendolyn and Washington entertained her throughout the season. Each time I called she was out. Even after the holidays were over, she entertained her new friends at Uncle Peppie's, often inviting them for Sunday dinner. Melbourne had a car, so some evenings he and Washington took Mama driving and to meet friends. They took turns inviting her home. Washington lived close to Glory, off St. Clair Avenue near Dufferin Street, and Melbourne lived in Parkdale.

Mama started to stay over at Melbourne's some weekends, returning to Uncle Peppie's on Sunday night. This wasn't to everybody's liking. Glory was the first to voice her disapproval.

"Peppie, it nuh look right," she said on the phone. "Mama should know better—him is a married man. It nuh right," she repeated. I thought that was ridiculous; Melbourne had been divorced some time back and didn't even have children.

When Mama's visits to Melbourne's became more frequent and lasted longer, Glory called a family conference at our house—without Mama. Uncle Freddie didn't care much one way or the other. "If Mama happy wid dat situation, dat fine wid me. Is less time in my business."

Glory looked at him, cut her eyes and sighed in frustration. She turned to Uncle Peppie for support. He agreed with her and the relief showed on her face. "It a little embarrassing, him being Val uncle and all . . . but you know how Mama is when she set on things. She won't listen . . ."

"So what if he is Val's uncle? Unnu too uptight," Freddie accused them. "Leave de woman alone—she lonely, she need some man company."

"You just hush," Glory said. "She is our mother and it just look careless. It's not so simple, you know. Melbourne is a drinker. Yuh never see him de night of de party? Dat is a bad influence on Mama. Look pon de little drinks Sid had in de cabinet—she nuh drink it out?"

"Glory, don't worry so much, yuh cyaan live Mama life."

"It going to come to a bad end," Glory grumbled. "She should act her age."

"What age have to do wid a little loving? Leave de woman alone," Freddie said again, looking at his watch. Glory sighed, looking at Uncle Peppie, but this time she got no support.

Since the Christmas party, I had been preoccupied with Justin. He called now and then to ask me out. Because I couldn't let Glory know about our relationship, I'd meet him at the strip mall, and he'd take me to a burger joint or a movie, telling me how pretty I was, then kissing me in the car before dropping me off at the mall. One afternoon he brought me to a friend's house in the east end. No one was home, and Justin led me to the bedroom. I wrote and told Punsie, swore her to secrecy even though she was so many miles away.

~ ~ ~

In June, Bella gave birth to a lovely, olive-skinned baby boy. They named him Vittorio Oliver Galloway. Freddie wanted his son to have his father's name. Mama didn't like it, but there was nothing she could do about it. She comforted herself by saying, "Ah thank de Lord dat is only de middle name, for ah don't know how ah could bear calling de pickney Oliver every day." By the time Vittorio was six months old, Mama had knitted him enough outfits to supply a set of quints.

Bella spent a lot of time on the phone with Mama, exchanging recipes. Mama was teaching her how to cook Jamaican food, how to shop for a good piece of yellow yam and a hand of green bananas; in turn, Bella showed Mama how to make pasta from scratch and what to do with each kind. Apart from Monica, I had never seen Mama so taken with one of her children's partners. It didn't go unnoticed by Glory and Aunt Val, whose relationship with her was strained and tense.

Mama proudly sent photographs of Bella and the baby to our old neighbours on the island and to Aunt Joyce in America. Grand-aunt Ruth got a thick package with photos, letters, aprons and pot holders. She even sent photos to

Uncle Mikey, but without a letter. To Monica she sent pictures and a postcard saying this relationship would teach
Freddie responsibility, and then he would start supporting
Freddie Jr. She continued to send Monica a little money for
him whenever she could, to help with school and books.

~ ~ ~

The day Mama received a letter from Grand-aunt Ruth, she
called her first family meeting. The following Sunday
evening we all gathered at Uncle Peppie and Aunt Val's, and
waited for Mama to tell us what the meeting was about.

"Mi get a letter from Ruth, and de contents is of grave
concern to mi. Ah want unnu to listen carefully, for mi need
all de help and support on dis one." Everyone nodded.

"'My dear sister,'" Mama began reading. "'I hope this
letter find you in peace. Freddie wife sound like a nice girl
and the baby pretty like money. With God's blessing and
guidance I hope they have a long and successful life together.
Little Freddie is growing into a fine young man, I only sorry
that Freddie couldn't see it in him to send for the boy and
take him off this island.'"

Mama paused and Freddie shifted uneasily in his chair.
She took no notice, her eyes glued to the papers in her hand.
Bella held baby Vittorio close.

"'Joyce moving back home next month, say she have
enough of foreign. When you coming back, you give any
thoughts to it? Icie and Ivan are doing fine and a real blessing to me, for I am now finding the restaurant business a
little tiring.

"'Maria what I have to say to you is not easy, but it have to be said. I waited this long because I truly believed that things would change with Mikey. Your house is the shabbiest on the street. The flower beds almost don't exist. The trees need shaping. People from all about come and jump the fence, trample on the grass that taller than me to get at the fruits on the trees. Mikey has not been spending much time there, it seem him taste in friends much higher than him can see. I try talking to him but you know how him can talk big sometimes. He let me know that everybody gone foreign and forget him, except for a letter every now and then from Glory. He say you forget you have a son out here.'"

Mama paused again, then went on. "'He come and give me the bank book for the house. Say him moving out. Praise the Lord that at least him collect the rent dutifully from the tenants. I am doing what I can with the help of Ivan, but talk to the children and see what can be done. Maria, the place really need care. I cry when I remember how the yard use to be a thing of beauty when you was here.

"'Give Molly a hug for me and tell her that her dear grand-aunt is still alive, so she can send me a little postcard from time to time. Kiss Glory and Freddie and Peppie for me. Greetings for Val and Sid. God Bless. Your sister Ruth.'"

Mama put the letter on the table beside her and waited. Nobody said anything, so she asked, "What yuh think we should do?"

Glory was the first to respond. "Sell de place, Mama. It don't mek sense to have it going to nothing when you can get good money for it."

"Is what yuh talking 'bout, gal? Sell? Yuh know how

much sweat and tears go in dat house? What yuh think mi was doing when you and Freddie in de country wid Mammy and Pappy?" Her voice grew louder and more impatient with each question. She waited again. She stared at Peppie. Peppie looked at his wife. Then Val spoke. Big mistake.

"Mama, I think Glory is right. Peppie and I will have to support her suggestion."

Mama gave her a killer look. "How yuh reach in dis conversation?" she demanded. "Yuh only sit in 'cause yuh married to mi son, but yuh have no voting privilege here. Yuh know de house? Yuh know Jamaica? Yuh know anything about our struggles?" Her words slapped Aunt Val hard. I felt sorry for Val, but I wasn't about to come to her defence, not when I knew my grandmother's pain better than anyone else in that room.

"So who going to go down?" Mama asked, this time looking at each of her children. "Somebody need to go down, and preferably is one a you bwoys."

Freddie spoke. "Mama I would love to go and help out, but ah can't leave Bella and de baby, and frankly I don't hold dat much attachment for de house. It would only be for you."

"Fi me? Yuh don't think Canadian government could run all of you out at any time? An weh di backside unnu going to run to if unnu don't even have a house? And what 'bout fi yuh poor bwoy chile down dere. You don't think that maybe one day it would pass down to him?"

"Mama, I done. Yuh live in de past too much," he said.

"Well, I'm sure we can work out something," Bella put in. "Mama is right, home is very important. My mother would feel the same way. I remember—"

Freddie cut her off. "Don't come in dis, Bell. Italy different and yuh family different." He didn't explain how or why, and nobody asked him to.

"Mama, me out of de picture," Glory said. "I don't hold no great attachment to de place, and is Canada we is now and we have to look to de future, not wallow in de past."

Mama glanced away and made to spit into her handkerchief, but thought better of it. Instead she said, "Then is forget, unnu forget so quick? Is amnesia unnu come down wid? Freddie, yuh don't remember de dead-end street? De parties, yuh kite-flying days, crab season? Peppie, yuh don't remember dat is de very yard you learn to fix yuh first car? Yuh forget dat when we get de house, it was just land, nothing never built on it? Yuh forget de buckets of water you and Mikey use to carry on unnu head? Glory, yuh forget de baking in dat house? De pastries and catering that pay yuh passage to come Canada? De Singer sewing machine in de front room dat sew yuh frock dem?"

My grandmother laughed bitterly, and now she did spit in her handkerchief. "Nobody want to remember where dem come from. Well, is one thing I know for sure and dat is ah will never sell dat place, not over mi dead body." Her voice boomed through the living room. "Ah won't sell it. I would rather mek de house dem rotten down. Mek people capture it, put up tent and live. Mek de house rotten," she repeated. "Ah know land can't rotten. One day when de house rotten down, ah will donate de land to charity, mek dem build a orphanage for all de pickney dem dat don't have fish nor fowl to mind dem."

~ ~ ~

Mama continued to visit Melbourne, and as Glory had fore-warned, they drank heavily every weekend. The family never visited Melbourne's house. Glory said, "Ah can just see de place, big and run-down, stink of liquor and in need of work."

Mama began to take a nip or two of drink at Uncle Peppie's, and soon she was drinking heavily there, too. Aunt Val was the first to complain to Glory about the burnt meat and the half-cooked rice. Glory sympathized with her, but that was all she could do. Val complained to Uncle Peppie, who did nothing, then she spoke directly to Mama, who responded by sucking her teeth and spending more time at Melbourne's. She cursed Aunt Val for interfering and cursed Uncle Peppie for being weak. One day, a Wednesday, I phoned her, and she answered with a heavy cough.

"Mama, what happen?" I asked.

"Nutten. What yuh mean?" she bellowed loudly into the phone.

"Nutten." I had never confronted her about her drinking. "Ah will talk to yuh later, Mama."

Later that evening when I called, Uncle Peppie answered the phone, his voice tired and disappointed-sounding.

"She in bed, Molly. She not feeling well."

The lies, I thought after I got off the phone, secrets that are not secret, those unspeakable truths.

~ ~ ~

It was inevitable, yet when it happened we were shocked. Uncle Peppie and Aunt Val got the call. Mama had been admitted to the emergency ward at a nearby hospital. She'd had a stroke at Melbourne's place. Fortunately it was minor, but she had kidney and liver complications. She spent seven days in hospital before the doctors decided they had to take out one of her kidneys. The family kept a vigil by her bed. Glory only left the room to talk to the doctors.

When Mama was discharged, we brought her to our apartment, where Glory, Bella, Uncle Peppie and I fed her soup and tended to her around the clock.

On her follow-up visit to the doctor, he told her she had to make some fast and hard decisions about cigarettes and alcohol. They put a strain on her heart, and her lungs would give out if she did not quit smoking. Glory had gone to the doctor with her, so I heard the entire report while Glory was on the phone with Uncle Peppie.

One night soon after, Uncle Peppie and Freddie came to visit. They sat down with Glory to have a talk with my grandmother.

"Mama," Glory started, "we worried 'bout yuh, and yuh have to change yuh lifestyle if yuh want to live. Yuh hear what de doctor say, dat if yuh continue to drink and smoke, yuh taking yuh life in yuh hands. De best thing to do under de circumstances is to stay here wid mi, where mi can take care of yuh."

My grandmother's eyes were as cold and hard as the marbles Punsie and I used to play with on Wigton Street. Uncle Peppie took her hand and squeezed it awkwardly.

"So what yuh have to say?" She swung her gaze toward him.

"Mama, we all want yuh to live for a long time. Glory have a point—why yuh don't come back and live with her, and yuh know yuh always welcome at my house."

My grandmother coughed heavily, spitting the mucus into her handkerchief. She fixed Freddie with the same cold gaze. He spoke before she could.

"Mama, everything up to you. Ah love you, but what else can I say except we all responsible for weself?" Glory gave him a cut eye, but he took no notice. Silence weighed the room again, then Mama turned to me.

"What you have to say, Molly?"

I was taken completely off guard, so rarely was I asked to give an opinion. I looked at my mother, then down at my hands.

"Talk, gal, mi grow yuh wid intelligence and sense," Mama said roughly.

"Mama, yuh should do what you think is best," I said.

Glory interrupted. "Mama, stop de games please. This is serious business. As a matter of fact, yuh should join Alcoholics Anonymous because yuh need help. Serious help. Yuh drinking is a major problem an' it go kill yuh if yuh don't stop."

A strained smile pulled at the corners of Mama's mouth. "But you have mi life all planned out, eh?"

"Mama, I am only thinking of you and you need help, you're sick," Glory pushed on.

"Go weh, gal," Mama replied, her voice razor sharp. "Who yuh think bring yuh on dis earth? Yuh think if mi couldn't tek care of miself, you would be here?"

Glory looked at each of her brothers for help, but none was forthcoming. Uncle Peppie looked off into a far corner of the room and Freddie at his watch.

"Let mi say dis one time. Ah not going to no Alcoholics Anonymous, dat is fi white people and weak-minded people, and mi nuh fit into any of dose category. Unnu mussi tek me for a damn fool." She paused, her breathing heavy. "And furthermore, mi ah go live wid Melbourne. Him is a good man and him need a woman to tek care of him."

"And who going to tek care of you?" Glory demanded.

"Yuh don't worry 'bout dat," Mama said.

"Then mi wash mi hands, Mama, do as yuh please," Glory said angrily.

"Ah have to leave soon—ah have to pick up Bella," Uncle Freddie said.

Glory's voice was resigned. "Well, go."

He kissed Mama on the cheek and turned to give Glory a kiss, too, but she turned away. "Sis," he said, "don't worry so much. Things will take care of themselves. 'Bye Peppie, Molly." And he was out the door.

Near tears, Glory escaped to her room. Uncle Peppie squeezed Mama's hand again and she held on to his. It was a tender and sad gesture. He loved his mother dearly, yet he couldn't speak up even for her own good.

Mama left our apartment a few days later and moved in with Melbourne.

Part Three

Around a Flowering Tree One Finds Many Insects

FROM THE DAY MAMA LEFT US she never took another drink or lit another cigarette. She never joined AA either. She slipped into the disorder of Melbourne's home and in time created a steady comfort. He was a man with a big heart. He had a genuine affection for people, and he liked nothing better than an audience. When Mama went to live with him, he was spending most of his time at the local community centre, where he relived his past as a boxer. An audience of young and old was always on hand to listen and to help him remember the story he had told many times. In the evenings he watched television with Mama, and their weekends were filled with friends and drinks and plenty of food. Visiting them, I felt like I was back on our dead-end street.

I'm still awed by Mama's strength. She continued to serve rum and other potent beverages to Melbourne's guests, and I never saw her begrudge them a drink or deliver an envious look. Even years later, when Melbourne's hands trembled from too much drink and his cough had turned to emphysema, she patiently rationed his drinks and cigarettes. By then it was too late for him to quit.

Glory never did come to terms with Mama living with Melbourne, but that didn't matter to Mama. What mattered was that she was once again mistress of her own house. Again she provided daycare for children to earn her own money. She did this for years, despite Melbourne's protests that they had enough to live on without her working. Over the years she stashed her earnings in several bank accounts.

~ ~ ~

One day Bella left. She left to save her life, and in so doing she gave up Vittorio. He was an absolute darling, a two-year-old with grey-green eyes, a butter complexion and sandy-brown hair. His lips were wide and thick like hard-dough bread under a spread of butter. He was not blessed with Freddie's strong jaw, but he had inherited his father's prominent nose and his mother's delicate, oval face.

We all knew from way back that Uncle Freddie was a woman-beater. We had crossed our fingers and hoped that with Bella, the wedding and the baby, things would be different. But twice I remembered hearing Glory on the phone, telling him he could be charged with assault if Bella ever pressed charges. He didn't listen, he never had. Even Uncle Peppie and Sid tried talking to him about it, but Uncle Freddie ignored their soft manner and brotherly pleas. Mama was his harshest critic, but because he had become so accustomed to her disapproval, she had no impact.

Mama really cared for Bella, and they spent a lot of time together. Even before Vittorio could talk, he knew all the rooms in Melbourne's massive three-storey house, for he and Bella were regular visitors. I, too, had warmed to Bella from the first. She was at most eight years my senior, the big sister I never had. I told her secrets and asked questions I would never have asked my mother. We laughed about silly things, tried out different hairstyles on each other and went shopping at the mall. She taught me Italian swear words and how to say, "I love you."

We had all seen her bruises, but we did the polite thing and kept quiet. Some nights she'd be wearing dark glasses. Sometimes I'd go to babysit Vittorio and she would make excuses about bumping into a closed door.

One day I was visiting Mama when she called. We were in the living room watching *General Hospital*, and Mama was trying to teach me to crochet, but my fingers wouldn't obey. The phone rang and when Mama answered, I heard Bella's high and trembly voice.

"Mama? Mama, I'm at the Toronto Western Hospital." Then I heard her crying. Mama didn't wait to hear anything else.

"Hold on, Bella, ah coming." And she hung up the phone.

We hurried to the hospital. What a sight she was. Swollen eyes. Bruised arms. A broken nose. Her beautiful golden hair chopped off.

"Mama, I didn't do anything," she said.

Mama hugged Bella, careful not to hurt her. She sat down next to her, her eyes pools of sympathy.

"Mama, yesterday was my mother's birthday." Bella struggled to speak.

"Tek it easy, dear, ah right here," Mama reassured her.

"I called her to wish her happy birthday. He was right there, he knew who I was talking to . . . and he just slapped me in the face for nothing."

She started to cry again, and Mama stroked her hand.

"So I said to him, 'What's your problem, Freddie? Do you have a problem?' and he just stared at me with his nostrils flaring like I said something awful. So when I hung up, he started in on me, kicking and slapping me around. He didn't stop until Vittorio started to scream, and the next-door neighbour threatened to call the police. Then he kicked the front door open and left. The neighbour helped me into a cab."

"Did the dutty dog say why he beat yuh?" Mama asked.

"He said I was talking to my mother in Italian because I didn't want him to understand what I was saying. Mama, he kept accusing me of telling her things about him. I would never do that, Mama, never."

She was in a lot of pain. Mama pressed her arm lightly, and Bella continued. "I said to him, 'How do you expect me to talk to her? In Jamaican? For Christ's sake, Freddie, she's Italian like me, remember? And she hardly understands English.' That just made him crazy."

She was shaking and sobbing hard. I got up and looked through the window at the streetcars and the night falling. For the first time Freddie held no magic for me. I wondered how this could be the same Freddie who was so gentle with me, the Freddie who taught me to fly kites, eat crab, took me to my first cockfight.

"Mama, I'm going to leave him," Bella whispered. "I can't take it any longer, it's not right."

"Stay, Bella," I heard Mama plead. "Stay, it important

for de child to have a mother. Stay and ah will help yuh, ah promise yuh that."

Bella didn't answer.

When Glory heard what happened, she told Mama to leave them alone. "Mama, cockroach no business inna fowl fight."

They quarrelled, of course, Mama protesting this wasn't a case of cockroaches and fowl—we were all family and it was our duty to take a stand.

Bella listened to her own mind and left without good-byes, without a trace. Uncle Freddie came home to find Vittorio in front of the television, happily eating a bag of chips. Freddie said she took nothing. Her clothes hung neat-ly in the closet. Her toothbrush, perfume and hairbrush were still in the bathroom. Even her nightgown lay peacefully under her pillow.

At first Uncle Freddie resisted any help from Mama. He made arrangements with his neighbour to babysit, but that didn't last long. Some nights he'd come home late and rely on his charm to wipe away the neighbour's irritation. One night he went too far. He didn't come home and he didn't call. When he hadn't turned up by morning, the neighbour called Catholic Children's Aid and they took Vittorio away.

Uncle Freddie didn't contact the CCA. When Mama found out—through a slip of Glory's tongue—she immediately called Freddie and demanded that he bring the child to her.

"Listen to mi, Freddie, yuh have to get dat child out of dat place. Yuh can't come to white-man country and put de little pickney in a orphanage, not wid so much family around."

He was stubborn and he held out. When she wouldn't let

up, he told her angrily that she was the last woman on earth he wanted to raise his child. Never one to give up easily, she ignored him and turned to Glory and Uncle Peppie and Aunt Val for help.

"Lord, how unnu can sit dere and mek de nice likkle bwoy go to government? Unnu nuh have no compassion? If him won't let mi tek de pickney, why one unnu nuh tek him? Why unnu cyaan do de right thing?"

~ ~ ~

Vittorio went to live with Mama and Uncle Mel when he was three years old. Uncle Mel, who loved Vittorio from birth, embraced him like his own son. Unrelenting, Mama demanded that Freddie come visit the child and show responsibility by giving her an allowance to take care of him. Of course, he did neither, and soon he stopped even calling her. Months later, after more stormy quarrels, he vanished.

Like Bella, he left without saying goodbye. For a time we received postcards tracing him to Calgary, then Vancouver and finally through Europe, but there was never a return address. Then the cards stopped. Later Glory told us that he was with a woman from Germany and was expecting a child.

Uncle Peppie and Aunt Val moved to Atlanta, Georgia, sometime afterward. Aunt Val had a sister living there who had encouraged them to make the move.

When Vittorio was about nine, Freddie made contact, and Vittorio went to Europe to spend a holiday with his father and his new wife. We all hoped that it would be a new beginning for both father and son, but much as I hate to admit it, especially now that Mama is dead, she behaved badly about the reunion, and instead of encouraging the relationship, she found fault with Freddie and laid open his past in front of Vittorio before he left. Freddie and his mother had one last dreadful telephone quarrel seven months before her death, and that was the last time they spoke.

~ ~ ~

Although I spent a lot of time at Mama's, I continued to live with Glory and Sid. I saw Justin regularly, going for rides in his Pontiac and visiting his friend's place in the east end. Justin was a sweet talker, and he spread his words like items from a picnic basket in front of me. I ate everything. I was sure that someday soon I would be his wife.

When I was nineteen, I received my high school diploma and landed a job with an agency, watering office plants. Glory didn't think much of it, but Mama gave me all the encouragement I needed. "Good gal. Yuh have to start somewhere. Nuh matter how little de pay. Hold on. Things will work out. Oletime people use to say, 'One, one full basket!'"

Glory had gone on to receive a nursing assistant diploma and was now working at a hospital near Keele and Eglinton.

~ ~ ~

Justin was the first person I told about the pregnancy. In my naïveté I had expected a quick and quiet wedding, our own apartment, our baby in a cradle next to our bed. Instead he acted like a bumbling idiot, offering me more promises "if only just this one time you get an abortion."

Next I confided in my grandmother. How sweet it was to be comforted by her. I sat with her in her kitchen and listened to the hum of her reassuring voice, which had calmed me since I was a baby curled up in our mahogany bed.

"Stand up and hold yuh head high, gal," Mama told me. "Is nothing fi shame. Is a thing what happen to better dan yuh and worse dan yuh. Face de challenge. Don't run from it. Keep de pickney, mek de dutty man go weh. Him will get fi him comeuppance."

I'd known not to speak to my mother about the matter. I'd vowed I would be Mrs. Somebody, with a thick, gold wedding band on my finger when I left Glory's home. Instead I left disgraced. In my foolishness I'd thought she wouldn't notice my swelling belly, just as I'd hoped she wouldn't notice my sudden craving for salt on ice cubes. One day she demanded to know who the father was, when and where it all happened.

"Leave dis house before dat belly start show! Either dat or get rid of it!" she shouted at the top of her lungs.

Sid sat with his head lowered, no doubt embarrassed for me. I didn't know whether he knew about Justin.

My mother started again. "Yuh is a blasted dutty wretch. A sneaking bitch, run round town wid every man."

I stared her down and a feeling of hatred heated up in me. "If mi is a blasted wretch and a bitch, yuh is a whore. Mi know mi father?" I challenged.

She slapped me with all her might and I fell to the floor.

"Yuh bitch, pack yuh clothes and get out of dis house. Ah only hope to God is not Sid . . ." She broke off.

I got up and went to my room to pack my things, then left for Mama and Uncle Mel's. I was thankful I had my grand-mother to teach me how to be a mother. Under her guidance, I concentrated on my unborn child. When I bathed myself, I washed my passage with care and used sweet oils. At night, wrapped in a blanket, I imagined my baby lying next to me, sucking milk from my breast. Mama cooked for me. I watched her moving about the kitchen, my worries and fears soothed by her humming and the smell of her cooking.

Mama knitted and crocheted just as she did for Bella's baby. We shopped together for things for the baby, and when I was too big and heavy to move around easily, she took great pleasure in shopping by herself. She bought the baby's first bath set and a brush and comb. She insisted that cloth dia-pers were best and got a full supply.

I loved my grandmother's pure and simple generosity, the return of the unconditional love I'd had throughout my childhood and now enjoyed again with my baby inside me. She knew I wanted a girl. She wanted a boy, for reasons I've never understood. Men had caused her so much grief, but if she were telling this story, she might tell it differently.

Without her, I don't know how I would have carried myself through those nine months. She held me in her arms if she thought I was slipping into self-pity, telling me I had a whole life ahead of me. With her by my side, I believed it.

My water broke in February. My daughter's arrival was swift and miraculous. I was still thin and small, and the pain sur-passed anything I'd ever experienced. Mama wiped the blood from my baby's body, and the midwife cut the umbilical cord and laid her in my arms. Her cry echoed against my chest when I cradled her, her black moss of curly wet hair cool against my skin. Her complexion at birth was a deep brown, like the bark of a tree, and at the base of her neck was a lighter, coin-shaped patch. Just like the one on Justin. She was the most beautiful thing I'd ever laid eyes on, and she was mine. I felt blessed. Had it not been for Mama, I'd never have known such beauty, never felt such love.

I named my daughter Ciboney Margaret Galloway. Margaret for my great-grandmother Mammy. Ciboney, because I liked the sound of it, and I remembered the old plantation with that name in Ocho Rios, where Mammy's mother grew up.

I made a pledge that day as I held Ciboney that I would never leave her.

Glory left Canada, following Uncle Peppie and Aunt Val to Atlanta. They told her there was more opportunity there, better prospects. Never one to stand in the way of progress, Mama gave her her blessing. When Glory decided to move, she broke up with Sid. She'd had enough of his extramarital affairs.

Sid came around to Mama's house a few times, bringing gifts for Ciboney. Once when he held her I was sure he saw the light coin at the base of her neck, just like Justin's. Mama fussed and looked after him, sending him home with large containers of food. In time his visits stopped, and it was just as well. Each time Glory called and heard that he had visited, she got angry.

~ ~ ~

The first time I met Rose was at a women's health clinic. I had gone there for a checkup after Ciboney, who was now six, had the chicken pox. Rose was sitting in the waiting room with a pregnant friend. We exchanged names and talked a bit about Ciboney. They left the clinic before I was called for my appointment.

Rose says fate brought us together. I say it was a simple cloth bag. I should have left the bag at the clinic's front desk for them to return to her, but her address was typed on an envelope in the bag and I decided to return it myself. I had an urge to take the bag home with me and explore its contents. Diagrams, designs of gardens large and small were scribbled on scraps of paper. Inside tiny notebooks were names of plants and flowers, some I'd never heard of. There were some university calendars in the cloth bag, too, one dog-eared at the pages listing horticulture courses. A small bottle of Japanese musk oil was in a corner of the bag, and I dabbed drops of it behind my ears.

I kept the bag for several days. To this day I still can't explain why, but I think I'd fallen in love with its contents.

I finally phoned Rose and told her I had found her bag. I apologized for the delay, and we made arrangements to meet midmorning at a coffee shop in Kensington Market. What was to be a brief exchange of a cloth bag and a cup of coffee turned into hours of talk. She was from Grenada, the Isle of Spice. Mountainous, lush, fertile. Grenadians say, "Throw a seed on de ground and fruits, vegetables, flowers spring up." Rose was all that: sensuous, lush, warm and generous.

That day in the coffee shop she wore cut-off blue jeans and a loose white cotton shirt, buttoned all the way down the front. Her thick, black, baby dreadlocks barely touched the nape of her neck. Her laughter was infectious, and I immediately liked that about her, for laughing didn't come easily to me. And her openness was refreshing.

"Did you go through my garbage bin of a bag?" she asked, laughing. I laughed, too, and avoided admitting to my curiosity. From the coffee shop we moved on to a small Caribbean take-out joint and then to Rose's house. She devoured the food in no time, talking all the while about her island and all that she missed. I wasn't as enthusiastic about the food as she was, and I promised her that soon I would let her sample my grandmother's cooking. Rose had no family here, except for an older brother she was estranged from. She'd left the Isle of Spice years earlier, coming to Canada to stay with her brother and his wife while she finished high school. She'd meant to stay on with them through university.

"It never worked out that way," she explained to me. "I finish high school with honours, but things so bad with mi brother and his wife I had to leave, too much confusion . . . and they never like my way of living my life."

"You just picked up and left?" I asked.

She laughed again. "What you want me to do, wait until they kick me out? Girl, I just get up and leave, and stay with a friend until ah get my own place," she said, waving her hand at the tiny bachelor apartment. "I couldn't go back home. I had to finish what I set out to do. Get a university education. Aaye." She shook her head, and despite the dance of her beautiful locks, her eyes betrayed her bravado. I learned later that she had just turned twenty-two, about four and a half years younger than I.

Lunch turned into dinner, then it was time for more

coffee. It was early spring and the evenings were still short. I called Mama to say I'd be late, and Rose and I talked long into the night. I told her about the dead-end street and my family.

Within weeks we'd become fast friends, sharing our love for plants and talking about travel, music and the Caribbean. In time we graduated from coffee and tea to rosé wine and mango-almond cheesecake, which Rose loved with a passion. We talked freely, though I skipped over my grandmother's binges because they were a thing of the past. I told her about Justin. And I told her about Myers and our garden back home, and about Grandfather Oliver, Punsie and Petal.

There were stories in her family, too: an uncle who'd sided with the Americans in Grenada in 1983, which resulted in hush-hush deaths and shame on the family name; a sister who ran off with a half-brother; another family member, an immigration officer, who was caught taking home goods confiscated from tourists. For Rose nothing was too serious for her not to find humour in, even if it meant digging deep. Of her mother and father she spoke with respect and gratitude, and I warmed to her even more. They were close to Mama's age.

Rose became as familiar with my household as I was with hers. Like me, Mama and Uncle Mel responded to her ready laughter. Ciboney and Vittorio loved to play tag with her, and she spent hours playing snakes-and-ladders with them. Rose was everything I had liked about Punsie and Petal. She had the same adventurous spirit. And of course there was her laughter, her scent and her flawless coffee-brown face.

With encouragement from Rose, I applied for a scholarship to study horticulture at the University of Texas. I had never imagined myself going to college. In high school I'd dreamt of working as an assistant in a plant or florist shop, but that was before Ciboney. I had devoted myself to her, harvesting all the joy that I could. Gardening was something I did in Mama's backyard, and I hoped that someday I would have a meadow of flowers of my own. But I had never been lucky with dreams, and if I hadn't met Rose, I would never have believed they could come true.

She had already been accepted to the University of Texas for the following fall semester, and she convinced me to go for a scholarship and join her. I didn't want to leave my daughter, but I knew I couldn't take her with me. For a brief moment I understood why Glory had left me with Mama to come to Canada. Had it not been for Mama, I wouldn't have taken the plunge; I would have stayed home and fulfilled my duty as a mother, keeping my pledge that I would never leave Ciboney in anyone else's care. But Mama remembered how I'd played in the dirt at Myers's elbow, and she believed in me.

Next to Ciboney, there was nothing I loved more than flowers and gardening. And so, with the promise of a better future for me and my daughter, I left her with Mama. It seemed the right thing to do and it was what I knew: to make a better life one had to go away. I made two promises to myself: that I would come back every holiday to be with my daughter, and that I would stay in Texas no longer than the required time.

I spent some of the best years of my life at university. It was my first taste of real independence. I could come and go as

I pleased. It was almost like being a child again. I was free from responsibility except to myself. Rose and I took our classes together, we ate together and shared a room. Soon we were inseparable.

Mama was still taking in children when I left for college, still cooking and tending to Uncle Mel. She visited Glory and Uncle Peppie a few times in Atlanta, and they tried to persuade her to spend more time there. She always refused. At first I felt guilty, knowing that Ciboney was part of the reason, but later I realized that Mama needed people who needed her, and her own children had long outgrown her.

I came back to Toronto for Christmas and over the summer, and even though I enjoyed the freedom and space Texas afforded me, I was always happy to be at Mama's house, to be fed, to listen to Uncle Mel's stories and, more than anything, to see Ciboney and Vittorio. I was glad they were growing up like brother and sister.

During the holidays I caught up on the activities of the family. Mama always had an earful waiting for me. Uncle Peppie had no guts, Glory didn't love her enough, Freddie had abandoned her, and Mikey was on the road to destruction. Mama encouraged me in my studies and assured me that all was well with Ciboney. Each time I visited, I brought games, educational toys and books for her and Vittorio. I took them to movies, to the park and the zoo, to give Mama a little holiday.

The second year, I began to be troubled by Vittorio's behaviour and the way Mama dealt with it. The day before Christmas I was sitting watching television with the family. The tree was loaded with gifts. An electric train appeared in one of the commercials, and Vittorio pointed to it, yelling, "That's what I want!" and jumped around excitedly.

"We bought you a lot of other things," Uncle Mel said. "Next year, if that's still what you want." Vittorio pouted and badgered. I sat there and watched Mama hushing him, telling him not to mind. On Christmas day he unwrapped a brand-new electric train.

There were other incidents I should have taken seriously but didn't. I trusted Mama and never questioned her judgment. One evening there was shouting in the living room and toys flying about. I heard a scream and the sound of a slap. Mama was the first in the room. "Unnu stop de fighting, what wrong wid unnu. Yuh both mus learn to live like brother and sister. Unnu clean up de mess." I would have been satisfied had I not overheard the rest of the conversation.

"It's not my fault, it's not me!" Vittorio shouted.

Then Ciboney's voice: "Mama, I didn't start it. He hit me first."

"Never mind, just clean up de games, don't tek no notice of him," Mama said to Ciboney. I heard Vittorio in the background, teasing Ciboney. Mama repeated, "Don't mind, put away de things, ignore him."

During the rest of the holiday I watched that scene play again and again. I reassured myself that I had less than two years to go at college, and I would make things right when I got back.

Each time I returned to Texas, I'd soon forget my worries. Rose had the ability to smooth them all away. Just being outdoors, sifting the dirt through my fingers was soothing. The campus was so beautiful, with its manicured lawns, mature trees, nature trails to get lost in, greenhouses, decorative beds and a full research farm. Were it not for Ciboney and Mama, I could have spent my life there.

~ ~ ~

In those first years Rose didn't come back to Toronto for the holidays. She went home to Grenada for Christmas, and over the summers she worked in Texas. Mama was fond of her and grateful that she had encouraged me to go to college. She always packed me off with a Christmas black cake, puddings and other baked goods to share with Rose. And with Rose's mother's cakes and jams and jellies, we had enough desserts to last us through the school year.

With each trip to Grenada, Rose came back with rich family anecdotes. I admired her dramatic flair and her openness. Though she adored her family, she did not shoulder their problems. I wished I could be like her, free of the responsibility of family history, free of its disappointments.

When did things change between Rose and me? I can't say precisely. At some point I began to take notice of her short, stumpy toes. Her large ears, which she hid with her locks. The smell of Japanese musk and sweat next to me in the greenhouse.

When I returned after one Christmas in Toronto, Rose wanted to celebrate her birthday by going dancing. And she wanted to choose the place. Where she took me that night wasn't really a surprise, though I would have been too shy to suggest a bar for women. Later that night, back in our apartment, Japanese musk was warm and sweaty on my tongue.

Her hands touched me everywhere. We soaked up glasses of rosé wine and savoured the taste of each other's tongues. I let her suck on my breasts and held my breath as her teeth grazed them. I pulled her up on me, caressed the nape of her neck and her black locks, rich with the smell of spice. I tasted her nipples, then rolled on top of her, my tongue tracing her sinuous body. I knelt between her legs to sweet pleasure. Spent, I luxuriated in her scent into the morning.

In our passion we promised each other that we'd be together forever. Someday we'd open a botanical garden, complete with butterflies, exotic tropical plants, caterpillars and even lizards. When we weren't making love or studying for an exam, we talked for hours about our future. We read up on new plants, ran experiments at the research farm and read botany as if it were poetry.

Though I continued to go to Toronto for the holidays, I was always eager to return to Rose and the world we had created for ourselves. But I couldn't pretend that things were not changing all around me, and where I least expected it, at Mama's house. During my third year away, she found religion and was attending the Open Door Pentecostal Church of Jesus Christ, which met in a basement around the corner from our house. That summer both Vittorio and Ciboney were going to services with her. She tried to get Uncle Mel interested, but he preferred to drink and entertain his friends. She seemed content with just the children going with her. Over the summer I went to one or two services with her, but I couldn't muster up much enthusiasm. She often sang hymns around the house, her voice rich and warm as always:

What a wonderful change in my life has been wrought
Since Jesus came into my heart!
I have light in my soul for which long I had sought,
Since Je'sus came into my heart!

More than anything I wanted to share my happiness with Mama, but I knew better.

Ciboney and Vittorio were growing fast. They had grown close, too, and were as inseparable as Rose and I were. I wanted time to talk with Ciboney alone, to discuss things that would set the stage for my and Rose's return. But Ciboney went nowhere without Vittorio. Whenever we planned to go out, she asked if Vittorio could come. It would have been selfish of me to say no, so I gave in every time.

It bothered me that Vittorio always wanted to be taken shopping for new clothes, new toys. Mama didn't share my concern. She laughed it off. "But, Molly, look how much clothes you use to have. Yuh forget? Mek de pickney dem enjoy dem youth." It sounded so simple that I felt like a grouch. I tried to ignore the two brand-new bicycles he had, the Nintendo games he insisted were his and would share with Ciboney if she was good, the drum set Uncle Mel had bought him and the guitar he now wanted, tired of the drum set, the piles of running shoes and clothes, the boxing gloves. Ciboney did receive the occasional gift from Mama and Uncle Mel, but not nearly as often as Vittorio. She wasn't as demanding as he was, and she didn't complain.

I returned to Texas and to Rose with mixed feelings. Soon after, Mama called and said she had given up taking in children and was embracing the church fully. She announced that she

was saved and was attending the basement service twice a week.
Vittorio was enrolled in a Seventh Day Adventist school.

"Ah don't like de marks him getting on him report card
and dem say him not concentrating, but ah don't believe dem.
Him say certain children in de class pick on him and dat de
teacher don't like him. Ah have to believe him, for a mi grow
him from him small. De Seventh Day school expensive, but
de discipline will do him good. Dem wear uniform, yuh
know," she explained.

I asked if it wouldn't be confusing for Vittorio to attend
a Seventh Day school and go to the Open Door Pentecostal
Church. He was thirteen then and I had genuine misgivings
about the mixed messages of the different denominations.
But Mama didn't seem worried. "Don't be a fool, Molly, is
one God, yuh know."

Ciboney was doing well in school and I was relieved that
there were no plans to move her.

Later that year I began to hear worry in Mama's voice.
At first she brushed it aside. "Mi just a bit tired, must be getting de flu," she said simply. But after I pressed her, she
slowly confessed that she was concerned about Uncle Mel's
health and about Vittorio.

"Ah don't know what fi do. Dem say him come late some
mornings and sometimes him don't come to school at all.
Dem seh money missing from de teacher bag and is him.
Dem seh dem catch him hand in her bag. Him seh is lie dem
telling on him. Him marks don't improve either."

"What about homework, Mama?" I asked.

"Him do it. Him even stop coming to the Open Door
Church so him will have more time. Ah try to help him wid

de lessons, but me and Mel don't understand much wid all dis modern-day teaching."

I reminded her that my graduation was close and I would be home soon to help out. My family had planned a grand celebration, for I was the first in the family to graduate from college. Mama, Uncle Mel, Ciboney, Vittorio, Uncle Peppie, Aunt Val and even Glory all planned to be there. I had done well and was the valedictorian.

The night before my graduation Mama phoned. Vittorio had been caught breaking into a car with a group of friends. He couldn't travel until the matter was cleared up, and under the circumstances she didn't want to leave him alone. Uncle Mel couldn't come either—he was not well enough to travel without her.

I wanted more than anything for Mama to be with me, to hear my speech, which I had dedicated to her, to watch the pride on her face as I received my degree. Glory, Uncle Peppie and Aunt Val flew in from Atlanta, and Ciboney flew in from Toronto. They took photographs and we went out to dinner, but it wasn't the same. I tried to hide my disappointment.

Ciboney spent a few days with me before she went back. Rose and I took her to the zoo and the movies, we fed her junk food, watched television with her, put on makeup, painted each other's toes in wild colours and generally acted silly. I was surprised how much she had grown. She was ten going on fourteen, and I was determined to spend more time with her. I didn't want to make my mother's mistakes.

I saw her steal glances at Rose and me. Even though we tried our best to act like just good friends, it was hard to keep words like "darling" and "love" and "sweetie" from coming out. She must have noticed how we looked at each other, seen the way our hands touched carelessly. Rose had wanted me to tell her about us, but I wasn't ready. I hadn't told Mama, and I didn't want Ciboney to tell her. I didn't know how to tell Ciboney not to tell.

"Do you think the girl is a baby?" Rose exploded just after Ciboney left. "How are we supposed to have a life together if you can't be honest with your own child?"

I didn't answer. There was nothing I could say; she was right. But Ciboney was my child, and though I didn't say it to Rose, I sensed that had Ciboney been *her* daughter, she might have thought differently.

On our last night together before I returned to Toronto, Rose opened me with her tongue and I vowed to her, trembling, "Ah give yuh all of me. Dis is forever."

"Hush," she said.

"Softer, softer," I murmured.

"I want you to burst with mi tongue and sing loud. I don' want you to forget tonight."

My voice was thick with want. "Forget . . . never . . ."

"Is dis love?" she teased.

"Yes, YES, water, air, de breath mi tek."

I rose to meet her full on the mouth. A swollen river found its way to the sea. I pushed her back on the bed. Her laughter was sweet and thick, like molasses.

"Ah love de feel of yuh nipples in mi mouth . . . is like raisins in ginger wine with all kind of spice," I whispered.

Her laughter became sweet murmurs. She moaned, then

sucked back her breath. "I not ready . . . not yet . . . don't want to. Oh Gawd . . ." She bit her lips.

~ ~ ~

I had fully intended to tell Mama about Rose and me when I returned to Toronto. I came back to find her in a deep religious fervour. She was attending church three nights a week, dragging an unwilling Ciboney with her. My daughter immediately saw me as an ally. I wanted to rebuild my relationship with her—I hardly knew her. Rose was spending a few months in Grenada visiting family before coming back to Toronto to find a job and an apartment. Mama often asked about her and spoke affectionately about what a good friend she was. I felt sure then that when I told her about us, it would be all right. But I wanted to wait for the right time. Cowardly as I was—and despite my vows—I never did tell Mama.

Uncle Mel's health was failing. The smoking and drinking had taken their toll on him, and he had trouble breathing. Though his cough was rough and crusty, he continued to smoke and drink. His memory wandered in and out, and he told his boxing stories over and over again.

Things with Vittorio had not improved, either. He'd done very poorly at the Seventh Day Adventist school and had been suspended several times for theft and fighting. The worry was etched on Mama's face. I tried my best to help. I took Vittorio and Ciboney to the movies and signed them up at the local Y. He became interested in boxing and we found a club not far away, but he soon tired of that, just as he had tired of guitar and drumming lessons. Once when he was caught shoplifting at the local corner store, I begged the woman not to call the police, reminding her that we had been regular customers for many years. She finally agreed on the condition that he never enter her store again. We didn't tell Mama, and for a while he kept out of trouble.

There were some good times. Some evenings we played cards, Monopoly or games we made up as we went along. We'd rent videos, make popcorn. I helped Mama as much as I could with the washing, which was too much for her now that she had arthritic pain in her right knee.

On the surface things looked fine. Rose decided to spend a few extra months in Grenada. Although I missed her badly, I was thankful in a way, for I still hadn't said anything to Mama or Ciboney, and I wanted to spend more time helping out at home and giving back something to Mama and Uncle Mel.

I found a job in the Department of Botany at the University of Toronto and settled into it. Mama was pleased and told all her friends that her granddaughter held a big position working and researching at the university. I was only an assistant to the researcher's assistant, but her face was so full of pride when she told people that I didn't have the heart to correct her.

Vittorio was asked to leave the Adventist school because of his behaviour, and we enrolled him in a technical high school. He had decided that he was interested in fixing musical instruments, not playing them. Predictably, after one semester he decided that he really wanted to be in electronics. He'd made friends with some older aspiring musicians, and they, no doubt, had filled his head with dreams of travelling and a job as their technician. Reports came from school about his absence and his behaviour, yet Mama steadfastly blamed the teachers and the school. I was thankful that Ciboney continued to do well.

~ ~ ~

Uncle Mel started to miss coins from his pant pockets and then bills. He complained about it, but no one owned up to taking the money. Mama convinced him that he was forgetful, that he had just misplaced it. Then larger bills went missing. She still told him that he was mistaken. One day he caught Vittorio in the act. When he complained to Mama she said, "Yuh mek mistake. Vittorio wouldn't tief from yuh—yuh is like a father to him." Uncle Mel was adamant that he'd caught Vittorio and it was no mistake. Mama called Vittorio into the kitchen. In front of Uncle Mel, Vittorio denied that he had stolen any money. Mama asked him to swear on the Bible and he did. I was upstairs in my room and her voice carried clearly from the kitchen.

"Mel, mi love yuh, and thank yuh for everything, but mi have to say yuh mek a mistake. Vittorio wouldn't steal from yuh. A de drinks turn yuh head. Vittorio have no reason to steal yuh money. Him could ask me for anything him want."

"Maria, I don't have any reason to lie, he's my son," Mel said. Then to Vittorio he said, "Vittorio, tell your mother the truth."

"I did," I heard Vittorio say.

For the first time since I'd known Uncle Mel, he spoke harshly. "Boy, you know I'm not lying. Why are you lying?"

"I didn't," Vittorio answered, meek and innocent as a small boy.

"Okay, mek it pass, him say is not him," Mama said
quickly.

Mama became more heavily involved in the church and continued to insist that Ciboney go with her. Saturday nights Ciboney
stayed up late with Vittorio in front of the television, and Sunday
mornings she slept late. No amount of yelling from Mama could
rouse her. "Molly, wake her up. Mek her get ready for church. Ah
doing this for her own good, not mine," Mama said.

"Vittorio don't have to go, why me?" Ciboney shouted
at me one Sunday morning.

"Why don't you go and ask Mama?" I said roughly. "Is
not me taking you to church."

Guilty at once, I promised Ciboney that I would talk to
Mama that evening.

"What are you going to say?" she asked.

"That you don't want to go to church and that I support
you."

Her response surprised me. "No, you can't say that."

"Why, isn't that the truth?"

"Yes, but Mama wouldn't understand. I don't want to
hurt her feelings." Ciboney looked sheepish. "Tell her you
have things you want me to help you with."

"Then I would get blamed," I said. "Do you have any
other ideas?"

"I dunno," she replied helplessly.

"Okay," I said, "I'll say you have lots of homework." She
seemed satisfied then. I hoped that this would bring us closer. I told Mama that evening while we were eating dinner.

"Ciboney can do her homework on Saturday. Three

hours of praising God caan tek away from her school books."

I looked over at Ciboney, hoping she'd say something about a project or something, but she didn't, and the conversation ended there.

Upstairs later that night she said to me, "Maybe I'll talk to Vittorio and get him to work on Mama. If anyone can get through to her, it's him." I felt my heart tear a little. I went to bed and slept badly that night.

~ ~ ~

Try as I might, I wasn't getting as close to Ciboney as I'd hoped. I hadn't succeeded in freeing her from attending church services, and I had begun to see little changes in her. She and Vittorio would stay up late and watch television on weekends. One night I crept quietly downstairs to the kitchen for some water. I saw them curled up together, her head on his chest, a small blanket half covering them. It was innocent—the door was wide open and the television on, and they were asleep. I woke her and she followed me, childlike, up the stairs to her bed. Still, I couldn't get the image out of my head. Over the weeks I kept thinking of young lovers—innocent, but lovers all the same.

That wasn't the only time I found them like that. I tried to talk to Ciboney—after all, she was my daughter and only eleven. I approached the subject one night when we were out at a little café. Aimlessly, uneasily, I started to talk about her changing body, menstruation, the whole bit. She sat and waited for me to finish. Then she said, "Mom, I am already seeing my period—I know about all of these things." I wanted to ask her why she hadn't told me, but thought better of it and said nothing. It might have been the right time to tell her about Rose, but I didn't. Instead I asked, "Does Mama know?"

"Yes," she answered.

"Why yuh didn't tell me?" I asked, crushed.

"Why are you making a big deal? It's nothing," she said dismissively.

"It just would have been nice to know."

She swirled the drink around in her glass.

"Vittorio know, too?"

Her ackee-seed eyes opened wide. "No, why should I tell him? That's sick."

I ignored her look and her tone. "I think you should be careful how you conduct yourself in front of him, especially when yuh watching television late at night."

"What do you mean?"

"Just that . . ." I fumbled. "He's a young man, and even though you are his cousin . . . his feelings could be misdirected . . ."

"I don't know what you're talking about." She stared me down.

"How is church?" I asked, eager to change the subject.

That, too, was a mistake; her response was to roll her eyes.

~ ~ ~

I spent more time at work, lost in the greenhouse. Ciboney stopped going to church, and when I asked her what brought about the change, she told me Vittorio was responsible. He no longer wanted to go to the movies with Ciboney and me,

or driving in the country, or even bicycling, the way we used
to do. Many nights he stayed out late, and Mama defended
him: he was a boy, it was only natural for him to want to be
around others his age.

Then my things started to go missing. First, little
things—a cassette tape, coins, a pair of sunglasses—but then
bills, my camera, a tape recorder and a Walkman. I talked
with Vittorio first, but he denied taking anything. It was hard
to believe he was the same Vittorio I'd watched grow up.

When my camera disappeared, I had a talk with Mama
about my suspicions, but she would hear none of it. "Check yuh
room again, Molly, maybe yuh misplace it. Vittorio wouldn't
tief from yuh." She paused, then asked, "Yuh ask Ciboney if is
she?" We both knew Ciboney had been away at camp when most
of my things had gone missing. After talking to Mama, my
watch disappeared and then a gold chain. I decided that the
only way to prove that Vittorio was stealing from me was to set
him up and catch him in the act. I put a few bills in my jeans
pocket and left the jeans on my bed while I pretended to take a
shower. While the water was running, I returned to the bedroom and there he was, digging through my jeans pockets like
a dog looking for a bone. He looked up when he heard me, and
I expected to see panic in his eyes, at least embarrassment, but
he stood there, cool and cocky, daring me to speak.

"What were you doing in my pockets?" I asked loudly
enough for Mama to hear downstairs.

"Nothing. I wasn't in your pockets." His tone challeng-
ing, he looked me straight in the eye.

"You were in my pockets," I insisted angrily.

"I was only looking for a pen."

"Get out! I'm sick and tired of you!" I shouted, surprised at my own rage.

Mama wanted to know what the shouting was about and I ran downstairs to tell her. Vittorio came as well, and he stood there, looking smug, Ciboney beside him, watching. I wanted to choke him, shake a confession out of him, but my fury and hostility should have been aimed at Mama, who asked calmly, in front of him, if I was getting forgetful like Uncle Mel.

I was careful to lock away my things after that, but my resentment grew. Vittorio could do no wrong in Mama's eyes, and my daughter saw that I had no power in the household. Not that Mama was unkind to me; she still encouraged me in my work and spoke of me to others with pride. I was sure that someday she would see Vittorio for what he had become.

He had long since dropped out of school and spent most nights in front of the television or in his room with the music blaring. Ciboney trailed after him like a piece of English ivy. I'd lost her. She would accompany me to the occasional flower show or movie, but he had the edge. I comforted myself by thinking that she would come to see that her smooth-talking cousin was a fake.

Whenever Vittorio was around, he'd pray with Mama, and for that she'd often give him money. Uncle Mel's health was deteriorating, and he spent more and more time in bed or glued to his television. There was no doubt that Vittorio was being groomed to take over. Mama never said, but we both knew it.

To say that I was disappointed would be an understatement, but there was nothing I could do. The woman who lived on her own terms, who was honest and never afraid to speak up, was turning to Vittorio for strength.

I dreamt often of Rose. In my sleep I could smell the perfume of nutmeg and other spices in the creases of her skin. Rose and I had been apart for almost a year, and it seemed like forever, even with the letters and phone calls.

Mama visited Uncle Peppie and Glory in Atlanta twice a year. They begged her to come live with them, but she wasn't interested. "A Canada mi live. Canada is mi home, not America," she'd say. "If mi go dere, what happen to mi church and all of yuh? Mi want to be in mi own kitchen wid mi own things. Ah don't want to be a burden to none of dem. Mi know everything here, how to find a doctor, hospital, mi know mi way around, and besides, what dem expect mi fi do wid Mel?"

Glory had never wavered from her position on Mama and Mel. Mama had done the wrong thing in living with him, she said, first, because they weren't married, and second, because he was Aunt Val's uncle. Uncle Peppie was a bit more tolerant. Unlike Glory, he'd accepted years ago that Mama would do what she wanted to do.

Truth was that though I missed her warm presence in the kitchen when she was away, I was happy with the space her absence brought, happy that Vittorio strutted less while she was gone. Mama always came back with renewed spirits. She had lots to tell and lots to criticize about Glory and Aunt Val. Their every mistake and smallest regret seemed to make her happy and eager to show me that had they listened to her wisdom, their lives might have been a bit easier.

~ ~ ~

Rose returned to Toronto in the fall. She stayed with us for a few months while she looked for a job and an apartment. It was good to have her in the house. She quickly settled into the family, doing chores for Mama, who now had arthritis in both knees. She helped Ciboney with homework and was even consulted about shopping for funky, second-hand clothes. She hadn't heard all of Uncle Mel's stories, and she listened with the patience the rest of us, except possibly Mama, had lost.

When Rose found a job and started making plans to move, Mama wouldn't hear of it. "Stay here and save up some money, girl. No need to rush into paying big rent, yuh like part of de family." We had no reason to doubt Mama's sincerity. Despite her religious fervour, she'd never demanded we get saved. For close to a year we lived happily.

Then Mama's health began to fail rapidly. Her knees were worse and she had to be fitted with a walker. In the beginning she could still make it to church and to the West Indian shops for groceries. I bought a second-hand car to drive her and Uncle Mel to the doctor. Her blood pressure was unstable and then there were problems with her lungs; she was at the doctor's two and sometimes three times a week. It was hard for me to drive her to so many appointments while I was working, but Rose helped out and Ciboney did her share.

One night we received a phone call. Vittorio had been arrested with three others for car theft. Mama swiftly calculated how much she'd need for bail and a lawyer. Uncle Mel's eyes looked dull and lifeless as he agreed to take the money from his savings. "But why did he have to steal?" he asked

helplessly. "He's our only son—all he had to do was ask."
Mama mumbled something about bad company.

I drove her to the police station, and she hobbled over to
hug Vittorio. He showed no remorse and said little. In the weeks
that followed, the ups and downs with his court date, the lawyer's
visits and keeping him off the street put a strain on Mama's heart.

What made things bearable were my nights with Rose.
We continued to plan our future together. Talked about saving money and getting a place of our own. We spent many
weekends at Uncle Mel's cottage in Muskoka, which became
our little hideaway.

~ ~ ~

It doesn't matter how Mama found out about my relationship
with Rose. She did, and all hell broke loose. Rose and I had
been away for the weekend and were coming through the
door on Sunday night when I heard Mama singing loudly:

If you are tired of the load of your sin,
Let Jesus come into your heart;
If you desire a new life to begin . . .

She stopped to greet us and then started up again. At first I
paid no attention—she was forever singing—but now she sang
the same lyrics over and over. Rose and I awoke to that hymn
each morning and heard it each time we came through the
door. Rose noticed a change in Mama. "I can't really explain
it, I just know what I feel." Forever the optimist—or coward—
I tried my best not to believe that anything was wrong.

The singing continued for more than two weeks. "I'm going to talk to Mama," Rose told me one evening. "Something is definitely wrong."

"Let's wait for a bit, maybe she'll say something," I urged.

"I'm not going to stay in this place and feel like a fish cast off on the shore. If you want to wait, you wait!"

"Talk quietly," I cautioned, but she wouldn't have it. Ciboney came to the bedroom door to find out what the commotion was. "Nothing," I said. She looked at me in disbelief. I was foolish, I know now, but I didn't know how much she knew. Though music was blasting from Vittorio's room, Mama surely heard the quarrel. Still she didn't say anything.

The next morning, Sunday, Rose left early on an errand and stayed away all day. Mama didn't go to church. She called me downstairs to the kitchen.

"Yuh know what ah want to talk to you about," she began quietly. "Ah don't have to tell yuh dat it nuh right, a Satan work. Him nuh mean yuh no good. Look pon yuh, a nice attractive girl, yuh can get any man out dere, even a husband, and yuh go tek up wid woman. It nuh right. It nuh right."

I said nothing, just stared straight ahead and felt like a fool. Then I was on my knees beside her.

"Lawd God Almighty, forgive me if is anything ah do to cause dis," she prayed. "Oh Lawd God, mi saviour, ah kneel down on mi old, tired, bruk-up knees and pray to yuh, Lord, every night. Lawd, me is yuh humble servant. Tek Satan off her. Oh Lawd, tell me what to do. Talk to me, Lawd, talk to me. Is whose sins mi paying for? Mi father? Oh Lord, dis is too heavy a load. First Mikey, now mi one and only granddaughter."

When she'd stopped praying, she appealed to me. "Molly, yuh have a daughter. Think 'bout her, if yuh won't think 'bout me. Mek friend wid yuh Bible, for a de only weapon dat can drive Satan away. Yuh know seh dat di wicked will not inherit the Kingdom of God? Neider di sexually immoral, nor idolaters, nor male prostitutes, nor homosexual offenders. So 1 Corinthians seh. Sodomite cyaan flourish inna God sight. It nuh right, it dangerous." Her breathing became laboured and she had to rest between sentences. "Yuh nuh 'fraid? Look at yuh Uncle Mikey. Yuh had sense and yuh was bright, so yuh know what was going on in we yard. Yuh see de destruction. Yuh see why we had to run. Never forget dat we had to flee because of Mikey and Frank."

I tried my best to hold back tears of humiliation. Ciboney had slipped in and was standing by the door. "Come, girl," Mama called to her. "Come sit down and mek we read de Bible together." Mama told me to read Psalm 51, to "wash me thoroughly from mine iniquity and cleanse me from my sin." At the end of verse 19, she turned to my daughter and had her read aloud Psalm 23: "The Lord is my shepherd . . ."

Rose came home late that night, looking tired and smelling of weed and wine. I curled myself around her and listened to her soft snoring. Morning came too soon. I hadn't told Rose about what had happened while she was out. While I was in the shower, I heard Mama calling for Rose. She offered her breakfast—she never tired of cooking, even though she had to use her walker to get around the kitchen. Rose loved Mama's cooking and couldn't refuse.

When I came out of the bathroom, I heard Mama's strong voice. "It nuh right, Rose. Dem is white-people ways."

"Mama, that is a matter of opinion. No disrespect but—"

My grandmother cut her off. "Rose, yuh is like another granddaughter to mi, yuh is like blood. Mi old and mi know what mi talking about. Yuh own mother would tell yuh if she know."

"She know," Rose said. "I'm an adult and I can decide what is right for me."

"All I know is what de Bible seh—man do not lie wid a man as one lies wid a 'oman. Read Leviticus." Mama hadn't been prepared for a debate. "And dat go for 'oman, 'oman thing. Destruction can only follow, an' mi nuh mek yuh ruin Molly—"

This time Rose cut *her* off. "Ruin? What yuh talking about? What yuh think Molly is, an innocent? Mama, ah don't want to disrespect yuh, but I can't sit here and listen to untruths. It not fair."

The last place I wanted to go that morning was the kitchen, but I had to go to work, and I had to keep Rose from talking about Texas and our life there.

Relentlessly Mama pressed on. "So is how long dis going on? Yuh meet Molly like dat?" she asked coldly.

I entered the room, and they both looked at me. Rose's eyes begged me to say something. I grabbed a fried dumpling off the plate Mama had set out for me and poured some juice. "Mama, ah have to go or ah will be late for a meeting this morning. Coming, Rose?"

"Yes, I'm ready," Rose said thickly, "but your grandmother wants to know if I corrupted you."

Trust Rose to be in a confrontational mood, I thought. In Mama's eyes was a heavy cloud.

"Ah don't know what yuh saying, Mama, but Rose didn't corrupt me, whatever yuh mean by dat. Mi haffi go, ah late for work." I grabbed my jacket, left my half-eaten breakfast and went out the door. I waited in the car for Rose, but she didn't come out. I left without her.

That evening I went out with a few friends from work, and when I came home, I smelled like Rose had the night before. She was in bed; the night lamp was on, and a half-full bottle of wine and a glass stood on the table. The classified section of the newspaper with "Apartments for Rent" was spread out in front of her.

Rose looked at me and smiled. "You're late. Mama got you walking and talking on streets?"

"Funny," I whispered, making a face.

"Come have a smoke. Let's get ripped. Mama went to church to cleanse us of our sins."

"Where's Ciboney and Vittorio?" I asked.

"Ciboney is spending the night with a friend, and Vittorio, who knows? Come." She stretched out her hands. "I checked on Uncle Mel—he's the only sane one around here, as far as I'm concerned—and he's okay. We had a few glasses together."

I sat on the bed, sighed, took a gulp of wine and a smoke from the joint she'd lit. "What's all this?" I asked.

"Molly, yuh truly amazing. I guess that is what I fell in love wid, that blindness. Even in the face of God you can't see Him," she said, laughing.

I stared at her. "What's all this?" I repeated, pointing to the newspaper.

"I'm finding an apartment."

"Just like that, without any discussion?"

"We're discussing it now, aren't we?" she countered. "When do you think I decided this, Molly? You think I decided months ago or last week? You think I wouldn't discuss it then?"

"What's happening wid us?" I asked.

"Why you asking me? Is me alone make decisions?"

I didn't know what to say. I couldn't up and move out. Rose poured me another glass of wine.

"I'm finding a place," she said. "If you want, we can look together."

"You know ah want that more than anything. That's what we always talk about, but ah have to wait a bit, ah can't leave now, not with . . . you know . . . things here . . ."

She sat staring into the wine bottle.

"What I'm saying, Rose, is that I'll live with yuh, I'll come, but ah need to settle things wid mi grandmother first, because she need mi help, yuh see that for yuhself, and then there is Ciboney." Frustrated, I stopped there.

"I understand," she said, squeezing my hand. "I understand, but I don't like it. I wanted you to choose me."

We made love through the night until a rose-tinted sunrise peered through the windows. By the weekend she'd found a one-bedroom apartment in the middle of the gay ghetto.

Believing she had scored a victory, Mama was beside herself with joy. "Girl, yuh doing de right thing mek Rose go," she said to me. "Nuh mek evil lead yuh astray. Dat . . . thing is so wicked dat inna Genesis 19, Lot offer him virgin daughter dem to some battyman radder dan give dem de decent man dem come fi get. Read dis, girl, it will help yuh through temptation," she said, handing me her Bible open at Psalm 51. "And keep de Bible, sleep wid it under yuh pillow fi seven nights. Yuh will draw strength from it."

Despite Mama and the guilt I felt, Rose and I continued to see each other.

~ ~ ~

Nine months from the day Rose moved out, Uncle Mel died. He passed away peacefully in his bed. I helped Mama make the funeral arrangements. We chose a casket and a burial suit, and planned a simple ceremony. It was a small funeral, just fifteen of us together in the chapel on a cold spring morning. Mama and I, Ciboney, Vittorio, Aunt Val, Uncle Peppie, his brother, Washington, and a few of Uncle Mel's old friends. His sister, Gwen, had left Toronto several years earlier and didn't come to the funeral. Rose attended, but briefly. Notable by their absence were Glory and Uncle Freddie. They sent condolences and wreaths, but they didn't come. I don't think Mama ever forgave them for that.

When the will was read, we learned that Mel had left all his properties to Mama. It was little consolation. His death took a toll on her, though she never spoke about it, and not even the Lord Jesus could light up the house. She continued to go to church, though the arthritis in her knees worsened. Sometimes they would swell up like jackfruit. I massaged them with Tiger Balm to relieve the pain. For this, she was always grateful.

One day her knees gave way completely. No longer able to go to church or do shopping, she had only her television and radio for comfort. Her failing health made her more dependent on me and put a strain on my relationship with Rose. I couldn't see her as freely as I had before, and there were times I was sure Mama was listening in on our phone calls.

Vittorio was hardly around. Immediately after Uncle Mel's death, Mama gave Vittorio the money for a sports car. It was a way of holding on to him, of making sure he stuck around. I hated to see Vittorio and Ciboney driving around, so carefree, while Mama made excuses for why Vittorio didn't have a job. It was always someone else's fault.

Whenever I could, I escaped to Rose's place. But it didn't take long for Rose to see that I was using her apartment to avoid facing the problems at home. She began to pressure me to make a decision.

"Is time to move out—you is a big woman. Vittorio getting all the benefits from your grandmother. Move out and let him take up his responsibility. Bring Ciboney if you want. When you going to think about yourself and your happiness?"

The truth was, I didn't know how to leave. But I didn't want to lose Rose, and she had begun talking about seeing other women. I moved some of my things to her apartment and offered to help with the rent. At the same time, I made sure Mama always had groceries, the house was clean, and she took her medication. There was no joy in my duties.

~ ~ ~

Mama started phoning her sisters more often than she had in the past, and she began talking about going home to Jamaica. She wanted to take a last sea bath, visit Port Maria, drink coconut water, sit under a mango tree.

"Everything turn out bad here," she said. "Look pon Vittorio, him don't even try to find work. Mi give him everything. Him just like him father, de tiefing, de womanizing, de night life. Still, him is mi responsibility. Ah tek him up when him was a baby and ah have to carry it through. Ah have business to fix, then ah want to go home."

She called Vittorio, Ciboney and me to a meeting. I think she wanted to let Vittorio know she was serious about leaving, but his mind was on his new girlfriend. He kept looking at his watch, and for a split second I saw Uncle Freddie sitting there. I felt a tear open up in my heart when I saw Mama look at him so lovingly.

Vittorio didn't say much. When she asked him what she should do with the house, he told her to do whatever she wanted. He said he wanted something new, a condominium, perhaps in Kensington Market or on the waterfront. Then he abruptly got up to leave.

Later, Ciboney told me that his new girlfriend worked in a massage parlour and was the mother of three children. Vittorio had told Mama that she was a bank teller.

Over the next few weeks Mama asked me several times, "What yuh think ah should do?" But she always answered her own question. She knew what she wanted and what was best for Vittorio. "Ah don't want to sell de house. Mel wouldn't want it so, and me don't believe in dem something name condominium. Yuh cyaan buy house in de sky."

Just after Uncle Mel died, Mama had bought herself a plot in the same cemetery, still resigned to finishing her life in Canada. She'd paid in advance for her casket and funeral arrangements. So, when she asked me to get a refund, I knew she was serious about going home.

She began her journey by giving away jewellery and personal possessions. She gave Ciboney a lovely gold chain and a single-band gold ring. Clothes she gave to less-fortunate church sisters, keeping only a few favourites. Then she called one more family meeting to find out what Vittorio's intentions were. "I don't want to take care of a house and garden," he insisted. "I want a loft."

His wish was beyond Mama's understanding, but she would do anything to please him. She agreed to sell the house and give him the money for a down payment, but only if he would clean out the basement and take away his old stereos, speaker boxes, car parts, electronic devices and other junk. Weeks went by and he did nothing.

She kept up her correspondence with her sisters, promising them that she would soon be home. She told Peppie and Glory that she was moving back to Jamaica. They asked her to reconsider and move to Atlanta, but she was dead set against that idea.

Ciboney, my hope and precious daughter, only fourteen years old, was pregnant. I didn't find out until she was five months along, and my heart broke. I felt betrayed when I learned that she'd told Mama. Ciboney wouldn't say who the father was. She wouldn't confide in me at all.

Things were happening very quickly in our family, and I wasn't seeing Rose as often as she wanted. She complained and pressured me, and I felt as though everyone was testing me.

~ ~ ~

Mama asked me to get someone to come in and clear out the basement so she could sell the house. I researched prices in the neighbourhood, discussed them with her and started contacting a few real estate agents. Uncle Peppie flew up from Atlanta to help me. We spent weeks preparing the house for sale and fixing up the yard. Uncle Peppie painted the kitchen and the hallway and had it ready for showing. The real estate agent and prospective buyers were in and out. Finally we had an offer. The day before Mama was to sign, she sent Ciboney to find Vittorio. He came almost immediately. They had a long private talk.

On the day of the signing, Mama, Uncle Peppie, Ciboney and I sat down with the agent and the buyer at the kitchen table. Vittorio was nowhere to be found. The agent explained the procedure to Mama and handed her a pen. Right there, without consulting any of us, Mama said, "Ah not selling." Uncle Peppie and I were stunned.

"Mama?" I asked.

"Not selling," she repeated.

We couldn't bring her to her senses. The buyer and the agent left in frustration. I felt such rage. "Mama, what going on? Yuh know how much time I waste wid dis shit? Where yuh dearly beloved Vittorio? I'm sick and tired of this. Yuh seh Vittorio like him father and grandfather, but yuh mek him dat way," I shrieked, near tears.

She sat there at the kitchen table and laughed at me. I was "delirious." "Stark-raving mad."

"Waste your time?" she shouted. "Yuh know about time? Yuh know how much mi put in you?"

Uncle Peppie got up from his chair and walked out the door. I went to my room and packed some clothes. On my way out, I heard Ciboney asking Mama if she wanted some tea and a slice of bread. On the street corner, I saw Uncle Peppie smoking a cigarette, something I'd never seen him do. He hugged me and we stood there holding on to each other for a long time. "Ah going back tomorrow," he said, "on de first flight out."

Rose was at her place, waiting for me. "How did it go?" I burst into tears. She led me to the kitchen and made a pot of tea. My hands shook as I held the cup. I spent that night with Rose, and the next, and the night after that, determined to leave my grandmother's house.

~ ~ ~

Things were never the same again between Mama and me. Something was dead, but I couldn't move on. They—she, Vittorio and Ciboney—were the family. I still did the cooking and cleaning and drove Mama to appointments. Listened to her complaints of Vittorio and her children and her lot in life while my life was tearing up like an old worn-out rag. Yet I stayed rooted.

Ciboney gave birth to a daughter. I was with her at the hospital and I stifled tears as I held my grandchild. A little miracle.

I looked into her fiery, screaming face and wondered at the cost of life.

Mama found new energy now that she had a baby in the house. She could no longer move around or make baby food herself, but she issued instructions to me and Ciboney. Vittorio showed up more often now that the baby was here. He carried her around in his arms with such tenderness that I had to stop myself from wanting to like him. Ciboney named the child Maud, Mama's middle name. That pained me, but then, Ciboney had never been only mine.

~ ~ ~

I encouraged Ciboney to go back to school; she had dropped out during her pregnancy. She said she wasn't ready. She wanted to take care of Maud full-time, and Mama backed her decision.

Vittorio turned up whenever Mama summoned him. Ciboney knew where he spent his time and acted as the messenger. When he came by, Mama gave him money for gas. I bought the groceries for the house without asking for a penny and paid the utility bill. My beat-up, eight-year-old car had been no gift from her.

My relationship with Rose was like a tulip bulb buried deep under snow. All I could do was wait, and hope, and believe in spring.

~ ~ ~

With renewed vigour Mama again made plans to return to Jamaica. Her church people came to see her, sang and prayed with her, and she looked forward to their visits. She talked about Uncle Mel, how much she missed him and what a good man he was. She looked so tired, and her mood was changeable and hard to live with.

One afternoon shortly after Mama had been complaining bitterly about Vittorio, he came home, bathed and put on a suit, white shirt and tie. Mama asked Ciboney to help her get dressed. She was in high spirits at the sight of Vittorio. In the afternoon light she looked the way she did back on the dead-end street, when we were getting ready to head off for the Ritz Theatre. She explained that they were going to see a lawyer. I watched them as they went through the door: mother and son.

Later that night Vittorio joined us in a family prayer. I cursed myself for sitting in with them, but I did. Tired from her own scripture readings, Mama soon fell asleep.

She was eager to leave Canada. Once again I'd become the worker bee, but this time I looked at it as buying my freedom. That was what I thought then, not knowing that I would never be free of her.

Part Four

He Who Is Free of Faults Will Never Die

WE'D BEEN PACKING BOXES, barrels and suitcases for weeks. Glory came from Atlanta to help out. Grand-aunt Ruth had asked us to bring lots of food—the cost of food in the supermarkets was outrageous, she wrote—so we packed barrels with canned salmon, tuna, flour, sugar, rice, boxes of cake mix, cereal and crackers, along with detergent, paper towels, toilet paper, candles, pots, plates and clothing. We made arrangements for a shipper to pick up Mama's bed, television set and VCR, commode chair, dresser, washing machine and dryer, a new fridge for Grand-aunt Ruth, a hairdryer for Aunt Joyce, car parts for Cousin Ivan and a new sewing machine for Cousin Icie. Glory and I would wrap and pack late into the night.

Mama couldn't do much except sit and give orders about what was to be put in barrels. She wouldn't listen when we begged her to go rest.

"Mi waan fi know what exactly going in de barrel," she insisted.

As usual, Vittorio was hardly ever at home. The day before Glory left, when the barrels were full and we needed help to lift them out of the kitchen onto the front porch, Mama complained bitterly. "Dat blasted bwoy, him should be here now helping. Instead him a walk street or a follow woman skirt. Just like him father. Him call and promise fi come and help, and up till now mi nuh see de wretch. Not even him own room him will tidy up. Rat and roach a fight fi space down dere."

Glory gave her a piece of advice: "Yuh shoulda kick de bwoy out long time. Yuh don't need to put up wid him shit, Mama, yuh too old fi dis."

Mama struggled for an answer. "Ah, mi dear, it nuh so easy. Old-time people use to say, 'What nuh dead, nuh dash way,' and none a we know what direction life will tek, only de Lord know, and him nuh worse dan any other bwoy."

My mother and I exchanged looks.

"Come, Molly, mek we walk down to de lake. Ah need to get some air," Glory said.

We walked out to the street and across the bridge over Lakeshore Boulevard to Sunnyside Beach. We strolled along the shore, the July sun glittering like false gold in our faces, the lake water dull and sluggish, mirroring our mood.

"Dat Mama need fi go see a head doctor," she started off. "For something wrong wid her head. All she do is cuss de bwoy and then in de same breath defend him."

"Him can't do no wrong," I said, sighing.

"She ruin so much people life. Give out bad advice and defend people failures. She shoulda leave Vittorio in de Children's Aid. Him mighta come out to something with adoptive parents. Just like she never have any right fi tek yuh out of mi house."

Her last words angered me, but I didn't say anything. It was one thing to talk about Vittorio and quite another to suggest Mama needed a psychiatrist and to compare me to Vittorio. After all, Glory had driven me from her home, and I had made something of myself, become the first in our family to go to university.

"Look pon Ciboney, pickney having pickney, and all she do every day is dress up and idle." She paused and then asked, "Anybody know who de father is yet?"

"No," I said in barely a whisper.

"Well, so it continue, another generation down de drain." *Just shut up,* I thought. *You should be one to talk.*

"Yuh can vex all yuh want, but someone have to talk de truth." She stared out at the lake. A heavy silence floated between us.

I made my face look like a stone and said coolly, "We should get back home. I have to start dinner."

~ ~ ~

Glory left for Atlanta the next day, and Mama continued to complain about Vittorio.

"Look pon de sink how it full a dutty dish and glass. As him use dem, so him just dash dem in and lef de house."

When it wasn't the dishes, it was the garbage, or money he stole from her hope chest, which of course he denied. One evening I came home from work to a mouthful of anger.

"Yuh see Vittorio outside?" she asked, sitting on a chair in the kitchen, crippled with arthritis. "Him just leave here wid him friends. Look out dere pon de kitchen how dem lef it. Full a dutty dish, and mi stove, look how de water and oil spill over, de garbage never tek out dis morning. Kool-Aid spill in de fridge and him nuh wipe it up. Dem use things from de cupboard and dem nuh put it back. Dem is a dutty set a dawg, and him tief out mi money."

Her smoker's cough cracked in her chest. She spit the saliva into a rag she carried in the pocket of her dress and went on. "And as fi Ciboney, she dress from early dis morning, dress up de poor likkle baby like dolly and gawn a street. Mi beg her fi clean up de washroom, and she seh when she come back. Of course yuh know dat mean when street lock down. Ah only wish ah was stronger in mi body, ah would just tek de baby from her. . . . Ah just dying fi leave here. Ah can't tek it anymore." She sighed in frustration.

She had gotten smaller over the years, and her face was lined and haggard. Her wrinkled hands were deep in the pockets of her old lady's dress.

"Mama is okay. Try to go rest. I will clean up," I said. I helped to set her hands steady on her walker and she went to her bedroom.

Despite my disgust at having to clean up Vittorio's mess, I pitied my grandmother. Looking back, I think loneliness and her lack of control over our lives drove her back to Jamaica. None of us had measured up to what she wanted. She used to say her Bible and God were her only companions, but even those companions could not take away the pain that often shadowed her face. I prepared her meals, washed her clothes, did the shopping and picked up her pills, but I didn't spend a lot of time comforting her. When Ciboney was home, she cut Mama's toenails, read her blood pressure and entertained her with baby Maud. Vittorio graced her with occasional smiles.

It brought Mama a little pleasure to sit at the kitchen door and watch me work in the garden. I planted her favourite annuals: strawberry begonias, scented geraniums, impatiens and dahlias. The forget-me-nots, purple irises, lilies-of-the-valley and large pink peonies were among her favourite perennials. I tended her hybrid, pink musk roses, which climbed a trellis in the front yard. Sometimes I read to her on weekends and treated her to take-out Chinese food. But there was never any real thanks for anything I did, and it was painfully clear that in her heart she wished Vittorio were the one helping her.

I remember, too, a weekend I spent with Rose. Ciboney had promised to stay home in case Mama needed help. Rose and I had just finished eating a delicious, candlelit supper. The mood was light and fun and so was the music. I placed a rose between my lips and was taking backward steps toward the bedroom. Rose mockingly followed, her nose lightly touching the rose. When the phone rang, she said, "Let the machine get it. This is much more fun." Later she played back the message.

"Molly, read Jude 7. Read Genesis 19. Tek heed before disaster reach yuh. Come home." She coughed into the phone and her breathing was audible. "Rose, lef mi granddaughter alone. Fi yuh own good read Romans 1, verse 26 and 27. Hell wait fi yuh."

"I can't take this any longer, Molly!" Rose shouted. "Something have to change. What give this woman de right to call my house and leave such a message, eh? Who she think she is, God?"

"Yuh don't understand," I shouted back. "Yuh just don't understand." I was groping for words.

"I understand all right. Molly, you just have to let go."

I was shaking. "Rose, it's not that easy. Ah can't turn mi back on her and ah can't cuss her. She been through too much. She going soon, remember?" I said, hoping to pacify her.

"And you just going to take the coward's way out. Wait until she leaves, and in the meantime I must put up with her abuse and insult." She looked straight into my eyes, as if she wanted to put a spell on me.

"You don't have to," I said. I got up from the bed, put my clothes on and began to pack my things.

"Where you going?" she asked.

"I'm going home," I said evenly.

"So this is how it is? Every time she say jump, you ask how high?"

I didn't answer.

"Talk to me, Molly, ah can't stand dis shit. This is how yuh communicate all de time—silence. Am I suppose to read dat?" she challenged.

I still didn't answer. I zipped up my bags and searched for my shoes.

"Molly, please stay," she said, her voice softer.

I didn't look at her. I didn't want to leave, but the simple truth is that I was afraid. Mama was upset and her breathing was laboured; I didn't want to be responsible for her having a stroke or worse.

"Please," Rose whispered. She was sitting on the edge of the bed. Her wild and curly hair had escaped the elastic band. She forced a smile and her dimples pierced deep into her cheeks. Her nut-brown skin glowed in the candlelight, and at that moment she was the most beautiful woman I had ever known. I quickly turned on the ceiling light to erase the image.

"Ah can't stay. We'll talk later, okay?" I promised.

"To hell with you. If yuh walk out de door, this is it."

I turned to go and a half-empty wineglass sailed over my head. I quickly closed the door behind me.

Rose got an unlisted phone number, refused to answer my knock at the door and sent back my letters unopened. For a while I told myself she wasn't right for me and tried to bury myself in Mama's affairs. Soon I was remembering her love-ly skin, her stumpy toes, her large ears, her dimples and care-free laughter, her touch on me.

~ ~ ~

I agreed to accompany Mama back home and stay with her for a few weeks to get her settled. I took a leave of absence from work, booked the flight, made arrangements for a wheelchair and seats near the bathroom, and ordered her special meals. Church members were in and out of the house, singing and praying for her safe journey. She was pleased with the atten-tion, and they promised to come visit her.

She awoke very early the morning of the flight and was dressed three hours before the limo came to take us to the airport.

"Well, kitchen, is goodbye. Yuh serve mi well over de years and yuh bring mi joy when mi could cook and move round." Her voice was light and clear. Her eyes lingered on the oven where she had baked so many cakes.

"Molly, ah leaving de cake tins and dem bottle of fruits fi yuh. Yuh can bake yuh first set of cakes out of it," she said, her voice gentle.

Vittorio and Ciboney awoke and got dressed minutes before the limo drove up to the house. Vittorio put our luggage in the car trunk, then helped Mama into the car. There was pride in her eyes at that moment, and I wished I had been born a boy.

We were all quiet as the car drove through the streets of Parkdale and onto the Gardiner Expressway. Mama peered through the window at the shops and streets that she would never see again. At the airport she asked us to join her in prayer. We found a quiet waiting area, locked hands and closed our eyes.

"De Lord comfort and shelter in Him flock even de greatest sinner. I thank mi God always on unnu behalf. Never lose sight of Jesus. Believe in Him, for Jesus will lead each of you by unnu hand."

Our flight was called. She kissed Ciboney and baby Maud and held them tight. "Come visit, yuh hear? Send Maud down fi spend some time wid her old granny. Ah want to spend little time wid mi great-great-granddaughter," she said.

Vittorio knelt by her wheelchair and she held on to him for a long time. "Son, don't forget fi pray even if yuh nuh believe. Just pray, in time de spirit of Massa God will guide yuh." Her throat went dry, she coughed and cleared it with discomfort. "Tek care of Ciboney and help Molly round de place. Nuh leave everything up to her, and remember fi tek out de garbage, for yuh is de man of de house now."

He kissed her forehead. "Yes Mama, I'll read my Bible," he said, giving Ciboney a playful wink. Then he pushed Mama's wheelchair through to the customs lineup.

As we waited to board the plane, Mama sat calmly, but there was a twitch of nervousness at the corner of her mouth. To steady herself, she smoothed her blue silk head scarf several times. Her black handbag—crammed with pills, religious cassettes, a washrag and a small Bible—was clutched tightly between her legs. She didn't eat much on the flight, but she hardly stopped talking.

"Mi stomach feel like mi have a baseball inside," she said nervously. "It too cold in yah. Mi feel like mi into a icebox." I asked the flight attendant for a blanket, and in no time Mama had thrown it off, saying it made her too hot. She kept looking at her watch and mumbling about the long flight ahead. I asked her if she wanted to listen to the radio or watch the movie. She only sucked her teeth and said, "Ask de stewardess for some tea wid a little biscuit—it might tek de gas off mi stomach." She eyed the bathroom a short distance away and sucked her teeth again. "A lucky thing mi wear mi Depends. How much longer we have up in de air?" she asked, staring at her watch again. She kept opening and closing her old lady's purse. Finally she took out her pills and removed four from their containers.

"Ask de stewardess for some water, mek mi tek dem pills."

The flight attendant brought the water. Mama drank it and pulled the blanket close about her. "Ask fi another blanket. Dis too small, and ask her fi some more tea. Mi feel cold."

The flight attendant couldn't move fast enough. I was glad that despite Mama's protest, I'd booked first-class tickets.

"What time now?" she asked again. "Get some juice fi mi." I got up and went to find the flight attendant. I tried to stay calm, but I was feeling irritated and tired, wishing that it was Vittorio here with her, or Glory, or even Ciboney.

Mama dozed off, and I leafed through a magazine to pass the time. Then she was awake again. "What time it is? Ah can't see a thing on dis watch, de numbering too small," she protested.

"Mama, yuh ask mi dat just twenty minutes ago," I said, my irritation unmistakable.

"Dis seat can't go back further?" she asked, ignoring me. I adjusted her seat and covered her with the two blankets. She closed her eyes and a soft snore followed.

I continued to flip through the magazine and then closed my eyes, too. Memories crowded my head, mostly of Rose and our failed relationship. Though I knew she already had another woman, like a fool I comforted myself with the thought that with Mama out of the way, we could try again when I came back.

"What time now?" Mama asked.

"We have another hour."

She looked at her watch again, then opened her purse and reviewed the contents. "Ah glad ah carry all dese tapes. Dem will be comfort to mi at nights, and Ruth will enjoy dem too." Then she turned and looked at me.

"Yuh hair look nice. Ah glad yuh mek it grow back. Woman fi look like woman, and when it too short it mek yuh look too mannish." Then she frowned. "A Rose did tell yuh fi cut it off, nuh?"

"No, Mama, she didn't tell mi to cut it off. She only suggested that cutting it would show off my eyes more," I said with measured patience.

She sucked her teeth. "Yuh is a real fool. Unnu mek people tell unnu all kind a foolishness fi control unnu."

"Yuh think ah don't have a mind of mi own?" I asked, meeting her eyes. She looked away. We lapsed into another bout of silence until she spoke.

"Ah hope Vittorio eat proper. Ah glad Ciboney leave behind, for she will mek sure Vittorio eat proper, between him and his new girl."

I swallowed hard. No point in responding.

I wanted to ask her why it was always Vittorio, Vittorio. What about me? Where did I fit in? Why was I taken for granted? Didn't I do good by going to school, learning a profession?

In truth, I knew she was proud of me, but I needed to hear it from her. I looked at her worn and tired face, the extra flesh at her neck, her old lady's scarf so tight against her skin, her wrinkled hands with the veins sticking out like snakes, and I couldn't ask.

The pilot announced that we'd be landing shortly, and excitement grew feverish like the heat outside. As the plane touched down, there was a round of applause from the passengers, Mama included. "Praise de Lord," she said.

I told her that we'd have to wait until the plane was empty and then they'd send two or three men to lift her. There were no wheelchair ramps on the island. She was so relieved to be back on the ground that it didn't seem to matter. We waited patiently. I removed her thick sweater, fixed her shoes on her feet, smoothed her blue print dress and loosened her scarf.

"Stop de fussing up wid mi," she said when I added a touch of perfume around her ears and dabbed my lipstick on her lips. "Mi is a old woman," she said jokingly, then asked seriously, "Molly, yuh sure dem out dere to meet we? Ah wonder if dem remember?"

"Of course, Mama. Dem wouldn't forget dat."

She nodded and fumbled nervously with the gold ring on her right hand. "Ah wish it was Wigton Street mi going back to," she said.

I had forgotten this vulnerable side of Mama, for I didn't see it often. "Mama, don't think 'bout dat. Grand-aunt Ruth and Aunt Joyce and everybody else looking forward to seeing you. In a few months when yuh get adjusted, yuh can move back there," I said, even though I knew it would take more than a few months.

We moved swiftly through immigration. I signed the necessary papers, answered questions and with some help collected our luggage. Soon we were outside in the heat. Grand-aunt Ruth, Aunt Joyce, Uncle Mikey, Cousin Icie and Cousin Ivan were there to meet us. We hugged and kissed and turned each other around, looking at what the years had left us.

"Ah glad fi see yuh, gal, yuh don't look a day older," Aunt Joyce joked.

"Welcome, mi sister, we glad fi have yuh back. Praise de Lord." This from Grand-aunt Ruth.

"Mama," Uncle Mikey said, and burst into tears as they held each other for a long time.

A street vendor went by yelling, "Coconut water, coconut water." Cousin Ivan called out to him and bought us each coconuts. Mama drank hers quickly and asked for another.

"Lawd, a long time mi nuh taste coconut water sweet like dis."

The last of the evening sun touched her face, and the hard lines at the edge of her mouth softened. We piled into Cousin Ivan's van for the ride home. We drove along the Palisadoes Road, the sharp smell of the sea, like raw fish, overpowering our noses and bringing back memories. The sun was setting on the Blue Mountains in the distance.

The ride to Grand-aunt Ruth's was full of talk, Mama wanting to know about everything. "What about Port Royal? Dem to do anything new wid it?"

"Dem talking 'bout new developments. More hotels, shops, beach area. It coming along. Is over dere ah work in de hotel as a waitress," Cousin Icie said proudly.

"Dat nice, Icie, ah glad to hear dat," Mama told her. "How 'bout Paul and Helen?" she said, turning to Uncle Mikey.

"Mama, dem leave de island long time ago an' dem settle in Chicago. Open de same business dere. Dem doing well."

"Yuh never think of going dere?" she asked.

"No, Mama. My visit to Miami every couple of months is good enough. Times change, yuh know. Anything in foreign you can get here for de right price."

Aunt Joyce cut in. "Enid come home, yuh know. She lef England about four years now. Looking real good. She bring home some fabulous clothes. She live up on de hills. When yuh settle, we can go visit her."

"Ah would love to see her. Ah always did like her, for she was a woman wid sense," Mama replied. "What about Connie Brown?" she asked.

"She also do well. She come home from America and build a fabulous house in Orocabessa. Yuh want to see it! It gorgeous, and it overlook de sea."

"Maria, yuh remember Inez Clarke?" Grand-aunt Ruth asked.

"Yes, nuh di gal we grow up wid in Port Maria?"

"She did leave Port Maria, yuh know. Her man send fi her. She go to America but she never mek it. She mash up bad. She a walk street and pick up cigarette butt." My grand-aunt sighed and shook her head.

"She nuh mash up, she mad," Aunt Joyce said. "Dem need fi scoop her up off de street and tek her to Bellevue. If it was America she would be in a institution."

Mama sucked her teeth and said, "Joyce, nuh talk fool-ishness, for America full up a mad people a walk up and down."

"Joyce, yuh think enough room deh Bellevue fi house all de mad people who a walk round?" Grand-aunt Ruth challenged. "Inez harmless, and she nah trouble anybody. When mi use to have de restaurant she use to come by dere, but since mi sell it mi lose touch."

Aunt Joyce shook her head. "She could a do better. She go foreign and mek white man tun her fool. Is a real shame when we set we sights high an' den we drop."

Mama asked Uncle Mikey about his other friends who used to come to the Sunday parties. He filled her in, but there was no mention of Frank.

"Myers come back to town, yuh know," Aunt Joyce said. "Him buy a house on Wigton Street."

"Ah so," Mama said without warmth or curiosity.

"How his children?" I asked.

"Dem abroad someplace in America wid dem mother. Dat relationship mash up long time, yuh know."

"It will be nice to see him again, after all these years," I said, remembering.

Once we got off the Palisadoes Road, the traffic slowed to a halt. Cousin Ivan cursed the roads, the traffic, the government, then the other drivers. We passed through neighbourhoods that looked like footage from a war zone, with one-room squatter's shacks that seemed too frail to hold back a high wind. Some didn't have enough zinc for the roof and were covered with heavy brown cardboard boxes.

"A Allman Town dis?" Mama asked.

"No, Auntie, dis is off Warika Hills," Cousin Ivan said.

"Oh," she said, as if remembering.

"It use to be nice place, yuh know, back when we was young, but de gunman dem move in and tek it over . . . but good people still live here," Grand-aunt Ruth said.

There were broken bottles, garbage, stray dogs in the road. The smell of stale urine seeped in through the open window. Men stood idly on the street corners. Children ran around shoeless, expertly dodging broken glass and dog shit. It was a free-for-all, with car horns sounding like an out-of-tune band. Everyone was in a hurry and Cousin Ivan was no exception, shouting and cursing through the window.

"Dem blasted deportees, dem come from foreign and bring back too much cars. Is dem cause de traffic jams," he complained angrily. Someone tried to overtake our van and came much too close. Cousin Ivan pushed his foot hard on the gas. The van let out a merciless screech and we were almost thrown out the window. Cousin Ivan yelled at the other driver, "Yuh buy yuh licence?" He criticized the man's beat-up car and raced ahead.

We drove a while longer, and as the car headed toward the Blue Mountains, the air got cooler. Trees and bushes and manicured gardens appeared in the distance. Cousin Ivan turned into Grand-aunt Ruth's driveway, and the dogs ran to the gate to greet us.

"Move out of de way, Brownie!" Cousin Ivan shouted. When we got out of the car, he said, "Hold on, mek mi tie dem up, dem sneaky, yuh know."

"Yes, dear, for mi never get a dawg bite in all mi life, an' mi too old fi get one now," Mama laughed.

We were up late that night, catching up on events and people before we finally surrendered to sleep. Uncle Mikey left, promising to call soon.

Next morning the crowing of the rooster in the backyard, the smell of roasted salt fish and breadfruit, fried plantains, ackee, fried dumplings and Jamaica Blue Mountain coffee welcomed us home. A rare smile flashed across Mama's face. She ate a portion of everything, though she kept saying that it was too much food. "Ah couldn't tell when last ah eat like dis. Mi have to go back on mi low-fat diet, but dis morning ah cyaan pass up dis food," she said.

Right after breakfast, I got ready to go and collect the barrels, bed, television and other goods from the wharf. Aunt Joyce insisted I go with Cousin Ivan.

"No, nuh bodder wid no cab. Yuh is a foreigner. And dem wretches out here know de foreigners and dem will tief yuh. Better yuh give Ivan de money fi de gas."

As Ivan drove, I had to hold on to the car door so as not to be thrown around. Now that the grand-aunts and my grandmother were not in the car, he was eager to show off his driving prowess.

We didn't return home with the barrels and the other items. The officials at the wharf told me corruption was rampant and they'd had problems with people pretending to be returning residents, coming in with valuable goods without paying sufficient taxes; then they would sell them and go abroad again and repeat the same process. They needed more proof that Mama was indeed returning, and they wanted to see her in person. Cousin Ivan spoke up before I even had a chance. "De woman cyaan come. De woman is a cripple."

They still wouldn't release the goods. We were told to go to the building next door and wait in line. We waited and waited, in the heat and confusion. Cousin Ivan grew impatient and began to pace the floor. "Ah don't have time for dis kind of crap. I is a busy man," he said loudly in the direction of the receptionist. The woman looked at him with indifference and said, "Sir, I don't control de storage, and I doesn't work at the wharf. I'm just de receptionist."

It was clear from her tone that this wasn't the first time she'd run into the likes of Cousin Ivan. He walked away from her desk, cursing the whole country—its inefficiency, the people in the office, customs. A woman sitting on a chair nearby agreed with him.

"Yessir, ah know exactly what yuh mean. Is seven weeks mi waiting for mi barrels. I have been in dis office every day since, and mi still cyaan get a straight answer 'bout mi barrels.

Dem think everybody is a tief when is dem is de real tief."

Another man, about fifty, wearing starched white pants and a white shirt, gave his piece. "Some a dem a more tief dan de prisoners in Kingston Pen. Last year dem tek away four turkey and five ham from mi. Seh dem cyaan come in unless dem cook. I sure dem never throw dem away—dem carry dem home and nyam dem."

The broker in Canada had given me his word that there would be no problem: "I will tek care of everything from up here. Mi have contacts wid people out dere, dat's why mi in de business." After I paid him he added, "Just show dem de letter from de doctor. De one saying she is a cripple and everything will be okay. Dem have more sympathy fi ole people."

I handed the receptionist the letter from Mama's doctor, which said she was disabled and couldn't move around with ease.

"Mi still have to see her—anybody could get a doctor's note from foreign," the woman said leisurely.

"How yuh a go see her and she cripple, yuh have wheelbarrow fi carry her?" Ivan asked. She ignored him, and I shook my head in slight disgust, hoping she'd see I was different from him.

"Get a letter from yuh grandmother and bring it in tomorrow."

When we were home and I told Mama what had happened, she wasn't happy. I assured her that I would write the letter and would go back early the next day. It didn't help much; her mood was downcast all through dinner.

"Mi want mi own bed to sleep in. Ah doubt if ah will ever see de television set and de VCR, or de hairdryer and all mi other things," she said gloomily. "Dem will probably tief dem. Dis country nuh change at all. Mi come back after all dese years and de same waiting game. Everything is a lineup."

Aunt Joyce joined in and said her piece about government corruption.

Next morning I left early with Cousin Ivan. I went back to the same woman, and this time I didn't wait long in the line. I handed her the letter.

"Okay, just go down de hall and out de door through to de other building. They will make arrangements for de goods to be delivered."

Cousin Ivan went off to get something cold to drink. I took a number and sat and waited. When my number was called, a man motioned me into his office. I handed him the papers, and he looked them over for several minutes, then set them on his desk and asked about the contents of the barrels. It was all written on the paper in front of him; nevertheless, I ran through the contents. Next he wanted to know my relationship to the owner, which was also in the letter right in front of him. Then he wanted to know how long I would be staying in the country.

"A few weeks," I replied in as friendly a manner as I could muster.

"Dat mean dere is enough time for me to show you what our country have to offer. How about tonight?"

"No, tonight is not good," I said, regretting my friendliness. "I have to settle all of this barrel stuff first."

He was persistent. "Come on, sister, yuh need to relax, enjoy de weather."

"I have someone," I said.

"Him on de island?"

"No, but . . ."

"No problem, den. How him going to know?" He laughed, exposing a chipped tooth. "Ah tell yuh what, give mi yuh phone number. Ah will see dat everything go through with these barrels."

A knock at the door saved me. It was another worker reporting a shipment gone bad, confusion about the billing, the woman outside cussing. I was quickly handed back my papers and sent off to another building.

Outside, the heat was sweltering. Cousin Ivan sat with a drink under a shady tree. I waved to him and pointed to the next building. There I was led into another small room, where I went through the details again. The official said I'd have to pay taxes on the goods. I told him I had already done that with the customs broker in Canada. "Dis is a different tax," he said confidently.

"But we're not bringing in excess goods. We're taking in less than an average returnee."

"Well, dat is true," he said, running his tongue over his teeth. "Dat true . . . but de lady old, and she coming wid washer, dryer, car parts; now what a old lady do wid car parts?"

"She can't carry gifts fi family members?" I asked.

"Yes, anybody can carry in anything. It will just cost them."

He sat there cool, while I wiped the sweat off my face and sat upright in the chair.

"How much is the tax?" I asked him in a tone that made it clear that I understood this was robbery.

He rubbed the corner of his eye sheepishly, then said, "Just give mi a money and mek we settle it right here. No need for a pretty lady like you going through all dis trouble." He gave me a broad smile.

We bartered until we came to an agreement. The money went into his pocket, and he stamped the paper and gave it back to me.

"All right, ah will send dese down to de wharf. Yuh things should arrive sometime dis evening. Walk good."

Nothing arrived that evening, and by the next morning Mama was vexed. "Just give mi a cup of coffee and a slice a bread, mi nuh hungry," she said at the breakfast table.

Aunt Joyce was ready to start up the talk about the laxness in the country, but a look from Grand-aunt Ruth changed her mind.

"Maria, yuh look tired. Why yuh don't go back to bed?" Ruth asked.

I went off to make phone calls. Before I got through to the right person, I'd talked to six different people. Each time I repeated the story. Finally the official I'd seen the day before came on the line.

"Hello, this is Molly Galloway. What happen to de delivery?"

He put me on hold, then the phone went dead. I called back.

"What happen, lovely lady? It might be dere dis evening, tomorrow morning or evening. It all depends. Ah can't guarantee delivery time."

"Mi granny need her things, her bed—"

He cut me off. "Listen, sis, ah doing mi best, but understand me is not de driver, and de driver have lots of stop fi mek. Everybody in de same rush."

"Okay, thanks," I said, defeated.

"What 'bout de phone number?" he asked. I hung up.

Mama sat in the kitchen folding some kitchen towels. Aunt Joyce whispered, "Any luck?" She could tell the answer from my face. "Dem blasted old farts, dem cyaan run business. Dem want fi go America and learn something 'bout business. Dat is why mi will forever love America, for dis shit couldn't happen dere. Once yuh pay yuh money everything all right, but dis blasted place full dutty tief. Even when yuh give dem something under de table, yuh still haffi beg."

Just then the dogs started barking, and we heard men at the gate.

"Shut up, dog. Settle!" Cousin Ivan shouted, tying three of the dogs to the mango tree. A truck backed into the yard and came to a stop next to the verandah. Mama's shoulders straightened as though a heavy weight had been lifted from them. She wheeled her walker onto the verandah and took a seat where she could see into the back of the truck. The four young men who'd made the delivery volunteered to break open the crates and help set up her bed and easy chair. I gave them a few extra U.S. dollars and they left happy.

That night the household was exhausted but content, and it was another late night with talk and laughter. The next few days were busy with unpacking boxes and setting things up. Our energy ran high and our mood was cheerful. Mama's religious tapes filled the house. She sat and watched and added her opinion here and there. Aunt Joyce was full of excitement. "All dese new things, ah love de foreign smell," she said.

"De curtains will look good in the living room on Christmas morning," Grand-aunt Ruth said.

I put Mama's clothes away and set her toiletries within easy reach on the dresser. The Depends went into a drawer close to her bed, her panties and merinos in another. I hung her dresses in the closet and set out photographs of Ciboney and Maud, two of Vittorio, a group shot of Peppie, Glory, Aunt Val, Sid and me taken one Christmas, a wedding picture of Freddie and Bella, and one of Mikey and Mama at his birthday party years ago.

The days passed peacefully. There was always music in the house or in the yard, drifting through the open windows, often religious tapes, too, but sometimes Cousin Ivan set up his stereo in the backyard and played reggae and rhythm and blues. Frequently my grand-aunts and grandmother would be in the house talking about the news or a soap opera on television.

Mama reacquainted herself with dasheen yam, negro yam, doctor fish, fried sprat, and her appetite grew daily. "Ah cyaan tell de last time ah eat susumba," she said, smiling. Or, "Some mackerel and banana would be good fi lunch." Cousin Icie promised to pick some up at the market, and it appeared on Mama's plate for lunch the very next day.

I was glad that I'd brought her home. I hardly thought about Rose. Every evening I helped Mama bathe, and then we'd sit on the verandah. We talked long into the nights about everything except Rose and Frank, and she rarely mentioned Vittorio or Ciboney. We talked about her banking and where to open an account.

My bedroom was next to Mama's, separated by the bathroom. Grand-aunt Ruth and Icie and Aunt Joyce had bedrooms on the other side of the house. The large living room, dining room and kitchen were in the centre.

From my room I could hear her old lady's snore, saw when her lights came on in the middle of the night and heard her turning and tossing. Some nights I heard the sound of her urine tinkling in the commode. Sometimes she'd call out that she had gas, and I'd get up and make her tea, talk with her until she fell asleep. One of those nights she began to talk about her father.

"Same way Pappy use to have de gas, yuh know. Sometime it have him curl up like a baby an' him would bawl. Me and Mammy use to look after him and when Mammy at work, me after him. We use to boil bush tea and give him fi drink. Sometimes mi haffi rub him chest and him stomach fi mek him belch and mek de pain go way. But him never really appreciate it—always love mi sisters more dan me. Maybe a true mi did look more like him, why him treat mi so. Him do mi some bad things. But mi forgive him, for him never know better . . ."

I hadn't taken any real notice, until that night, of the devastating change age had handed to her. Her face had grown more severe with age, her skin blotchy and lined, her jaw loose. When she talked about her father, she looked even worse. Mornings, she'd sit with my grand-aunts, and the three would recollect having only one pair of shoes between them and that pair being for Sunday school. They walked to school barefoot, helping Mammy with chores after school, setting bundles of clothes on their heads and walking miles to deliver them. The talk was never dull and never sad, even when it came to Pappy. Yes, Pappy was a womanizer and, yes, sometimes he didn't bring all his money home to Mammy. But he never drank, smoked or gambled. Grand-aunt Ruth and Aunt Joyce remembered his tenderness, the sweets he passed to them behind Mammy's back, the piggyback rides he gave them.

Some nights I sat with Cousin Ivan and Cousin Icie after Mama fell asleep, watching B-grade movies on television, the ones that don't make it in North America. Sometimes we played cards and listened to the various deejays on the radio and the latest in dance-hall music.

We settled into a routine. Every morning I boiled water for Mama's bath. I emptied and cleaned her commode, made her bed. Every night, I read to her, sometimes from *The Daily Word*, other times from the scriptures or a bit of Louise Bennet's poetry.

Grand-aunt Ruth did a little handwashing every day for herself and Mama. She wouldn't put panties and slips and bras in the washer, firmly believing they must be washed by hand. She, too, was getting on in years, but she was strong and steady on her feet. Cousin Icie took charge of the kitchen and cooked most meals, except when her job didn't permit it, and then Grand-aunt Ruth took over. Aunt Joyce supervised the kitchen, made the menus and wrote out the shopping list. She also put up new curtains and changed the furniture around. A woman came in once a week to give the house a good cleaning. Cousin Ivan looked after the yard, but his garden did not have half the magic of our old garden under Myers's care.

There were scheduled times set aside for television. Aunt Joyce watched *Good Morning America* at six every morning.

The television woke us at five-thirty when she turned it on to warm up. She liked to keep up with what was happening in New York. At breakfast she'd talk about all the designer clothing worn on the show that morning. Not to be out-done, Mama talked about *Canada A.M.*, but the grand-aunts paid little attention, because there were no Canadian television stations in Jamaica and not much news of Canada. Mama quickly changed to talking about *60 Minutes* and CNN.

"Dem program more intelligent, mi never have time fi listen to fool-fool talk," she said.

Aunt Joyce laughed. "Maria, serious news is not all there is in life. Mi come in dis world fi enjoy miself. Ah don't care what yuh say, I love to keep up wid de fashion and news of society people."

Then Grand-aunt Ruth laughed, too, and said, "Well since mi never go foreign yet, ah will just stay out of dis."

"Mi can talk, for mi in Canada long time, and de U.S. was just cross de way," Mama maintained. "We get a lot of dem programming and mi never rate *Good Morning America*."

Grand-aunt Ruth had Mama's serious and practical bent—she always thought of making provisions for tomorrow—while Aunt Joyce lived for the day. She wasn't ashamed of say-ing that she'd take her last penny to buy a new pair of shoes or cloth for a new dress. Her stories about her boss in America became an inside joke for the rest of us. "Dat woman," she'd say, "don't wear nutten but designer clothes, and yuh should see her jewellery. Everything real. Age don't have nutten on dat woman. Yuh name it and she is dere every summer—Paris, Rome, France, Italy."

Then she'd go on about the foods she had tasted at her employer's house. "A pure rich-people food she eat, yuh know. Smoked salmon, de very best. Mi nuh mean nuh fool-fool salmon, kosher and de best. Caviar, champagne. Is right dere mi learn what wine and what drinks go wid which food."

Mama would interrupt about then. "Ah glad yuh employer treat yuh so good, mek yuh eat caviar, drink champagne and all dem fancy things. Yuh lucky, for dem is not de story mi hear in Canada. Girls come Canada and work hard in domestic service, and mi never hear dem talk like you. An' is not dat mi read in de papers."

"Mi talking about my experience," Aunt Joyce maintained. "Ah don't know 'bout anybody else, ah just know some of dem don't get anywhere because dem go foreign and tun fool. Dem come America wid de same 'no problem' attitude and expect too much. America is a good place. Yuh can mek life."

Occasionally Grand-aunt Ruth threw in a neutral comment. "As mi never go to America and taste dem deh breed a food, mi nuh have much to say, except mi nuh feel deprived of de caviar or smoke salmon, or even Paris. Thank God Him bring we out of poverty, and we comfortable."

Two or three times a week Mama held Bible studies on the verandah. Those days, I took myself to the garden in the backyard or went to visit Punsie, who now had six children and had moved to Molynes Road. Grand-aunt Ruth and Aunt Joyce had been going to a Baptist church every Sunday for years, but Grand-aunt Ruth also studied with a group of Jehovah's Witnesses every Wednesday on the verandah, and

Mama, never one to pass up the opportunity to debate, joined in. Cousin Icie was Roman Catholic and went to a church nearby, and Cousin Ivan was a "turn-back" Seventh Day Adventist. Thursday evenings, Mother J, a member of the Church of Redemption (Pentecostal), came to hold prayer meetings, and everyone but Cousin Ivan and me joined in. Given the tolerance shown to all these different beliefs, I found it unforgivable that they wouldn't accept Mikey's difference. I won't say my difference. The grand-aunts and cousins knew little about my personal life back in Canada, for Mama had not mentioned anything about Rose.

~ ~ ~

We didn't see much of Uncle Mikey for the first two weeks. He called and was always cheerful, but he had visited Mama only twice since her arrival. The rainy season had begun, and he came with flowers and fruit and a large bottle of fresh coconut water. Patches of his hair had turned silver and shone about his face. He wore a well-cut blue suit and sport-ed handmade brown leather sandals with a matching brown leather handbag.

Mama was happy to see him and it showed in her face. "A so you look prosperous!" she exclaimed, allowing him to kiss her and make much of her. My grand-aunts also complimented him. Light talk about the rain, the garden, plans for Christmas, the rising gas prices and local government followed.

"Dis government need fi come outa power, for dem curry favour too much. Dat is why de country a mash-up," Aunt Joyce said with authority.

"But dem all stay dat way. Yuh tek one outa power and put in de other and is de same thing," Grand-aunt Ruth said.

"Dat's not what ah talking 'bout. Mi know all of dem curry favour dem party supporters, but mi get fi understan' through reliable sources dat dis government give de benefit to de battyman dem who in a business. Mi hear one businessman cuss, seh, him cyaan get no contract, tru him nuh part a de battokrisy."

Uncle Mikey's smile faded. Grand-aunt Ruth cleared her throat uneasily. I looked down at my lap and didn't say a word.

It was Mama who came to the rescue. "If de government corrupt, it have nutten to do wid dat. From we a pickney we use to hear Mammy and Pappy talk 'bout de government, for when we revolt and de British back off, a fi we own people, de one dem train in a fi dem England school who tek over and dem continue to give job to friend and company, nutten fi do wid what you talking about."

"Well, if yuh want to believe dat, go ahead. Mi sure Mikey can tell yuh dat times change," Aunt Joyce said.

"How him fi know, him in a government?" Mama asked, talking over Mikey's head.

"Den him must know, him in business wid one of de biggest hotel owners who reputed to be one a dem kinda man?" Aunt Joyce pressed on.

"Dat's why mi nuh talk politics, yuh know, for is not God's way and Him tell yuh so in de scriptures." Grand-aunt Ruth tried to smooth things over.

Mama said, "Whether dem in bed wid de politicians or not, yuh can't judge dem. De Bible tell yuh dat as plain as day. For dem nuh worse dan de robbers and murderers. And even dem God forgive, dat's why Him put Him son pon de cross fi all a we sins and Him tell we, 'He dat is widout sin among you, let him cast de first stone.'"

My face grew hot with anger. Still I offered nothing. Uncle Mikey looked at me, his eyes pleading. I looked away. I'd never told him about myself.

"Ah think it's time to leave," he said.

"Hold on, Mikey, mi want to talk to yuh," Mama said.

"Come help me wid something inside," Grand-aunt Ruth said to me and Aunt Joyce.

We went inside the house, leaving her and Mikey on the verandah. It wasn't hard to hear their conversation.

"Sit down," Mama said. "So who de bwoy yuh live wid and in a business wid?"

"Mama, dat is not any news to you. An' mi cyaan tek de throw mud an' all de susu."

Mama's voice grew louder. "Den yuh nuh 'fraid a de talk, unnu nuh 'fraid people shoot unnu? Or a unnu so powerful? A so unnu bold-face?"

"Mama, don't shout at mi! I am not a likkle bwoy, an' mi nah beg unnu anything."

She sighed. "Yuh have to start read yuh Bible, it nuh too late." She lowered her voice, but it was still audible. "A sin, yuh know. A sin. De world nuh love mampala man, an' God nuh have no room fi unnu in a fi Him kingdom. A only fire waiting fi yuh."

"Mama, let mi tell yuh something, ah never come here fi dis. Mi come fi see yuh, spend likkle time. Not—"

"Mi nuh care what yuh come for, me is yuh mother, a

mi mek yuh, and yuh fi listen, for mi nah tell yuh no lie. And if yuh nuh stop dem kind a life, it will destroy yuh." We heard her pause and cough.

"Mama, ah love yuh, but a lot happen over de years since yuh left mi, and mi survive without any help from de family." His words carried a bitter edge. "Mi not walking and begging on de streets. Me nuh wear tear-up clothes and mi nuh walk and holler and mi nuh tief."

Mama said nothing. Grand-aunt Ruth started to sing.

He pardoned my transgressions,
He sanctified my soul,
He honors my confessions,
Since by His blood I'm whole.
It is truly wonderful . . .

"Ah leaving Mama," Uncle Mikey said. "Mi nuh have time fi dis."

We heard footsteps, followed by the loud screech of car wheels.

"De blasted bwoy feisty, eh?" Aunt Joyce said when Mama entered the house, leaning heavily on her walker.

"Ah tell yuh," was all she said on her way to her bedroom. She shut the door behind her.

~ ~ ~

One night shortly before I was to leave, I said, "Mama you should have come back long ago." We were sitting on the verandah, watching the people passing by on the street, listening to the laughter of the children playing next door. It seemed like a different world from the one we left behind.

"Ah mi dear," she sighed, "everything have its course. It wasn't time yet." She coughed and her chest rattled. "Bring mi some tea and some water," she said.

I brought the glass and cup and set them down on a small table. She fumbled in her purse for her pills and swallowed two. Then she drew out a sealed envelope and handed it to me.

"Give dis to yuh mother when yuh see her."

"But . . ." I started to protest, knowing that Glory wasn't likely to be visiting me.

"Nuh argue, Molly. Tek it and give it to her whenever dat might be. Is mi will. It nuh urgent, for with God's blessing mi will live a few years longer. Go put it in de bottom of yuh suitcase."

~ ~ ~

At the end of the rainy season, when the dogs were in heat, Mama began to have trouble sleeping. She tossed and turned and talked in her sleep.

"Man, let mi alone, mi nah talk. Release mi. Jesus, help me," she would cry out, often till dawn. Sometimes her lights went on and off all night. Then the dogs would start up. Her feet were swollen by then, and she was tired in the mornings. We blamed it on the dogs.

"Ah tired, ah cyaan fall asleep," she finally admitted one morning at breakfast.

"Maria, relax. Yuh nuh need fi sit up wid we and talk or

even watch television. We will tell yuh what happen wid the soaps, and furthermore yuh have a television in yuh room, yuh can lie in bed and watch it," Grand-aunt Ruth suggested.

"A nuh nutten, yuh know, a de blasted dawgs race up and down a nighttime," Mama said, trying to find some explanation for her tiredness. There were six dogs in the yard, one female among them. She was in heat, and every night brought vicious fights in the yard, with all five males trying to mount her. We heard her yowling. Some nights were worse than others. Other dogs in the neighbourhood would jump the fence to have their way with her, setting the ones who lived in the yard fighting for their territory. Poor Brownie had already had five litters.

"Is when de season done?" Mama asked. "A mi window dem come all de time wid dem noise. Mi really born unlucky."

"Mating time soon done, Maria, and everything will settle down," Grand-aunt Ruth assured her. "Yuh soon see. But in de meantime try fi sleep in de day, for no one demanding anything of yuh. We glad yuh return and we want to look after yuh and mek yuh feel at home."

"Dem blasted dogs need neutering, dat is what dem do in America," Aunt Joyce said.

"Neuter, Aunt Joyce, how dem fi neuter?" Cousin Ivan asked. "What dem doing is natural, yuh know, and dat bitch Brownie lucky, after so much litter, de neighbourhood dawgs still vote her number one." That got him a severe cut eye from Grand-aunt Ruth.

"Aunt Maria, ah think is jet lag. Ah hear people at de hotel ah work seh it tek time to wear off, " Cousin Icie offered, looking pleased with herself.

"Maria, is probably de heavy food dat yuh body not accustomed to. Joyce, from tomorrow mek we start Maria pon some pumpkin soup and callaloo and mix-vegetable soup. Tek her off de heavy food," Grand-aunt Ruth said.

Uncle Mikey came to visit again. He brought a beautiful white orchid plant for Mama. There was no unpleasant talk and I prayed that this day would be a new beginning.

"Mama, when yuh feel a little better, we'll tek a ride to Wigton Street. De two house in need of repair, but now dat you here, we can work on dat," he said.

"Dat would be nice, son. Yuh don't know how I miss dat little dead-end street." She gave a smile.

"Mama, it not like how it used to be," he warned. "But we can fix it up. Is not a place to consider living, though. Too much gunman and dutty nega—"

"Time will tell," she said, as if she were a seer.

~ ~ ~

That night I heard Mama call out, "Molly, come. Molly!"

I hurried into the room and sat by her bed.

"Molly, bring mi some tea, de gas a tek mi over."

I brought her the tea, and she took one sip. Her face exploded with pain.

"Molly, tek mi to de doctor, de hospital, anything, but mi cyaan tek dis pain," she pleaded.

"Mama, is after two in the morning, mek we wait till de sun come up. Mi want yuh to get a good doctor and mi nuh understand de hospital system here." I was also afraid that the city streets were not safe then.

"Molly, mi cyaan wait. Oh Lawd, de pain. Call de cab, mi will go miself," she said defiantly.

"Aunt Joyce, Icie, Grand-aunt Ruth!" I called, but they were dead asleep.

I opened Ivan's bedroom door and shouted, "Wake up, wake up!"

I put a housecoat over Mama's nightgown and a pair of socks over her swollen feet. Ivan and I lifted her into the van. By then, the others were awake.

Icie said we should take her to the Seventh Day Adventist Hospital on Hope Road. Ivan sped to the emergency entrance. We ran inside and found the one attendant fast asleep on a bench.

"Wake up man, emergency, what yuh getting paid for?" Ivan demanded roughly.

A young nurse approached. "Medical cards?" she asked. "It will cost some money to admit her, and additional for de doctor to look at her."

"Yes, yes, how much, money is no problem," I said impatiently.

She led me to an office while Mama lay there, struggling to breathe.

"Name? Address? Kind of payment? Cash? Good."

A doctor was examining her by the time I was through with the paperwork.

"It's heart failure, m'am," the doctor said. "We have to do more tests, which will cost money, and de bed will cost, and other things."

"It doesn't matter," I said to him. "I just want her to get better."

I paid for three days in a private room, with private-duty nurses.

"Okay, everything taken care of, we'll get her to her room, get her comfortable. Come see her tomorrow, everything will be fine," a nurse reassured us with a smile.

We left, exhausted and relieved.

Aunt Joyce and I arrived early the next morning. Joyce launched right in.

"Nurse, nurse, come in here, is what dis—mi sister stink a piss. Look how de bed soak and unnu seh unnu a private hospital and mi niece pay big money last night. Fi what? Dis?"

A young nurse ran into the room. "We just changed her not too long ago," she said, caught off guard.

"Change just a while ago? Is who unnu a try fool? Unnu think we a blasted idiot? She nuh change since last night, and mi demand good treatment for mi sister. Give mi de rass diaper, mi will change it."

"It's okay, m'am, I will do it. I'm sorry, I just came on duty and was just getting de medical records. Her doctor will be in soon. We'll call you when he comes in."

Aunt Joyce stood firm. "Ah not leaving until mi see mi sister clean and de bedsheet change."

"Okay, m'am." I was worried about Mama, but I felt sorry for the nurse.

When Aunt Joyce was satisfied that her sister was in good hands, we went home and waited for the doctor's call.

"Relax, Molly," Grand-aunt Ruth said. "She at de hospital, everything okay or dem would call."

We waited. No one called, so I called.

"Come immediately. Your mother must be transferred to the University of the West Indies hospital. We don't have the facilities to deal with her needs," an officious-sounding woman informed me.

I saw the doctor at the Adventist hospital when I arrived.

"Tek this letter to U.W.I. Hospital at Mona," he said. "It is the best hospital on the Island. Dr. Nadash will meet you there."

I sat next to Mama in the ambulance, and a male nurse sat opposite us, keeping watch. It was rush hour, and the traffic was at a standstill. The road was too narrow to allow for passing, but the ambulance driver put on the siren. Mama was fighting hard to breathe and she held my hands tightly.

"Is de ambulance equipped with an oxygen mask?" I asked.

"Yes, mi have one here, but it will cost yuh extra. Dat is in addition to de ambulance fee."

"Dat's okay, ah don't care. I just don't want her dead in dis ambulance."

"Nuh worry, sis, everything under control. Yuh a foreigner, right? Mi like how yuh mix de Jamaican."

I refrained from sucking my teeth and glaring at him. Fine time for him to be telling me about my accent.

The nurse fit the oxygen mask over Mama's face and her breathing came more steadily. The traffic eased a bit and the ambulance slowly moved forward.

Mama tossed and turned, clutching at the mask. I grabbed her hands, and fighting back the tears and the tremble in my voice, I whispered to her:

The Lord is my light and my salvation
Whom shall I fear?
The Lord is the strength of my life;
Of whom shall I be afraid?
Though war should rise against me, in this will I be confident—

The driver cut into my prayer. "Listen, sis, hold tight, ah going to cut thru one of dese side streets, or we won't mek it wid dis traffic."

He turned down a side street and drove on the sidewalk, almost hitting two pedestrians. He stopped abruptly and shouted, "Unnu nuh hear ambulance wid siren? Unnu nuh know fi move outa de way? Mi will ride right over unnu, yuh know!"

He slammed on the gas. The group scattered, some climbing over people's fences. They knew he meant business. The ambulance picked up speed, bumped over potholes, dodged cars and bicycles, its siren blaring all the way to the hospital.

When we finally came to a stop at the private wing of the University of the West Indies Hospital, the attendants were waiting for us. But there was no doctor. He hadn't arrived. The receptionist said she'd page him. Aunt Joyce and Grand-aunt Ruth arrived with Cousin Ivan and Cousin Icie. We waited and waited.

Aunt Joyce cussed. "Dese blasted people in dis country, dem don't know a blasted thing. Dis is de worst country to get sick in. Where dis doctor deh?"

The receptionist played deaf. My grand-aunt kept cussing. When it got too loud for her to ignore, the receptionist mouthed, "Mi nuh responsible."

"Mi nuh care if yuh nuh responsible. But weh de doctor, how come yuh nuh know where him is?" Aunt Joyce demanded. "Yuh nuh work here? You people never responsible for anything yet."

Grand-aunt Ruth said quietly, "Lady, please admit her, she is mi dear older sister and we want de best care for her."

"Ah can't do anything, m'am. Dis is a private hospital and nobody can be admitted without a doctor's signature."

"Den unnu going to mek mi sister dead in de hospital hallway? Ah so unnu wicked?" Aunt Joyce was shouting now. Visitors coming in and out of the hospital paused and watched. Grand-aunt Ruth tried to quiet her.

"Quiet? Quiet? Mek dem finish kill mi sister? Not a rass. Ruth, if mi ever sick, yuh just put mi on de next plane to America. Mi nuh waan fi sick out here. Dem know nutten 'bout medical care. Look pon mi poor sister. She a go dead in a hospital hallway because of dem blasted idiot who claim dem is medicine people."

"Aunt Joyce, come mek we tek a little breeze outside," Icie offered.

"No, Icie, yuh gwaan. Mi sister a dead and mi can't keep quiet and see it." Then she yelled, "Murderers, murderers, unnu is murderers."

Two security guards approached to ask her to keep her voice down, but she turned her wrath on them. The nurse who'd come with us in the ambulance asked the receptionist for a quiet waiting room off the hallway. We wheeled Mama in and closed the door.

"It not good for de patient to hear all of dat. Even though she confused, that kind of talk won't help wid her recovery. She might look like she nuh conscious, but she hearing everything," the nurse said to me.

I went outside and asked Aunt Joyce to cuss more softly. The receptionist kept paging the doctor.

"Is what kind of doctor dat? Dis is sheer irresponsibility. Him probably in some woman's bed right now and turn off him beeper."

The receptionist took offence. "M'am, Dr. Ford is a very respectable and responsible man. Ah beg yuh not to say things like dat."

"Beg mi? Yuh can say anything yuh want about yuh Dr. Ford, and I will say what comes to my mind. All I know is dat mi sister a dead. De other hospital say come here, dat dem arrange wid Dr. Ford to admit her and now we cyaan find him. A better wi did tek her down to Kingston Public Hospital 'mongst de gunman and tief. She woulda get treatment long time."

The phone rang. "Dat was de doctor," the receptionist informed us when she hung up. "He didn't know that dere was a patient waiting and he cyaan take on the old lady. Him have too many other cases."

Aunt Joyce started in again and now I was thankful that she was there. "Imagine in dis posh hospital nuh doctor not around fi look pon mi sister. What is dis, a hospital or a rass claat morgue?"

"M'am, yuh upsetting de patient. Please quiet yuh voice," the nurse said. "Dis won't do her any good. I have to ask you to be considerate of her."

Helplessly I looked at Grand-aunt Ruth and the others. Cousin Ivan was pacing the hallway. I went back to Mama. Her frightened eyes were searching the room.

"Molly, mek mi dead. Mi life done," she said in a bird's whisper. "Come closer."

Her eyes had no focus. She was dying. "Mi only have one wish and dat is fi you and Vittorio and Ciboney fi live good."

"Mama," I said, "yuh not ready fi dead. Peppie and Glory and everybody else soon come."

I leaned down and held her. My tears fell on her eyes.

"Mi only have one regret, mi sorry mi never get de chance fi tek Maud and tell her about de glory of de Lord," she whispered. I stroked her hair and another tear fell. Her grip on me loosened. She was struggling to breathe. I looked over at the nurse, my eyes begging for a miracle.

"She not in grave danger," the nurse said. "She'll pull through."

I went out to join the others. Aunt Joyce's shouting had become even louder and had attracted the attention of several people passing by, including a young doctor.

"Doctor, mi poor sister almost dead. She in a little room off to de side and we cyaan get nobody to look at her. Ah tell yuh, doctor, something radically wrong wid dis country. De government is piss—"

The doctor laughed. "I will take her on. Where she is, mek mi check her."

I led him to the little room and he examined her.

"Okay, I will admit her and tek de case."

We couldn't thank him enough.

"Check wid de receptionist," he said, "and mek her show yuh de administrator's office fi discuss payment."

"Semi-private or private room?" the woman there asked. "De private room will cost two thousand dollars per day and we need a deposit for a minimum of a week. Mek mi read out other costs. De medications is separate money, de oxygen separate. De doctor service is another fee. De specialist is another separate money." She paused for me to take it all in.

"Now here is a list of things for yuh to bring for de patient," she said, handing me a sheet:

Soap
Towel and washcloth
Powder
Nightgowns
Toothpaste, toothbrush
Hand lotion
Vaseline
Comb and brush

"As yuh know is a private hospital, so we will provide de sheets and diapers."

~ ~ ~

The private room was very basic, very spare, painted a dull lilac. Its saving grace was its view from the window—the Blue Mountains. When Mama felt better, she would enjoy it. The doctor was in the room with the others when I got there.

"Miss Galloway, I need to ask some questions about de medications your grandmother was taking."

I told the doctor that her pills were in her purse at home. I didn't know the names. Mama's eyes were closed, but she mumbled, "Vasotec, Adalat, XL." He thanked her. She kept repeating the list. "Vasotec, Adalat, XL. Vasotec, Adalat, XL. . . ."

"Thank yuh, m'am," he said, and chuckled.

"Vasotec, Adalat, XL. Vasotec, Adalat, XL. . . ."

Aunt Joyce said, "Mi sister is a real comedian." We all laughed.

Later the doctor told us to go home. She was in good hands, he said.

The next morning we arrived to find Mama staring up at the ceiling, her hands in tight fists.

"Maria, a me, yuh sister," Grand-aunt Ruth said, but Mama didn't respond. I went to her and held her hands. She turned and looked at me but there was no sign of recognition.

"Mama, Glory on her way," I said. "She coming in from Atlanta today, and Uncle Peppie coming tomorrow." Mama turned and stared through the window at the Blue Mountains. She was hooked up to an IV drip, and an oxygen mask covered her face. She pulled it off and said, "Get mi out of here. Ah don't want to stay here."

"Mama, let mi put de oxygen back on. Yuh need it."

She resisted, so Aunt Joyce and Grand-aunt Ruth held her still while I put the mask back on her face. She calmed down for a moment, but wouldn't look at us, only the ceiling, folding and unfolding her hands. Then she tried to take off the mask again.

I rang for the doctor. "Please, what is wrong with her?" I asked. "She not acting herself."

"We had to give her some medication last night to quiet her. She was fighting the nurses. She's a strong woman, yuh know, and the nurses couldn't control her. She kept climbing out of bed. Next time, we will have to restrain her. Is a dangerous situation."

I nodded. "Yes, I understand."

We sat beside her until the medication wore off and recognition came back. She looked around, but there was no smile.

"Unnu tell Glory and Peppie?"

"Yes, Mama. Glory coming tomorrow and Peppie on the weekend."

"Yuh tell Vittorio and Ciboney?"

"Yes," I said.

"Where Mikey?"

"Him coming soon," I lied. I had called Uncle Mikey that morning. He hadn't come.

"Freddie, yuh get in touch wid him?"

"Yes," I said, not knowing what else to say.

"Tell dem fi come soon."

"Yes, Mama."

An orderly brought a tray of food for her, but she wouldn't eat. "Aunt Maria, let mi feed yuh, yuh need yuh strength," Icie coaxed, but Mama's lips remained tight. She slipped in and out of sleep only to stare at the wall. She wouldn't talk to us. She began to recite the names of her medicines again. Aunt Joyce and I looked at each other and smiled, easing our anxiety.

"Unnu go out and get some air," Grand-aunt Ruth advised. "I will stay here."

We walked out into the sunlight and through the peaceful grounds of the university. Once we were back inside, Aunt Joyce began to cry.

"Come, Joyce, mek we go home and rest. We come back later. Molly, you come eat some food and come back," Grand-aunt Ruth said.

"Is okay, Grand-aunt, ah not hungry, and when ah get hungry ah will pick up something in de cafeteria. You all go."

They left. "Glory coming soon," I said to Mama, hoping to get her talking. She pulled off the oxygen mask but didn't respond; she was still reciting the names of her medicines.

At last she stopped and looked at me. "Close de door," she whispered.

When I had, she said, "Molly, ah waan fi leave dis place. Help mi."

"No, Mama, dis is where yuh will get better."

"Ah waan fi leave here. I waan to go home to mi own bed."

She tried to climb out of bed, and I held her down, but she was too strong for me. I pressed the buzzer and a nurse came, followed by the doctor. They gave her another injection and the bed rails were pulled up. I sat and watched her sleep as the blue sky turned grey, then charcoal black.

Morning came and a gentle breeze greeted Mama through the windows, but she still looked trapped and unhappy. Glory would be coming soon, and I didn't want her to see Mama like this. I combed and plaited her hair in cane rows. I sang to her as I wiped her face with a damp washcloth, rubbed on a little face cream and put Vaseline on her dry lips.

"Mama, Glory coming today," I said. I had hoped for a response but got none. I started to sing softly.

My Bonnie lies over de ocean.
My Bonnie lies over de sea.
My Bonnie lies over de ocean
Oh bring back my Bonnie to me. . .

There was a moment of recognition as if she was trying to remember where she had heard the song.

"Mama, Glory coming today," I repeated. She didn't answer. I filled a basin with water, washed between her legs, changed her diaper and got her into a fresh nightgown.

Glory arrived, exhausted but happy to find her mother alive. She hurried over to the bed and kissed her on the cheek. Mama didn't hug her back or talk to her. She looked irritated and pulled at the oxygen mask.

"Mama, don't," Glory said.

Mama's hands went back to her side.

"How yuh feeling, Mama? Yuh hungry? Yuh want water or anything?"

Mama just lay there on the bed looking at the ceiling, folding and unfolding her hands, looking at them as if they had not been with her all her life.

I told Glory about the medication, and she went to find the doctor. The nurse told her he would be in later and explained why they had to put Mama on that medication. We waited and waited. The doctor didn't come that night. Finally I called a taxi to take us to Grand-aunt Ruth's and made arrangements for the cab driver to pick us up early the next morning.

~ ~ ~

Mama looked dead when we arrived. Her eyes were shut tight; her hands were lifeless, and there was no movement in her feet. Only the oxygen mask told us she was alive. Glory quickly went to the nurses' station, hoping to find the doctor.

"What is wrong with my mother?" she asked.

"M'am, yuh will have to wait until de doctor come," the nurse said.

"I can't wait anymore. I have been waiting since yesterday. I need to know now."

"I'll get the supervisor."

He went through the same routine with Glory, told her she had to wait until the doctor came. Glory wasn't satisfied with that and persisted till the supervisor gave in.

"Dat dosage too high," Glory said. "Nuh wonder she look like a zombie. Ah want to talk to de doctor now. Dis is a private ward and we paying 'nuff money."

"I will contact the doctor," the supervisor said.

We went back to Mama and opened the window to freshen the room. The bed was soaked in piss, and she lay there like a stone in a puddle. The nurses were busy and said they wouldn't be able to get to her for three hours. Glory got a container of water and we took off Mama's soaked nightgown and wiped between her legs, where she was chafed like a baby. Glory dried her gently, powdered her and snapped on a diaper. Then we changed the bed linen.

The doctor finally arrived and told Glory what he had told us the day before. "She gets very restless and fights the nurses. She tries to climb out of bed. I'm afraid we will have to give her medication again tonight for her own good. She is strong and there is not enough nurses to watch over her at night."

"Ah don't like that," Glory said. "How will ah get to talk to her if she all drugged up? She don't even know mi."

"Ah tell yuh what," he said. "We have sitters here at the hospital that yuh can rent from midnight to 8 a.m. Check with dem at the desk to make arrangements, because if she have a sitter I won't have to prescribe any more of this drug."

Glory thanked him and made arrangements for a sitter. We waited late into the night, but the sitter never showed up. A nurse at the desk told us that some sitters called in sick when it rained. Glory stayed with Mama that night and I took the cab back to Grand-aunt Ruth's. "Yuh late tonight, sister," the cab driver said. I mumbled something about the hospital and the sitter and that my mother was staying the night.

The radio was turned low and some slow rhythm and blues throbbed from the beaten-up speakers. The music eased my mind and I relaxed a bit. The driver didn't talk much. He seemed to sense my mood, and for that I was grateful.

~ ~ ~

The next morning I found Glory sitting in a chair next to Mama, coaxing her to eat her cereal. She looked over and smiled at me. "Is a lucky thing mi stay last night. Mama try fi climb off de bed. We had to put up de rail. If ah wasn't here, dem would have injected her again."

Later Aunt Joyce and the rest of the family came to visit. Mama didn't say much, but she listened to us talk. Glory left with the others to go get some rest, while I stayed with Mama.

She kept trying to climb out of the bed. I rang for the nurses and Mama began to cuss and shout at them, demanding to be let out. Three nurses held her down and a fourth injected her.

"We sorry to have to do that, but we don't have no choice. I cut down on the dosage. She will just sleep a bit and be up in a few hours," the head nurse said.

When Glory returned, Mama was still asleep. I told her what had happened, and she sat down next to me. Mama opened her eyes and looked around the room, a frown etched into her forehead.

"What yuh doing here?" she asked Glory.

"Mama, I'm here because yuh sick. Ah here to tek care of yuh."

Mama looked off through the windows to the Blue Mountains, then at the bed railing, which was pulled high. She narrowed her eyes at it and stared out the window again. "Is what dat?" she asked, pointing.

"Is de Blue Mountains, Mama. Aren't they beautiful?" Glory said.

Mama grudgingly agreed. Then she looked at me. "De door open?"

"No, Mama," I said.

"Open it, and look if anybody out dere. Look both ways down de hall."

"Nobody out there," I said.

"Good," she said. "Pull down de railing and let we go."

That made me laugh.

"Mama," Glory said, "Dis isn't a jail. We bring yuh here to get better."

She sucked her teeth and commanded us to pull down the railing.

"Mama, no, yuh here to get better," Glory persisted.

"Unnu a idiot? Dem fool unnu? A kill dem wawn fi kill me in here."

"No, Mama," Glory tried again. "Dis is a hospital."

Mama pulled the mask from her face. "Dis not nuh hospital. Dis a hell itself. De bed feel like it deh on fire. Dis is a iron grave. Mi haffi come out! Mi nah mek dem kill me so."

"Mama, calm down," I said.

She glared at me, and Glory tried once more. "Mama, de bed cyaan be on fire. We sitting right here next to yuh. De railing is for your own protection," she said patiently.

"Okay," said Mama, "if yuh so sure 'bout dat, why yuh don't come and tek mi place here on de bed?" For such a sick old woman her voice was harsh and mean. Glory didn't answer and left the room quietly.

"She gone?"

"Yes, to get juice," I said.

She turned her face to the window.

"Mama yuh shouldn't talk to Glory like dat, yuh know," I ventured. "She really love yuh."

She sucked her teeth. "Love? Unnu know love?"

I didn't answer.

"What about Peppie and Freddie and Mikey?" she asked when Glory came back to the room.

"Peppie coming tomorrow, and Freddie trying to get a flight . . . Mikey will come soon." My mother was lying. We knew by then that Freddie wasn't going to fly back from Amsterdam where he was now living, and Mikey, well, that was another story.

"Mama, de sitter coming tonight," Glory said.

"Mi nuh want nuh sitter. Ah want to get out. Ah want to sit down wid mi sisters and watch we likkle programs."

"Okay, Mama, we'll get dem to bring a television to de room."

"Nuh bodder spend up any money. Is not de same like sitting wid mi sisters. Yuh think me leave Canada fi come here and lie down in a hospital bed surrounded by strangers?" she asked angrily.

A nursing assistant brought her supper, which she refused to eat. "Mama, have some of de soup," I said.

"Dis a piss food. People can nyam soup, juice and tea fi dinner?"

Glory pointed to the window. "Mama, look out and enjoy de beautiful Blue Mountains."

"Mountain? Blue? Which part of it blue?" She sucked her teeth again. "Why yuh nuh come tek mi place on dis iron bed and you can look at de fart mountain."

"Mama, yuh want mi to read to yuh?" I asked.

"No, mi nuh want no Bible reading in a dis place. A hell dis."

With that she closed her eyes and drifted off to sleep.

"Ah glad Peppie coming in dis evening. It will be good to have him here wid we," Glory said.

"So there is no chance of Freddie coming?" I whispered.

She shook her head and put a finger to her lips. I left before Glory did and waited outside until the cab driver came. He asked me if I would like to go for a drink that night. I had almost forgotten there was life beyond Grand-aunt Ruth's house and the hospital.

It was early December, there were stars in the sky and the weather was balmy. The smell of the city was unpleasant. We found an open-air bar with music and ordered two beers. The cab driver, Philip, asked the usual questions. "Yuh married?"

"No, but I am involved with someone," I lied.

"Yuh live wid him? Any children?"

"I have a daughter," I said. "How about you?"

"Well, I is what yuh call a baby father," he said with a grin. "Ah have four youth, and dem have three different mother. But don't cast no judgment on mi yet, because ah look after every one of dem. Ah not one of dem careless man."

I laughed. I took a quick look around the bar to see if there were any women alone. None. Every woman was paired off with a man. I thought about Rose for the first time in a long while and wondered what it would be like to be here with her.

"Want to dance?"

"Sure, but I'm not too up on de latest dance," I said.

"Just follow de leader," he said pleasantly. "Don't worry, dis is a uptown establishment. Yuh don't have nuh downtown dance-hall competition."

~ ~ ~

Mama's health began to improve, and she was due to come home. Peppie arrived from Atlanta, and she was glad to have her favourite son there with her.

"Only Vittorio and Ciboney and de other two mi want fi see now. Yuh tell Vittorio fi come?" she asked, turning to me.

"Yes," I said, but I hadn't.

Two days before she was to leave the hospital, she took a turn. She started hearing voices.

"Dem waan fi kill me. Dem waan fi kill me. Get mi out a dis iron coffin. Ah don't want dis coffin," she screamed one morning when Glory, Peppie and I visited. Her eyes were wide open as if she had seen a ghost.

"Peppie, shut de door," Glory said.

"Mama, who trying to kill yuh?" I asked her.

"Ah can't tell yuh, him say if ah tell anyone, him will kill mi. Mi cyaan tell."

Glory said, "Mama, yuh hearing things, nobody want to kill yuh."

"Yuh think yuh intelligent?" she threw back. "Yuh not intelligent, yuh is a damn fool. Continue fi let dem fool yuh. Yuh come in a dis iron coffin and let me go. You tek my place."

Peppie and I held her to the bed, while Glory ran to get the doctor. Mama was fighting us hard. There was no choice but to let the doctor inject her. We sat there in silence. She awoke some hours later, delirious.

"De man, him coming fi me. Him waan fi kill mi," she started again. "Him say him ready, him say if mi talk, him will kill mi. Mi want peace, mi cyaan keep de secret any longer, it a burn mi up inside."

Her eyes were wild and unfocused. "Adalat, Adalat. Go weh, Satan. Lef mi alone. I won't tell de secret, so jus' lef mi alone."

"Mama, it okay, it's all right," Peppie said, stroking her arms.

Her mouth was pressed tight. Such pain on her face.

"Tek mi out a dis iron coffin! Tek me out!" she shouted, her voice carrying out the open windows and through the door. She began to cough and vomit. Thick, slimy mucus, like a mixture of dirt and water, spilled from her mouth. Glory wiped it away with a towel, but Mama kept vomiting.

"Get de doctor!" I shouted.

Peppie rushed out of the room. The doctor came in and began pounding on her chest. He spoke rapidly to the nurses in medical language that we couldn't understand. They rushed in and out of the room. Mama's face was like ash. I couldn't look at her, not like that. I ran from the room and found a bench outside. The tireless blue sky, the sunshine, steadied me. Students from the campus walked by, laughing and talking, unaware that inside an old woman was dying.

In the distance I heard Bob Marley singing "Natural Mystic" from somewhere on the campus. The record sounded like a lament played just for my grandmother. As the song wound its way up the mountains, Mama died.

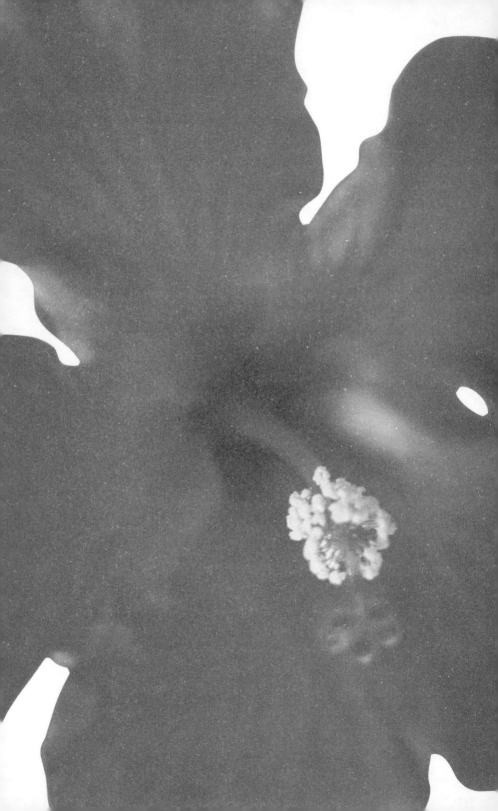

Epilogue

The Heart Is Not a Knee;
It Does Not Bend

CHRISTMAS IS COMING, but we're not sure how to spend
the holiday. Grand-aunt Ruth insists we respect the memory
of her sister by celebrating the birth of Christ. Aunt Joyce
couldn't agree more; she's already bought a few fancy dresses
and shoes and has tickets for a stage show at the best hotel in
Kingston. I guess we'll go through the rituals of Christmas,
soothing our pain with the traditional songs and what
precious memories we can scrape together.

Glory, Uncle Peppie and Aunt Val and Vittorio have
left the island. I convinced Ciboney to stay for Christmas,
see a bit of Jamaica and get to know her great-grand-aunts.
We're both not ready to face home—the snow, the cold,
the emptiness.

I call Rose several times. Leave messages. She never calls
back. One day she answers, as unforgiving as I suspected
she'd be. She loves me, that I know. She understands that I've
come back needful, but she's not willing to take on the burden left by a dead woman.

I decide to take Ciboney to see the dead-end street. I want

to see our old house, the Ritz Theatre and the Chinese pastry shops once more. Cousin Ivan offers to drive us there, but I want to travel by bus, to smell, to breathe, to remember at my own pace.

"Careful, Molly, Kingston change, yuh know," Aunt Joyce says. "A pure duttiness left down here. Ah don't know why yuh want fi tek de dutty bus and mix wid—"

"Joyce, leave de girl alone, nothing won't happen to her. After all, she not a fool," Grand-aunt Ruth interrupts. Then she turns to me. "Molly go wid God's blessing, and hold yuh handbag tight."

To appease Aunt Joyce, I allow Cousin Ivan to drive us as far as Half-way Tree. We take the bus along Maxfield Avenue and in no time are caught in a frenzy of commuters pushing and shoving and jostling for space. The smell of fresh perspiration is strong, and the sounds of reggae and patois fill the air. We bake in the heat that presses in through the windows. There is no room for conversation between Ciboney and me, so we simply bask in the sounds and smells until the driver calls our stop and we push our way out.

The old neighbourhood has really changed. The streets feel boxed in now that small grocery shops and houses made of zinc and corrugated boards have been built in people's front yards. The sidewalks are littered with garbage, broken bottles and dog shit. Skinny stray dogs circle each other, vying for chicken bones. Barefoot children in tattered clothes run about the streets, while women carrying baskets of fruits and vegetables skirt the sidewalks and piazzas, selling their goods. I point out a betting shop to Ciboney; it used to be a Chinese shop that sold Mama's pastries. I don't point out the bars Mama frequented. They're still selling rum, though their names have changed.

We turn onto the dead-end street and I hardly recognize it. The pavement is full of potholes. Additional shacks have been added to weathered brick houses, and most of the gates are broken. Young men hang off fences like soiled rags on a line. Two or three girls in bikini tops keep them company.

Petal's old treehouse still stands. It's painted in beautiful Rasta colours, and hardcore dance-hall music spills out from it with a violent intensity. The smell of ganja reaches our nostrils. The fruit trees have all been cut down except for one in front, which shades a makeshift shop selling single cigarettes, cigarette paper and candy.

Suddenly Ciboney tugs on my arm, interrupting my thoughts, and asks, "How much further?"

I slow at the next house and point it out to Ciboney.

"This? This? This is the house all the fussing was about?" she asks in disbelief.

I shrug, disappointed. "This is not how it used to be."

The flower beds are gone, the trees cut down, and concrete covers the yard. The barbed-wire fence is naked without the bougainvillea vine. The paint on the house is badly flaked, and the stairs leading up to the balcony are lopsided. I bang on the old, broken-down gate. A pack of scrawny mongrels rush to greet us, followed by children. A woman looking as tired as the house comes out to the verandah.

"Come in, don't mind de dogs!" she shouts.

"Hold de dogs," I tell the children.

Ciboney cautiously follows me to the verandah, where I introduce myself to the woman.

"Ah know. Ah heard about de landlady. Ah sorry fi hear." She invites us into the house and lets us wander freely through the rooms. They're clean, but the walls are in need of paint, the floors are chipped, and the ceiling is stained with brown water marks.

"De roof a leak, de floor chip up, mi use dis big pot fi catch de rainwater. The water all blow thru de window. And look," she says, pointing to a dripping pipe.

"We'll try to make some repairs," I say, before remembering that Vittorio is now the owner of this house.

"This was Mama's and my room," I tell Ciboney. "And this was Uncle Mikey and Uncle Freddie's." Ciboney looks around, her eyes indifferent.

I ask to see the backyard.

"Nutten much to see, everything chop down. Is pure concrete dere," the woman says.

Ciboney sighs and rolls her eyes. I ignore her.

The only familiar thing in the backyard is the fowl coop. A few hens and a rooster strut around, followed by half a dozen yellow chicks. The vegetable garden is gone, and only a stubborn hedge of mint remains.

Before leaving, I climb the steps to the balcony. "This used to be the fanciest house on the street," I tell Ciboney.

"Yeah, I bet," she says derisively.

My heart boils, but I smother my anger. "Come, let's go visit Myers."

Myers had been at Mama's funeral, and I promised him that I would visit before leaving the island.

From a distance, it's easy to tell which house is Myers's. His yard is the only green one on the street. Mango trees laden with expansive leaves envelop the house, but as we go through the gate and up the path, we can see him sitting on the verandah, smoking a pipe.

"Yuh really come back fi visit me?" he asks, smiling, as we join him and sit down. Myers's hair is silver-grey, but his face shows little wear for his years.

A woman named Violet, not much older than me, comes out of the house and offers us a drink. At Myers's insistence I take a cold rum-and-lime drink and Ciboney has a long glass of lemonade. The mango trees block the ugliness of the street and muffle the dance-hall music.

"Yuh dear ole granny gone to rest," he said. "A de Father call her home. Nuh fret yuhself. The flesh gone, but de spirit still present." A whiff of ganja floats through the mango tree. "Cyaan get away from dat, yuh know. Rum and dat a we staple," he says matter-of-factly. He turns his attention to Ciboney.

"And how are you, foreign princess? I see you have yuh mother same ackee-seed eyes. Watch dem Jamaican man, yuh nuh, for dem love ackee." Ciboney laughs and appears more relaxed.

Myers calls out to Violet to bring another round of drinks.

Violet looks anxious. "Myers, remember, de doctor—"

He brushes away her last words with his hands. "Doctor kill people every day. When God ready fi mi, no one have any control. Mi father use to say, 'whey nuh broke nuh fix it.'"

"Myers, you ever visit America?" I ask.

"Never had no desire. Mi love Jamaica, doh it not paradise. Yuh cyaan ever seh who running dis country. Sometime it look like a foreigners and gunmen in control. Dem own we coffee, dem build up dem resort, dem control de ghetto area and dem bring every kind a drug in de country fi kill de youths. And de damn politicians 'fraid fi dem." He takes a large gulp of rum.

I ask Myers to show us his garden. His backyard is filled with fruit trees, flowers and a large vegetable patch. He takes Ciboney by the hand and leads her down a stone path, pointing out callaloo, susumbés and the cho-cho vine. I sit on a stool outside the kitchen door and wonder how things would have been had I not written that letter to Uncle Peppie so many years ago.

Violet comes out of the house. "Ah never know yuh granny, but Myers say she was a strong-minded woman. A good friend. Somebody who never throw stone pon other people. Him seh, she did like her drinks every now and then."

I ask her if she works for Myers and she gives an embarrassed laugh.

"Things hard in de country. Myers kind enough to take me in."

She offers me another drink. I hesitate, but the disappointment on her face makes me change my mind.

Ciboney's voice draws nearer. She sounds happy. Her face is animated and brims with new discoveries.

"We should go now," I say. "The sun going down. Myers, ah will come back and see you again soon."

"Ah not sticking around much longer—ah see enough of life."

"Don't mind Myers, him talk like that all de while," Violet says, laughing.

Ciboney and I both hug him and say goodbye. I hold him a bit longer and feel his heart thumping softly in his chest.

Walking back down the street, I pause at our old gate and take another look at our house. The sun is going down and the sky is a rainbow of yellow, blue and rose pink. I can see Mama sitting on the verandah, holding court, a flask of white rum, water, lemon and ice set before her.

"Ciboney, I say, "I can't take another bus ride today. Let's get a taxi." She holds my hand and we walk like that for some time.

~ ~ ~

The next day Ciboney and I visit Port Maria. I want her to see where her great-great-grandmother Mammy's house once stood. We walk over to the district of Jericho, where Mama's cousins live, and eat a lunch of fried snapper and hard-dough bread, washing it down with lemonade. Then we grab a couple of towels and walk down to the beach to bathe in the sea. Afterwards we stretch out on the sand beneath a mangrove tree, letting the lazy waves lull us into near-sleep.

"You loved her, didn't you?" Ciboney suddenly asks.

"Of course. Even though there were moments when I found her hateful."

"I don't mean Mama."

I hesitate, searching for words, then say, "Yes."

"Why did you let her go?"

"I had no choice."

"What do you mean you had no choice?"

I search the sea water for an answer. "Yes, I did have a

choice. I chose Mama," I finally say.

"You have to live your own life, Mom," she lectures, as if I were a schoolgirl.

"Ciboney," I say tiredly, "we don't live our lives independent of others. It's all a give and take, and when you take, you have to give back." She is quiet. "Rose is fun and adventurous, and totally free. All the things I'm not. All the things I love about her. But she has a blind spot. She forgets that in some small way we are all dependent on each other."

Silence stretches before us. Children romp along the beach, playing tag.

"What about Vittorio?" she asks. "Did you ever love him? Or was there always this thing between you?"

"What thing?"

"I don't know. Dislike . . . I don't know."

"No," I answer slowly. "When he was a baby, I loved him like a little brother. Changed his diapers. Sang him songs. I adored his mother. I still have a photograph of her. Don't you remember when I used to take you and Vittorio to the movies, the botanical gardens, the park, zoo? Everywhere."

"I don't remember."

I flinch at her reply and remember Mama asking her children, "Unnu have amnesia?"

"Mama turned him into a spoiled brat," I say impatiently.

"That's not true. She was understanding and patient. Isn't that how grandmothers are supposed to be? I don't know what I'll do without her. I miss her so much it hurts."

"'I know, baby . . . I miss her, too, and things won't ever be the same." I try to pull her into my arms, but she swiftly moves away. "Please," I say. "Let's try."

She shrugs, jumps up and runs into the water. Her tiny frame seems so fragile in the sea.

I follow her and shout, "I'll race you to the buoy and back."

She easily beats me. When I reach the shore, I fall to my knees, gasping for air.

"You need exercise," Ciboney says, glad to have won.

We return to our spot under the mangrove tree and watch the soothing movement of the waves. I try to absorb their serenity, but I'm on edge.

"Looks like we'll get rain," I say, looking at the patches of cloud forming above our heads.

"Yeah," she answers absently.

I'm thinking of buying a house when I get back home," I say.

Ciboney takes this in with measured interest.

"There'll be room for you and Maud."

"I'm comfortable enough," she says.

The sky grows as dark as night and there is a burst of thunder. Lightning as dazzling as fireworks flashes from the heavens, and rain suddenly gushes from the black clouds. Ciboney and I dash for cover under a thatch-roofed shelter, and I wrap my towel tight around me to take the chill away.